My Boyfriend Merlin

Book 1, My Merlin Series

PRIYA ARDIS

Ink Lion Books

Published by: Ink Lion Books, LLC. http://inklionbooks.com

Visit the author website: http://www.priyaardis.com

ISBN-13: 978-0-9848339-2-4
ISBN-10: 0984833927
E-BOOK ISBN-13: 978-0-9848339-0-0
First Trade Paperback Edition, November 2012
Juvenile Fiction / Legends, Myths, Fables / Arthurian

For my Nani and Dadi, we miss you.

CONTENTS

ACKNOWLEDGMENTS

I would like to thank my family and friends. This book has been truly a community effort and I am grateful for all their support, encouragement, and numerous- not to mention often repetitious "first reads" over the years. I would like to thank the writing organizations that do their best to encourage every writer to climb out of the basement once in awhile. I dedicate this book to them and a great English teacher, Mrs. P., who let me know when something sparkled or it was only so-so.

In addition, I would like to thank my editors, ER, WM, and CMcC. Thank you to CM at Phatpuppy Art for giving me such a gorgeous cover picture. Thank you to Kat, my real life fairy godmother, for pulling the cover, book, everything else together.

THE WORLD CHANGES

I remember exactly what I was doing when I heard the news...

I'd always heard the phrase from older people. They remembered they'd just ordered a cup of coffee when JFK died. They remembered they'd been folding their leg warmers when the Challenger blew up on takeoff on national TV, or that it was a Tuesday when terrorists crashed a plane into the twin towers...

I'd heard about such life changing events, but like anyone, I didn't really believe it would happen to me.

I was sitting in school when the story broke. A text message made my phone vibrate in my pocket. Making sure the teacher's back was turned, I snuck out the phone.

RYAN, WE NEED TO TALK. It blinked with a number I recognized, even though I'd deleted the name from my contact list. *Matt.* I felt his eyes boring into the back of my head. I refused to look.

I drew my sweater around me. A line of windows across the top of the basement classroom did nothing to retain warmth. Our school district may have been well funded, but you couldn't tell from the bland grey floors, whitewash walls, and standard issue combination desk-chairs.

My name is Arriane Morganne Brittany DuLac—you can imagine why I go by Ryan instead.

I doodled on my notepad and tried to concentrate as our Advanced European History teacher droned on about Queen Elizabeth. It was hard to be interested when I knew more about the subject than she did.

"With one decision, she changed the course of history. Her ships defeated the Spanish armada—Ryan, what year did the Spanish armada try to invade England?"

I blinked at her. Switching off the phone without replying, I snuck it back into my pocket, but I was pretty sure Ms. Bedevere saw me. I quickly said, "August 8th, 1588. The fleet was stopped in the English Channel near a place called Gravelines."

Ms. Bedevere slowly nodded. "Near northern France—"

"Actually, it was part of the Netherlands—"

The door to the adjoining classroom flung open. We all snapped to attention.

"You've got to see this." Mr. Hainey, our bald, munchkin-sized Physics II teacher, burst inside with a wild look behind his round glasses. "They're showing it on every channel."

Hainey housed a permanent TV in a closet in his classroom that he called the "lab." He grabbed Ms. Bedevere by the hand.

"You have to see. You'll never believe it."

"Peter, I can't leave the classroom. What's happened?"

Everyone knew Hainey had a crush on the petite redhead. After an unfortunate pipe leak orphaned us, he'd convinced the principal that the empty biology room down the hall from his classroom would be the best spot for our history class.

"This is a once in a lifetime chance. You're a history teacher. History is happening now." He hurried her to the door. "If you don't see it, you'll never forgive yourself."

Ms. Bedevere's eyes fixed on me. "Ryan?"

Feeling the other kids looking at me, I squirmed, but nodded.

Someone coughed. "Kiss-ass."

"Class, stay put until I get back. No matter what." She tossed the words over her shoulder as she left. A sudden gust of wind slammed the classroom door shut after her.

Across the room, Grey Ragnar stretched and drew attention to the broad shoulders under his football letterman jacket. He sauntered over and sat on my flimsy student desk, making it sink. Model-like brown hair emphasized a chiseled jaw. "Hey, DuLac, I have two words for you—*casino prom.*"

Grey's buddies hollered enthusiastically.

I resisted a groan. "I'll bring the idea to the committee."

Grey smiled broadly. "I knew you and I would be on the same page, Ry."

I was saved from answering as a muted vibration made the windows shake. A boy stood up to investigate.

His name was Matt. Matt Emrys. He'd started school just this fall, two months ago... long enough for every girl in the school to fall in love with him—not that I knew why. Okay, I knew why. He was hot. Six foot, lean muscles, pretty face, and he rode a shiny new yellow-and-black Ducati that had more curves than I did. He was a little eerie, a little dangerous, and a lot irresistible. Who wouldn't be in love with him?

I sighed. I thought his dark amber eyes were his best feature. The rest of him looked seventeen, but his eyes looked grown-up... as if they'd seen lifetimes. I'd been enthralled as soon as I'd laid eyes on him. I'd moved not too long ago, too. After my mother died, I'd been brought from sun-soaked Texas to the cold Boston suburb of Concord. In a life of dull grey, Matt Emrys stood illuminated in full color.

Matt flung open the window. A screeching sound filled the room. He slammed the window shut. In an odd mix of southern US and British accents, he calmly said, "It appears to be the city siren."

One of Grey's football buddies shouted, "Let's get out of here."

Beside me, our soon-to-be valedictorian, a quiet girl, wheezed and pushed aside the thick brown hair that usually veiled her face. You had to be really nerdy to be valedictorian at Acton-Concord High School. Five out of the top ten kids had gone to Harvard last year. "Ms. Bedevere said to stay in class."

"I'm not going to stay here just because she said so. Learn to make up your own mind, Bennett." Grey scowled at her.

His buddies nodded along with him. Bennett blushed under the male scrutiny.

I rose. "Leave her alone, Grey. It's what Ms. Bedevere said."

Grey gave me an irritated look. "And what do you suggest, Madam President?"

"Ragnar is right. We should go." Matt's deep voice washed over me from the back of the room.

Grey looked at Matt in surprise. I could see in Grey's face he wanted to take back his words, just to spite Matt. Since the first day Matt had started school, he and Grey had been going at each other. Grey could be overbearing. He pretty much ruled our class. Then, Matt had transferred in and the *battle royale* had begun. I hadn't seen it at first—I became a blubbering idiot at the sight of Matt—but the antagonism between them was mostly Matt's fault. He needled Grey, and only Grey, purposefully. I didn't know why.

The other students' heads swiveled back and forth between the three of us.

"Emergency procedures state that we should go to the nearest safe room." I straightened to the full length of my five-foot-two-inch frame. "Ms. Bedevere will be in Hainey's room. We'll all go there."

Like horses released from the gate, the class scrambled to close up their backpacks and rush out the door.

We went down the hall into the long physics room. It turned out we weren't the only ones Hainey had alerted. Kids from the Chem II class next door had already beaten us there. Even though the class sizes for advanced placement classes were fairly small, fifty or so students crowded the room.

Ms. Bedevere smiled at me winningly. "Good work, Ryan. I

knew I could depend on you to handle anything."

"Right, as if you would have remembered to come get us," Grey muttered behind me.

High tables and bench seats made up the physics room. Hainey pointed under them. His class was already huddled beneath. "Get down. They say it will be here any minute."

Grey asked, "What's going on?"

A rumble shook the building. I lost my footing and stumbled.

A pair of male arms wrapped around my waist and stopped the fall. A smooth voice spoke into my ear. "Don't panic. I have you."

I took a breath. *Matt.* I should have pushed him away, but I couldn't. A sense of calm encased me. The building trembled, but it seemed far away. Lights flickered off and on. He pulled us to the side of the room behind a tall bookshelf filled with Hainey's science knick-knacks.

The building gave a slight shudder. A few glass beakers tumbled off the lab tables and broke. The knick-knack shelf wobbled. Instinctively, my body moved to get away from it.

Matt's arms tightened around me. "Stay still."

My heart raced. I wanted to stay with him. *Pathetic.*

I tried to pull away. He held me in place.

"Are you crazy?" I pointed at the tables where everyone else was huddled. "We need to get under—"

But it was too late. The building gave a violent shake. A model of the galaxy crashed to the ground. I heard a few gasps.

Most of the knick-knacks flew off the shelf. I braced myself.

None of the knick-knacks touched us. A microscope, a floating ball as heavy as twenty-pound weights, and numerous other models tumbled down... and over us. I watched as they fell all around Matt and me. It was as if an invisible bubble was keeping us safe.

I glanced at Matt, flabbergasted. Half a minute after it started, the tremor stopped. No one moved for what seemed like another ten minutes. Although, with Matt holding me, I wasn't sure if I wanted to move... ever.

There was loud shuffling as the kids under the tables started to emerge. Matt let go of me. I grabbed his arm and pointed to the fallen knick-knacks. They made a neat circle around my feet. "Why didn't they hit us?"

Dark eyes fixed on me, but then let go. Matt shrugged. "Guess we were lucky."

"Ryan?" Grey said from the other side of the shelf.

I could hear the anxiety in Grey's voice. My soon-to-be brother's voice. The Ragnars had taken me in when I had no one left. Now they wanted to adopt me to make it official. I wasn't entirely sure how I felt about it. It had always been my mom and me against the world, and I'd lost her, too. Being part of a family was as thrilling as it was scary. As much as I didn't want to let Matt off the hook, I couldn't let Grey worry. I stepped back around the shelf into the open part of the room. "I'm here."

A few kids stared when Matt walked out behind me. One snickered. "Hope the earthquake didn't distract you two."

Grey looked at Matt with an unhappy expression. I walked closer to Grey, leaving Matt behind.

"Was that it?" someone murmured. "I thought an earthquake would be bigger."

"Joey's car shakes worse than that," one of Grey's buddies said and made an old jalopy glug-glug sound. His friends laughed.

"But we don't have earthquakes," another kid said.

"Boston had a 3-pointer not too long ago," our valedictorian intoned. "I don't know if one's ever come all the way out to Concord."

Hainey waved his cell phone in the air. "It's not an earthquake. They're calling it the Total Tremor. And it wasn't just us. It went around the whole world."

Everyone crowded around the "lab." Hainey had managed to cram a TV, floor-standing speakers, two videogame consoles, and a mini-fridge into a closet at the back of his classroom. Conscious of Matt watching me from across the room, I stood on my tiptoes. My lack of height only let me make out a corner of the TV through the crowd.

Hainey flipped on the news.

Ms. Bedevere squealed like a five-year-old on a sugar high. "I don't believe it!"

"I knew you'd love this." Hainey grabbed a potato chip bag and started stuffing chip after chip systematically into his mouth. "It came down in a big explosion. Everyone thought it was a bomb. But then… poof. The giant stone just appeared. That's when the Total Tremor started."

Out of the corner of my eye, I saw Matt make his way toward me.

"What appeared? What stone?" Grey muscled his way through the crowd to the front. His buddies followed close after him, edging everyone else out. Avoiding Matt's seeking gaze, I squeezed in behind Grey through the crowd.

Near the front, I stopped beside Ms. Bedevere. "Is that what I think it is?"

In a thick Bostonian accent, one of Grey's buddies exclaimed, "It's a metal cross."

Another teammate guffawed. "It's a sword, doofus."

On Hainey's flat screen, the tagline read "Trafalgar Square." Smoke and broken concrete littered the scene. A few pigeons persisted in hanging around the destruction. British policemen had closed off the square and stood on guard around the perimeter. Crowds of people gathered around them. They all looked wide-eyed at the spectacle in the middle.

"It's not a meteor, folks," said a cheery blond reporter in a fitted suit. Her nametag read Anders. "But it has caused a sensation. It has been confirmed that the epicenter of the Total Tremor began at the giant stone. Wait—" She touched the microphone piece in her ear. "I have a clip coming in. We have an amateur video… a tourist in the square today filmed the entire thing." Anders waved to a crewperson on the screen. "Let's roll this."

A grainy video clip showed the giant rock appearing out of nowhere a few feet above the big fountain. It seemed to poof into existence. Gravity realized around it and it fell to the ground. A big boom and flying dust went everywhere. People screamed—no doubt thinking *"TERROR ATTACK."* But the whole square shook. The video jostled at this point. People rushed past the tourist who was filming. The video righted again, this time on the surrounding buildings. Like a wave radiating out from the square, the buildings shook in sequence. Once the wave had traveled through, the tourist turned back to the center of the square.

Mammoth lion statues, who perched on the edges of Trafalgar Square, stared impassively at the wreckage. Half of a fountain dedicated to Lord Nelson, the hero of the Battle of Trafalgar, lay broken. Water sluiced off the crushed fountain, flooding the square. Droplets fell on the hilt of a long metal object sitting embedded halfway into a massive obsidian-black rock, the size of a pick-up truck.

"It's a sword," Ms. Bedevere repeated, not taking her eyes off the television.

"Not just any sword," I murmured. If I hadn't known the King Arthur legend, the stone would have looked like something dropped by aliens—or some other higher power. The camera zeroed in on one side of the rock. On its otherwise smooth surface, the stone had one jagged side extending from the bottom to the top, almost like steps.

"Certainly the Total Tremor is no laughing matter." Anders gave an over-bright smile. "Thankfully, a minimal number of lives have been lost—mostly due to panic. Still, the globe is abuzz. There hasn't been an event this widespread since the meteor that caused the extinction of the dinosaurs. And it all rooted from here."

Images from around the world flashed across the TV. Paris. Madrid. Berlin. Times Square. They all had one thing in common—they had all trembled under the force of the tremor.

"But is it some sort of elaborate hoax? We have set up a panel to ask just that. Dr. Latimer, an eminent physicist from the Massachusetts Institute of Technology. Dr. Vivane Northe, a noted King Arthur historian and lecturer at Essex University in the United Kingdom, a man in very high demand today. They are both calling in to share their expertise."

The picture changed to a white-haired man in a too-expensive suit, Dr. Latimer, and a second man, Dr. Vivane Northe. His lean yet gorgeous face filled the screen. With a rakish smile that said he knew exactly how attractive he was, Northe appeared more underwear model than mole-like university lecturer. He also seemed really young—about twenty or so. But that wasn't why I gaped at Northe.

He could have doubled for Matt.

"*He's* a professor?" murmured a girl beside me.

Northe said, "The myth of King Arthur starts with Arthur pulling the sword from the stone, and thus, claiming his right to the throne…"

My jaw dropped lower. He also spoke in the same eerily familiar accent as Matt.

"Talk about hot for teacher," purred a girl from the Chem II class.

"He's not that handsome," Matt muttered.

We all turned to Matt.

"Missing a twin, Emrys?" Grey asked with a sneer.

"If we were, would not our surnames match?" Matt's accent emphasized the droll bite to his statement.

Grey glowered at him.

"You *do* sound just like him," Ms. Bedevere ventured.

Matt's tone softened. "Yet he is not my twin."

"Of course—" Hainey rubbed a hand over his bald scalp and gave a fake laugh. "Of course. Let's leave Mr. Emrys alone."

Everyone dutifully turned back to the TV. Hainey gave Matt an I've-got-your-back thumbs-up sign. I don't know what it was about Matt, but the teachers all treated him like he walked on water.

Anders said, "We have yet to see how the British government will respond. The question we must ask here is not just why, but why now? And what do we do next?"

"Closer scientific study should begin immediately," intoned Latimer. "The impact crater suggests the stone could not have fallen more than a few feet. It alone could not cause a worldwide tremor—"

Northe interrupted, "You're missing the obvious. We should gather other historians—"

Everyone jumped when the class bell rang.

Hainey muted the TV. "Back to your rooms."

We all hurried out.

I was throwing my notebook into my backpack when a couple of pep squad girls tried to get my attention. One held up a scribbled sign on notebook paper. "Princess Prom. Perfect

Party."

I tried not to laugh. *Princess Prom. Really?* But I didn't have the heart to crush them. Instead, I smiled and gave them a thumbs-up. The girls nodded happily.

Matt came up from behind my desk. He gave the Princess Prom sign a pained look. "You're not serious, are you?"

My smile froze. I wanted to ignore him. Why did he have to wear that black leather jacket? It was the slim kind without a collar. It made him look so... intense. "I bring every idea to the committee."

"Of course you do. You're very... conscientious."

I zipped up my backpack with a snap. "I'm student president. I have to be."

"No. I don't think so. You just don't like to say no."

"What do you want, Matt?"

"Plenty of things." *From you,* his eyes suggested. His hand reached out to smooth a few stray tendrils of hair. I jerked away. His hand dropped. He smiled almost wistfully. "Odd day, don't you think? This strange tremor and all—"

"I'm sure there's a scientific explanation for the tremor."

"A scientific explanation," he said slowly. "Is that what you really think?"

"Sure, why not?" I pulled on my backpack and put one foot out from the desk. "Look, I've got to get to gym."

He blocked my exit. In a wounded tone he said, "I saw you switch off my text."

My cheeks puffed. I seriously debated throwing my

backpack at his head.

"You have nothing to say that she wants to hear, Matt Emrys."

In a staccato of thigh-high boots and bouncing brown curls, Alexa stomped up to my desk. A boy in the desk beside me nearly swallowed his tongue at the sight of her in avenging-angel mode. Alexa didn't notice. Her usual carefree expression was set to protective bulldog.

"Pardon me?" Matt stared at her in confusion.

"Pardon me," Alexa mimicked. "You sound so polite. Too bad you don't act it."

She grabbed me by the elbow and started pulling me toward the door. "Let's go or Coach will skin us for being late again."

"Ryan, wait," Matt started. "It's important. I need to talk to you."

My traitorous heart fluttered. I wanted to say yes. But I'd been saying yes for two months. We'd been talking for two months. I thought we were friends. I'd been wrong. It still hurt how wrong I'd been. I shook my head. "You dumped me, Matt. Remember? You don't get to talk anymore."

ATTACK

"I can't believe you even let that jerk near you," Alexa said as she hurried us down the hallway. "After the way he treated you—"

"It was only two dates," I muttered.

Alexa snorted. "He texted you to break up. How weak is that?"

"I text all the time," I defended.

The hallways of Acton-Concord High were crowded with kids. Everyone took the few minutes in between class to check their phones, which were supposed to be kept in the lockers. It was the one rule I couldn't make myself follow. I couldn't bear to be parted from my scheduler and with all the activities and clubs I'd signed up for, on top of taking a full AP course load, a paper scheduler just did not work for me.

My phone vibrated in my pocket. "We're going to be late."

Alexa rolled her eyes. "Do you sleep with that thing?"

We ran across a small courtyard, barely glancing at the

gloomy sky, to a side entrance of the gym that led directly to the girl's locker room. Alexa stopped at the door.

"Grey and I just want to look out for you, Ry. You've had a tough year. Don't think we don't know you still have nightmares."

My jaw dropped open. "You hear me?"

Alexa's generous lips turned down into a sad smile. "We're on the same floor and you're not exactly quiet." Her perfectly symmetrical eyes narrowed. "And I'm not letting Emrys take advantage of my way-too-sweet sister."

I felt my cheeks heat. The white knight routine happened to me a lot. The combination of possessing a petite frame, curly dark-blond hair, and big eyes seemed to land me in the role of the damsel in distress every time. They all thought I needed rescuing.

But it wasn't like I was a basket case. Well, not totally. I lost my mother last year, my only family, and sometimes it became a little hard to breathe. Blinking back the pain, I forced a smile. "Let me remind you, Alexa Ragnar, that when your mom adopts me, you're officially going to be my *little* sister."

"Only by age." Alexa snorted.

I opened the door to the gym. "I can handle Matt—or anyone else for that matter."

Alexa raised curved eyebrows. "Really? Have you decided on the prom theme yet?"

"It's a committee decision," I protested.

"It's *your* committee, pres."

I chewed my lip. "What if everyone hates what I pick?"

Alexa went into the locker room. "You can't please everyone."

"I just want it to be perfect," I muttered before following her in.

***

Behind the gym, the mossy field smelled sharp from rain. Crisp blades of grass crunched under my cleats. Wind tried to penetrate the leggings under my blue skirt and chilled the skin exposed by my tied-back hair. I held my lacrosse stick tight against the fabric of my yellow shirt. We scrimmaged against girls wearing green shirts.

We were up two-to-one. Alexa passed me the ball. With a speed I only seemed to possess on the field, I ran down to our goal, sidestepping through the other team's defensive net as easily as if they'd laid out a path for me. I had almost made it to the goal when a girl the size of a bulldozer charged me.

I blinked. Her face twisted. I froze.

A protruding forehead. Long teeth. Hulking body—the beast stared at me.

I blinked again. Her face returned to normal.

It was too late. The girl knocked me to the ground, grabbing the ball from me. She turned to pass it off, but Alexa intercepted it and lobbed the ball at the goal. It hit the pole, and I saw it turn to fall back outside, but a sudden shift of wind pushed it in instead.

The girls on our team cheered.

Alexa sauntered over to me. "It's a good thing you have me to back you up."

She held out her hand. I slapped it.

I grinned at her, my heart filling. To both our surprise, I hugged her. "Sisters are forever."

***

After school, I walked past the curb packed with lower-classmen waiting for the buses to come. A '70s red Corvette roared up the curb from the student parking lot. The freshmen stared at the fancy car with awed eyes. We lived in one of the wealthier towns just outside of Boston. A Corvette wasn't an uncommon sight in the student lot, but Grey's happened to be a vintage restoration. It screamed for attention.

Grey rolled the driver's side window down. "I've got to take Alexa home. Her car won't start. I told Mom not to let her buy that European scrapheap."

Alexa leaned toward me past her brother. "Tell him it's a classic, not a heap. And he should get something other than a two-seater. There are three of us now."

Grey turned red in the face. "I already asked Mom for a Land Rover—"

I rolled my eyes. "I'll take the bus. I'll be fine."

A mammoth yellow bus turned into the school lot. It grumbled up the lane, but had to stop just a few feet from the Corvette that blocked the whole lane. The door of the bus opened with a bang and the harried driver came bustling out wearing a thick coat and Bruins wool cap.

"Whaddya think you're doing?" He stopped short when he

saw it was Grey. Tommy had been driving Grey and Alexa since they were in kindergarten.

Tommy gave them a huge smile. "How's that gorgeous mother of yours?"

"Working too much, as usual, Tommy." Grey smiled his most charming smile. He glanced at me. "Ryan's going to need a ride out to the manor."

The deafening rev of a high-powered engine filled the air. Like a rocket, Matt's sleek Ducati thundered up the drive.

Matt took off a top-of-the-line Arai helmet and quirked a brow at me. "I can take her. Save the bus a trip up to the manor."

"No one is going with you, Emrys." Grey bit out. "Haven't you noticed it's raining?"

Right on cue, a giant whooshing sound hissed from below the bus. The bus tilted as its back tires deflated in front of our eyes. A cacophony of groans filled the air.

Matt extended his hand. "Please, Ryan."

I hesitated. I should say no. Why did I want to say yes?

Fat raindrops slid down from the grey sky like wriggling worms.

Before I realized it, my hand was slipping into his. He didn't have on gloves. Big, warm hands wrapped around mine. The warmth seemed to spread through his hands all the way into my bones. I climbed on the bike behind him and sank against his back. A thrill of pleasure shot through me. My fingers curled—and probably my toes. Not that I could see them to confirm.

"Ryan!" Grey and Alexa protested at the same time.

"It's only drizzling. I'll see you at home," I said.

The Ducati's steel heart roared to life. The next thing I knew, I was plastered to Matt's back, a white helmet on my head, as the bike flew out of the school gates and onto the street.

The streets of Concord dipped and rose, making the ride more akin to a roller coaster than a steady skate. Painted with fall leaves of red, brown, and gold, the picturesque town of closely-knit buildings, upscale Victorian houses, plus the occasional patriotic red farmhouse, complete with horses, looked like the perfect New England town. The chill of wind seeped through the crevices of my coat. We stopped at a red light under an antique-looking streetlamp that marked the end of the main part of town.

"How can you drive this in the rain?" I asked.

Matt shrugged. "Rain doesn't fall on me."

Oddly, he was right. Droplets seemed to fall around us, but not on us. The light turned and the Ducati took off. My cheek slammed into Matt's shoulder. The scent of sandalwood soap and synthetic leather filled my senses—Matt didn't like real leather.

We turned off onto a one-lane road marked by a plain red mailbox. Small gravel paths splintered off the main road and through the woods, eventually leading to grand, isolated houses. The sky grew dark as a cloud moved over us. Matt cursed and swerved the Ducati. If I'd been plastered to him before, now I could have been a second skin.

Matt jerked the Ducati to and fro.

"What are you doing?" I said.

"We're being followed."

I glanced behind us. There was nothing. A prickle at the back of my neck made me glance up. My breath hitched. A diaphanous shadow the size of a big rig swarmed over us. It swooped down.

Matt muttered, "Why did I get you a white helmet?"

Matt said a word I didn't recognize. A strange wind swept over my head and my helmet buzzed. My ears hurt. In the bike's side mirror, I saw the color of my helmet was now *black...* I blinked. Was I seeing things? My arms tightened around Matt. "Matt, stop the bike!"

He ignored me. "Hang on."

The Ducati swerved again. We slipped in oil-slicked black ice that ran along the road gutter. I screamed when the Ducati skidded. The bike started to overturn. We dipped so far that my head should have scraped the ground, but Matt put out his hand and somehow the bike righted itself.

We sped down narrow streets off the well-worn paths and further into the countryside. Crossing a sleepy cemetery just outside town, we pulled off the street. The Ducati zigzagged in and out of trees, but the shadow stayed with us. Branches and tree limbs hit back at us as we burst past them.

Matt pulled the bike to a screeching halt inside an isolated clearing.

The shadow landed in front of us. It was about five times as tall as us, with a long serpentine body and two giant wings. The wings had no feathers. Instead, their surface seemed as blank as an abyss. As if sensing my gaze, the shadow looked down. Round, glowing, red eyes locked on me like those of a hungry dragon finally catching sight of its prey. Its beak opened.

"What is that?" I screamed.

Matt pulled out a sword from a saddlebag on the Ducati—a saddlebag I'd never noticed until that moment. He threw the sword at me. I grabbed it out of reflex.

"What am I supposed to with this?"

He dug around in the saddlebag. "You used to take fencing lessons—"

"How did you know that?" I hadn't fenced since my mother died.

"I'll tell you later." He pointed to the shadow while he pulled out a book and some plastic packets.

"Are you serious? You're going to read?"

Matt flipped open the book. "Just keep it occupied."

I debated running off into the woods. I debated slapping myself to get out of whatever nightmare I was having. But I couldn't leave Matt.

Then, the shadow swooped down, solidified somehow, and took shape—into the shadow of a giant dragon. Not knowing what to do, I hacked away at it without any sort of plan. The shadow-dragon swiped back with wings like claws. I ducked and hacked again as its teeth snapped at me. Every time the sword connected with the shadow-dragon, my arms rang in pain, as if I swung against solid rock.

The shadow-dragon opened its mouth and a stream of fire roared out. Instinctively, I raised the sword above my head. Fire blasted the sword, but instead of burning me to ashes, it redirected back onto the beast.

The dragon screamed as the fire singed its side. It swiped a hand at me. Deep claws shredded through the skin on my right side. I screamed. Blood oozed through my clothes. I dropped the sword.

The dragon poised for its final attack. I was going to be burned alive.

Grey's Corvette roared through the woods.

I heard Alexa shout, "I see Ryan. Get closer."

The Corvette turned directly into the path of the shadow. Grey rammed the car into the shadow. The dragon screamed, but didn't retreat. Its wing slammed the Corvette like a batter hitting a giant red ball. The car flew into the air, flipped, and then crashed back into the snow.

"No!" I cried.

The dragon's seething eyes turned back to me. The Corvette's door opened and Alexa jumped out. She started to head to me, but stumbled on the sword I'd dropped.

"Alexa!" Matt held a packet in his hand and ran to her. "Give me the sword."

The dragon opened its mouth and a blast of fire scorched the leaves just beneath my feet. I tried to back away, but, in a step, it had reached me.

"No!" Alexa ran in front of the dragon with the sword.

The dragon swiped her away with little thought. The sword went flying… and landed right at Matt's feet. Matt grabbed the sword. He sprinkled something on the blade and yelled, "*Sarati!*"

The word scraped my ears and spun around the glade, bouncing off the trees.

The shadow-dragon swooped down at him.

Matt threw the sword. It landed in the middle of the shadow's chest. The beast let out an outraged bellow as the sword slid down the beast's black belly, cutting cleanly through half the beast's body. By the time the sword had reached the ground, the shadow had evaporated.

Matt rushed to where I lay on the ground. He swung me up in his arms.

"Why didn't you just do that in the first place?" I demanded.

"I needed the dissolving powder or it would just get angry instead of dead."

Pain blurred my vision. "Alexa. Grey. Make sure they're okay."

"First, you." Matt laid me on my side.

My head lolled against his chest. A drizzle of rain slapped my face.

"Stay with me, Ryan."

I tried to protest. A warbled sound came out of my mouth. Lethargy made my body weak.

"Wake up, Ryan." Matt opened my shirt roughly. "Damn

beast. This is going to take all my strength."

A sharp pain spread out like creeping vines from the wound on my side. With small clawing tentacles, it shook my body. I writhed on the ground.

I'm pretty sure I drooled.

Just as I thought I could take no more, a hand yanked away the vines. They shrunk back. Pain receded.

And it was over.

Matt flipped me onto my back. I stared at him dully. He looked normal… not even winded… except for the slight sheen of blue fire that seemed to dance in an outline around him.

I blinked. The blue fire disappeared, leaving me to wonder if I'd imagined it.

His hand slid down my bare ribs. "That was the easiest healing I've ever done."

I sat up shakily. "Alexa. Grey."

Matt ran to the upside-down Corvette and forced open the driver's side door.

"He's fine." Matt pulled a shaken Grey out of the car.

"R-Ryan?" Grey said groggily. "Alexa?"

I slowly got up and glanced around the eerily quiet clearing. All around us trees with leaves of orange and red swayed in silent rhythm. But I saw no sign of Alexa. My body shook with the effort of staying upright. Matt came back and caught me before I dropped back to the ground.

"Matt? Where is she?" I said hoarsely.

Setting me on a waist-high boulder, Matt closed his eyes.

Leaves around us shifted. A huge stack of them moved to reveal a limp Alexa on the ground.

My heart stilled. I pushed myself up. Grey and Matt were already sprinting to her. Grey reached her first and picked her up. Her head flopped at an odd angle. Grey's cry tore through the clearing, clawing at my ears.

I fought to breathe. "M-Matt?"

Across the clearing, he looked at me with sad eyes.

I hobbled over to Alexa. "Help her. Like you did me."

Matt closed her eyes. "It doesn't work like that. I can't heal her. She's too far gone."

I dropped to my knees. The ground, wet and soft, gave way to my weight. My knees sank into mud. Wet drops streamed down my face. My body hurt, feeling all at once every hit and every cut.

In the sky, fast-moving clouds crashed and collided with each other. Droplets of rain and wind-ravaged leaves fell here and there in jagged bits with no particular pattern.

I fought to stay upright.

How could this happen again? I couldn't handle it. Not again.

Matt knelt down beside me. He put a hand on my back. Warmth seeped into my numb skin. It burned, molten fire into solid ice.

Pulling at the last vestige of my strength, I jerked away from him.

"What are you?" I demanded.

BETRAYED

Amber-brown eyes stared into my soul. "Are you sure you want to know?"

"Alexa—" I swallowed. Hard. "I need to know."

Matt said a soft word. A breeze whirled around us. He waved his hand at the trees that canopied us from the bleak sky. They rustled as they opened to show the clouds. They parted just enough to let in a few rays of sunlight. Light streamed down and illuminated the Old North Bridge. The place of the first battle of the American Revolution—the shot that was heard around the world.

Matt took my cold hands and pressed them in his. "I'm a wizard, Ryan."

***

Matt put the helmet back on me and slung me up on the Ducati. I don't know how he held me in place, since I couldn't seem to focus on anything, but within minutes, we were bursting through the thicket of trees beyond the clearing.

Clouds raced us as we sped past the quiet graves at Sleepy Hollow Cemetery. The cemetery reminded me of the aftermath of a great battle, like the one I felt I'd just fought. The Ducati sped down the narrow road, balanced so delicately that any moment it could fall off the sharp edges of the road.

The red Corvette followed us as if it had a mind of its own. Matt had put a zombie-like Grey inside. Upon reaching town, we plunged down a gravel lane through another barrier of thick brush. There, nestled against a backdrop of long-limbed trees, under a single ray of sun in an otherwise grey sky, stood Ragnar manor.

The first time I saw the gothic monstrosity, nothing had seemed more foreign from the two-bedroom townhouse under the scorching Texas sun that I had grown up in. Matt drove the Ducati down the lane, pulled the bike halfway around a circular driveway, and stopped in between a gurgling stone fountain and the front door.

I scrambled off the bike. My knees folded. My helmet would have met concrete, but Matt caught me about the waist. He tugged the helmet off with one hand.

"You're still weak," he said. "Try not to move too much. I've told your body to heal, but it's not instantaneous. The Ragnars enchanted the manor long ago. We should be safe here... for now."

The Corvette rumbled up behind us. Matt had done something to it to make it follow us to the manor like a faithful puppy.

The front door of the manor opened wide as Sylvia, Grey and Alexa's mom, stepped outside. My chest squeezed with anxiety—as usual Sylvia looked immaculate. I'd known her forever. She had been my mother's best friend since they were children. They could have passed for twins.

Unlike anything my gym-teacher mother would have worn, Sylvia had on an expensive navy business suit with padded shoulders. Yet she pulled it off. The president of Ragnar Bank and Commodities projected smooth control. She seemed ready for anything.

Sylvia's assistant, Marla, a thirty-something with one long streak of white in her otherwise jet black hair, followed close behind her. She spoke accented English into her cell. "…who cares about a tiny tremor? We're still here, *yes*? The markets will quiet."

Sylvia marched toward us. "Ryan, are you all right?"

Her words were uttered calmly, but there was steel underneath. Tears sprung into my eyes. I pushed away from Matt. Sylvia came closer… and noticed the scratches on the Corvette. The broken side faced away from us.

"What?" she muttered.

The Corvette's engine cut. It sat silent in the courtyard— beaten and broken. Sylvia's heels clicked in sharp staccato as she strode straight to it and pulled open the driver's side handle.

Grey stumbled out of the driver's side with a wild look. "It wouldn't open!"

Sylvia caught him by the shoulders. "Grey! Are you okay?"

Grey shook his head. "Alexa."

"Where is your sister?" Sylvia said sharply.

Matt stepped forward. "There was an attack, Mrs. Ragnar. I'm sorry."

Sylvia paled. She ran to the Corvette's passenger side. I heard her yank it open, but I couldn't look. She let out a horrible mewling cry.

The wounded sound pierced through me like a knife in the gut. I swayed in place.

Matt put an arm around my shoulders in support.

I shook him away. "Just don't, Matt."

"What happened?" Sylvia demanded.

Matt went to the Corvette. He put his hand on the passenger door to shut it again. Sylvia stopped him.

"Who are you?" she barked at him.

Although not much taller, Matt seemed to tower over Sylvia. "My name is Matt Emrys. I have been sent from the Council."

"Council," gasped Marla. She came up beside me.

"What council?" I asked.

"The Council governs all of wizard-kind," Matt said.

Marla crossed to the car. Digging out a spare blanket from the trunk, she brought it around and smoothed it over Alexa. Sylvia bit into her own fisted hands. For the first time since I'd known her, she didn't seem in charge of the world. She looked lost, alone, and out of her depth.

"W-what happened to my daughter?" Sylvia asked.

Matt bowed his head. "We were attacked. By the time I got to her, it was too late. I am sorry."

Grey's head jerked up. "Ryan had blood all over her. That thing nearly shredded her, but you fixed her."

"Yes," Matt said. "She was only wounded. I could heal her."

"Heal her, but not Alexa." Grey blinked. "You're full of shit, Emrys."

"Grey," I said faintly. "I'm so sorry."

Grey gave me a bleak look. "She made me follow the bike. She wanted to protect you."

My legs heavy under a crushing weight that seemed to have overtaken my entire body, I crossed the cobblestone driveway one stone block at a time. I put a hand on Grey's arm. "She did protect me."

He flinched.

I dropped my arm.

Grey walked to Sylvia. She leaned back against him. I doubted either one could have stood on their own.

Sylvia's eyes remained fixed on Matt. "Who attacked them?"

Matt returned a steady gaze. "Gargoyles."

"Gargoyles?" Marla repeated.

"Have you lost your mind, Emrys?" Grey said.

"Enough, Grey." In a tired voice, Sylvia said to Matt, "I'm sorry. I haven't kept him familiar with our family history."

Matt nodded as if he was used to such deferential treatment—something I wasn't used to giving. With effort, I pushed away the lethargy overtaking my body.

I let out a pained laugh. "Gargoyles? That's ridiculous. I suggest you trade in the biker jacket for a straight one."

Matt looked back at me with utter seriousness. "Is it as ridiculous as a dragon?"

Deep in my gut something uncomfortable stirred. A small gust of wintry wind flew through the driveway. I glared at him. "Why would anyone attack us?"

"What do the gargoyles want with us?" Marla asked.

"Not you." Matt said. "Grey is the candidate—"

Grey's head jerked up. "What?"

Sylvia hugged herself. "Grey has never shown any wizard traits. Alexa—" She stopped and swallowed. "Alexa had shown some telekinetic abilities. But not Grey."

"Candidates need not have magic. King Arthur was not one." Matt paused. "I have been watching Grey for a long time."

"What do you mean *watching*?" I said.

Matt didn't look at me. "If he wishes to live through the next few months, he must be protected."

"Mom." Grey turned to Sylvia. "I want to know what is going on right now."

"I know." Sylvia put a shaky hand on her son.

"Since the manor has some protection, I've asked the other candidates to rendezvous here. They will be here tonight," said Matt.

"No one is coming inside my house," Grey shouted.

"It's not just your house," Sylvia snapped.

Grey took a step back, as if she'd slapped him. I was surprised, too. I'd never so much as heard a cross word from Sylvia to Grey in the entire year I'd been living at the manor. Grey was her darling—the one who could do no wrong. Alexa and I had commiserated about it more than once. My chest tightened as I realized we never would again.

"Sylvia, what is going on?" I asked.

She looked at me as if she'd forgotten I was there. "I will tell you and Grey everything. Right now, I have to make arrangements." Her voice broke on the last word.

Marla put a hand on her shoulder. "But of course, I will do it."

I said, "We have to call the police."

Marla shook her head. "You can't—"

"Everyone knows Grey and Alexa drove off together. You can't hide this," I said.

Matt stared at the Corvette. "I think I can help."

Matt flicked his wrist. A giant gust of wind swirled around us like a tornado. It picked up the car and smashed it upside-down into the fountain. The passenger side had been completely crushed.

Alexa was still in the car.

We all gaped at the wreckage in stunned stupor.

Then, Sylvia let out a hiccupping cry. She crumpled into Grey's arms.

As he held his sobbing mother in his arms, Grey shot Matt a furious look. "Bastard."

***

It was almost evening by the time the police finished taking our statements. We stuck to the story that the Corvette lost traction coming down the lane into the driveway.

We gathered in the Ragnar's majestic living room. Mammoth brown-leather couches dominated the space, Rajasthan rugs softened hardwood floors, and floor to ceiling French doors opened to the woods outside. A stone hearth—fireplace was too bland a word for it—stood in the corner and went all the way up the thirty-foot wall. The living room opened to the second story of the house.

I sat in my favorite chair—a wood rocker next to a jeweled lamp where I could watch the gorgeously tall evergreens sway with the breeze. I pulled a cashmere throw around my shoulders and huddled into it. The smell of pumpkin bread lingered on it. Alexa and I had cooked and decorated the house last night. A wave of depression struck me, and I struggled to push it back.

Out of the five couches in the room, Grey sank down on the couch next to the rocker. I held his hand. He had remained stone-faced through the whole process.

A ruddy-faced detective asked Grey, "Mr. Ragnar, one last time. The car slid down the drive and overturned, crushing your sister, but you were able to pull yourself out without even getting a scratch. Is that exactly what happened?"

Grey looked at Matt. "No."

The detective's gaze sharpened.

Matt touched his arm.

The detective blinked, looked confused for a moment, and then stared at his notepad. "Forgot what I was saying," he muttered. He wiped a hand over his face and closed the pad. "It's been a pretty crazy day with the Total Tremor and all. Too many accidents. I hope they find out what's responsible quickly." He gave us a brief nod. "I think that is all, Mr. Ragnar, Miss DuLac. And again, I am very sorry for your loss."

A few minutes later, the police had all cleared out of the manor. Grey went to stand at the window to watch them carry Alexa away.

Matt watched him. "The Council has entrusted me with the task of finding candidates. I have been traveling the world for over a year now. Only a candidate can lift the sword from the stone. It's part of the sword's protection. One must be worthy."

Sylvia drew a sweater around her. Her fingers trembled and I could tell she was trying to hold it together... for Grey, for me. "Grey is a Regular. He can't be a candidate."

"Let me get this straight." I cut in. "You think Grey is some King Arthur candidate. You came here to scout him."

For the first time since I'd gotten on the Ducati—just this afternoon, but it seemed like a lifetime ago—Matt the mighty wizard looked uncertain. He said hesitatingly, "Y-Yes."

I leaned back hard in the rocker. He'd become friends with me to get to Grey.

Matt cleared his throat. "Once the candidates arrive, we will leave. You may take one bag."

"I'm not going anywhere, Emrys—not on your say so,"

Grey bit out.

Sylvia said, "Grey, why don't you go rest? You need time to yourself—"

"There is no time." Matt pushed a button on a large remote and a hidden panel opened to reveal a flat-screen TV. He switched channels until he found one covering Trafalgar Square.

A reporter in a fitted suit stood in front of a long line of people. "Speculation about the Total Tremor continues. From all over the Isles, they have traveled to London. Tourists and residents are lining up for one purpose—to wait their turn, their chance, to pull the sword. Yes, that is correct. You know how the story goes—King Arthur pulled the sword from the stone and became the king of England."

The camera panned to the line of soldiers, wearing heavy Kevlar and carrying long machine guns, who stood guard around the square.

"The British government has been flooded by demands. Countries all around the world have sent delegates to be present for whatever the stone may yield. They believe—as the Total Tremor indicated—whatever happens with the sword here will affect the whole world."

The camera cut to a bearded man in front of the crowd. In a thick British accent, he declared, "I'm not leaving until I get my chance. You can tell the minister. You can tell the queen. It's my right."

Others around him murmured in agreement. They held up signs ranging from "OUR SWORD. OUR CHANCE," "IT'S

THE END," to "SAVE THE WORLD. PULL THE SWORD."

"What do you think will happen if someone does pull the sword?" the reporter asked him.

"Not sure. Something. Nothing. Who cares? No one will forget the bloke who pulled the sword. Point is—you won't find out if you don't try."

Another man leaned in front of him. "The end is here. Listen to the legend. Arthur won't come back until the land needs him. It's the end. The sword is our one chance. We can't just sit back."

"It can't be real," I murmured.

Matt muted the sound.

Sylvia clasped her hands together. She sighed. "It is real. It is also our heritage. Everything you know about the legend is true—to a certain extent, that is. King Arthur. Merlin. They were all real." She pointed to the TV showing a close up of the giant stone.

"Heritage?" Grey scowled. "We're all descended from Merlin?"

Matt let out an odd, choked cough. "No. Many families had magic. Merlin just happens to be the most famous."

A shadow crossed Grey's patrician features. "All those times Alexa knew who was at the door. The night Dad died. She dreamt about him on the plane."

Sylvia bowed her head. "The night your father died… everything changed. The family has run the bank for centuries. I never knew until then that its main commodity was…"

"Magic," Matt finished for her.

Grey jumped up. "Do you know how crazy you sound?"

Matt pointed to the TV. The jagged black stone, half the size of a semi-truck, took up most of the screen. "What about that? Is it real?"

"I. Don't. Care," Grey said.

Matt made an impatient sound. "Haven't you ever wondered why you've succeeded in every sport you've tried? You have incredible reflexes—almost as if you see the action before it happens. It's because you are a candidate."

Grey scowled. "I'm not anything to you."

"Our race is called Keltoi. Some called themselves druids. Not Merlin, but a fringe group of wizards. Mostly, we were just like everyone else—struggling to survive. Except we had one advantage. We could control the natural elements. Magic, as you would call it. During Arthur's time, the Keltoi were quite numerous, but everything changed after the Battle at Mt. Camlan." A shadow crossed over Matt's face. "When Arthur died at Mt. Camlan, the age of wizards and man living together passed. Eventually, the wizards formed their own society away from those they called the Regulars. It was at the same time that the gargoyles disappeared. Both races have been blending into the background of civilization for millennia."

The large windows in the living room showed swaying trees, hovering like gargantuan guardians over the house. I didn't want to ask, but I did anyway.

"Why did the sword appear now?" I said.

"Something very bad is coming—"

I knew Matt well enough to read a lie on him. "You don't know."

His lips twisted into a small smile. "It doesn't matter. The gargoyles want it. And they are willing to kill whoever stands in the way."

Sylvia hugged herself. "I can't believe the gargoyles would do this. They don't have that much magic…"

Matt pinned her with a derisive look. "Except what merchants like you sell to them. The gargoyles have been amassing power without us even knowing it. We are at war and because of you, we're losing."

Sylvia lowered her eyes. "The Council never stopped me."

"The Council has been shortsighted. They don't want to take up the problem of regulating the sale of magic. I'm trying to change that."

"Mom, you're a *banker*," Grey said. "Magic is not real!"

Matt flicked his hand. The whole sofa floated up a few inches. Grey jumped up as if he'd been sitting on a bed of lava. He leaped across it at Matt. His agility impressed me. Grey hadn't become a jock by accident.

Before Grey reached him, Matt flicked his hand in the air again. Grey flew back. His shoulders hit the wall with a forceful thud. This time, Grey got up much more slowly.

I stepped in between them and faced down Matt. "You've proven your point."

"I wanted to show him what would happen if a gargoyle came bursting through the door right now." Matt locked eyes with Grey. "Believe me, it would be the last thing you'd ever see. You're no more than a pup—one easily culled."

Grey's nostrils flared like a bull about to charge.

Marla burst into the room. "You need to see this."

She hit the volume button on the remote. The clipped voice of the bubbly reporter blared through the flat screen. Yet, this time her face was a mask of sorrow. "This just in—we have had a death in Trafalgar Square. Twenty-five year old Gianni Russo traveled to London from Venice, Italy, to try his hand at the legendary sword. But he will never return home again." A scene of medical vans and police in the square filled the screen.

The reporter continued. "At approximately nine-thirty this morning, his turn at the sword came up. He stepped up onto the rock and touched the hilt of the sword. Those in the line behind him said nothing happened. He stepped off the rock and was on his way out of the square."

The camera panned to bring the reporter and a middle-aged man in focus. The reporter stuck a microphone in the man's face. "Can you tell us what you saw?"

"He was there at the edge of the square." The man pointed to where police had set up ropes to funnel an exit out of Trafalgar Square. "Almost out. Then, he gripped his arm tight, and I saw him fall to the ground."

"Thank you, sir," the reporter said. The camera panned back on him. "We don't have confirmation yet. It appears to be a heart attack. However, relatives who'd come on the trip with Gianni Russo said he'd been in perfect health—"

I muted the TV. "Gianni was a candidate?"

"Yes," said Matt. "There is risk in trying for the sword."

My voice rose. "And you want Grey to do this?"

"Yes." Matt pointed at the long line of people on TV who surrounded the stone. "We must find the sword bearer. Imagine the power it gave to King Arthur. With it, he reshaped the world. We must make sure it doesn't fall into the wrong hands. Why do you think the gargoyles sent the dragon? To wipe out any candidate that is not theirs."

"How do you even know Grey's a candidate?" I demanded. "Who says so?"

"I do." Matt's crystal-hard gaze locked with mine. "I am the one person in the world who can seek out candidates and I am not wrong. I have foreseen it."

"You are a seer." Sylvia looked at him with a half-scared, half-awed expression. "There has only ever been one with name the *Emrys*. You are his descendant?"

I frowned. "What is a seer?"

Matt's lips twisted into a grimace. "I see the future."

***

I rested my elbows against the ledge of the balcony outside my room and tried to breathe. In the middle of the driveway, under the artificial light of the driveway lamp, sat the dry carcass of the fountain. Half of an ugly stone creature stared up at me. A wrinkled forehead, a dog's face, outstretched wings—it was a gargoyle, I realized.

The front door flew open below me. Russet-brown strands of Matt's hair gleamed in the fading light as he hurried to his bike. Despite myself, my chest gave an odd squeeze at the sight of him. As if he could read my thoughts, his head snapped up. I stepped back into the shadows of the balcony hoping he wouldn't spot me.

"Ryan." Matt stood on the ledge of the balcony.

My mouth opened and closed. Against the backdrop of the sinking sky, his silhouette seemed to be surrounded by a faint blue glow.

I said inanely, "How did you do that?"

Matt raised an amused brow. "I *am* a wizard."

"Great. Why don't you wizard yourself back down?"

Matt jumped off the ledge and onto the balcony. "I know you're upset."

"That doesn't begin to cover it." I stepped back farther into the shadows.

He inclined his head. "Are you hiding from me?"

I didn't answer.

"Why are you out here?"

I hugged my arms to myself. "I couldn't sleep. I keep thinking about—" In a rush, I said, "The dragon. It's like it lives behind my eyelids. Just waiting for me to fall asleep."

In a blink, Matt had his arms around me. He pulled me tight against him. Warmth surrounded me, pushing out the bitter chill. For a second, I let it seep into my frigid bones. I let it reach inside me, a lifeline out of the icy abyss that threatened to swallow me from within.

"You'll be okay," he murmured into my ear. "You're not alone."

I pulled away from him. "I am alone, Matt. Because of you.

I lost my sister. You're trying to take my brother. Tell me, Matt. How am I not alone?"

Whirling away from him, I stomped to the door and back into my room.

"Just go away."

"I can't." The words seemed like almost a sigh.

My heart stilled and then restarted. The guy was a lying liar. *Lying liar?* Even in my head I sounded like a baby.

I burst out, "You used me to get to Grey."

"Yes," he replied without apology.

There was a pause. A long one. I was the first one to break. I turned my head to look at him. "So what's left to say?"

Matt got up. Heat radiated off his body. His gaze caressed my face. "I need you—"

I cocked a brow. "You're looking to hook up?"

He chuckled. "Not exactly."

"I need you, Ryan," he said softly. "You're a candidate, too."

A NEW ROAD

My jaw dropped open. "What?"

Matt bluntly said, "I had hoped never to tell you."

"You said every candidate needed to come forward."

"There has never been a female candidate chosen before this ascension."

I gaped at him. "I'm excused because I'm a *girl*? What kind of ass-backwards thinking is that?"

Matt gave me an affronted look. "We haven't had an ascension since Arthur's time. Things were a little different back then. I'm only trying to protect you—"

"I'm the only one—the only girl?"

Matt ground his teeth. "No, we have identified others."

"Did you tell the others?"

"No. Not yet."

My eyes narrowed. "Did you plan to tell the others?"

Matt's cheeks turned a guilty red.

"Why not me?" I demanded.

"You're just so… nice," he muttered.

I sighed. *They all thought I could do nothing.* "Are these gargoyles going to stop coming after me because I'm a girl? When were you going to tell me that I was putting everyone around me in danger?" I took a step toward him with murderous intent.

"I understand you need time, Ryan, but we don't have much." He backed up all the way to the ledge and jumped off the balcony.

I couldn't help it. I ran to where he'd jumped off, half expecting him to be splattered on the ground. He'd landed nimbly on his feet. He looked up, saw me, and grinned.

My heart did a yo-yo.

I stuck out my hand and flipped him off.

***

The house sat silent in pitch dark. I lay awake. The bedroom doorknob turned. I sat up.

Matt burst into the room, stopped midstride, and gaped at me.

I only had on a skimpy nude camisole. And one side had slipped down to expose most of my cleavage. I snatched up the bed sheets.

Matt colored. "They are coming."

I flew out of bed. Going to the window, I threw aside the curtain and heard… crickets. Nothing moved in the early morning light. The driveway stood completely empty.

"I don't see anything." I frowned.

Matt tapped his forehead. "I do. I just saw it."

I touched the windowpane. The glass was a sheet of ice. I shivered and turned back to look at Matt. His gaze fell on me and lingered. I shivered again, but this time it had nothing to do with the cold. Matt adroitly turned away, only to meet my gaze through the reflection of a dresser mirror next to my bed.

Light glinted off the gold-brown strands of my hair. Bits of refracted green shone from the pendant necklace I wore.

"Your necklace is broken," he commented.

I touched the chain around my neck. I moved closer to stand behind him and look into the mirror. The emerald pendant had a deep crack through it.

"The dragon must have broken it during the fight," I murmured. "Guess it wasn't real."

"It compliments your eyes," he said. "How did you get it?"

"Sylvia. She said it used to be my mother's. They'd traded it long ago. But she said that I needed the charm now more than her."

"Charm? I imagine so." Matt let out a small cry and clutched his forehead. His eyes pinched shut. His face twisted in pain.

I put a hand on the broad expanse of his back. "Matt?"

Instantly, Matt's face smoothed. He shook off my hand. His eyes opened and fixed on my skimpy top. He made a strangled sound. "Do you think you can put on some clothes?"

In the mirror, I saw my cheeks turn red. He looked big and

hulking behind me. His eyes still dark with pain and…
something else that I didn't trust myself to identify. Next to
him, I looked more waif than woman. But the intense way he
stared at my reflection made me want less clothes, not more,
and for a moment, allowed me to hold back the horrors of the
day.

I went to my closet. The custom walk-in closet Sylvia had
built for me—no small feat in a hundred-year-old manor. I
eyed the shelves crammed with clothes. I admit, I might have
let Sylvia spoil me just a bit. Okay, maybe a lot.

I grabbed a pair of corduroys and a long-sleeved shirt. I
pulled on the clothes and picked up some boots. As I came out
of the closet, I asked, "What did you see?"

The relieved expression he'd gotten after seeing me dressed
disappeared.

"W-what do you mean?"

I gave him a suspicious look. Had he been peeking? "You
had a vision, didn't you?"

"Oh, yes," he said with a quick grin. He leaned back on the
dresser.

"And you saw?" I prompted.

His expression closed. "It's better you don't know. The
things I see… aren't always understandable."

"Have you ever been wrong?"

"It's possible, I suppose. But, no, I've never been wrong."

I crossed to him. "That doesn't sound bearable."

He glanced at the window. "Sometimes it's a relief when it

finally does happen. Until then, I alone have to live with it in my head." His expression became bleak. "If the gargoyles get what they want, Ryan, if they get the sword… what they can do to the world is unimaginable."

I stilled. "Try me."

"Worse than World War III. Worse than a thousand Hiroshimas. It will be the end."

I blinked. "Even if I believe that this sword is that powerful, why would they do that? Why would anyone?"

"They won't mean to. But it will be their fate. If they get Arthur's sword, they will have no one to guide them—"

"Like you," I said shrewdly. "Merlin complex, much?"

"I admit, I may sound a bit dramatic." Matt smiled. As if he couldn't help it, his hand reached out to brush across my hair. After a brief hesitation, I leaned into the comfort his touch offered.

Time seemed to stand still for a long moment as we stood in the warm confines of my bedroom. For a second, I could forget everything, and he was just… Matt. The boy from school.

He pulled me closer. His hand tightened in my hair.

Sirens began blaring all over the house.

ENEMY MINE

Matt and I ran out into the hall.

Grey burst out of his room in sweatpants, his hair stuck to one side of his face. "What's going on?"

Marla came out of her room. "What is happening?"

Sylvia hurried down the hallway. "It's the perimeter alarm—the magical one. We've got maybe ten minutes until they reach the house."

Matt's phone beeped. He pulled it out. "It's a text from the other candidates. They are coming down the lane. But the gargoyles are not far behind, by what I've seen in my vision. We're going to need decoys." He looked at Sylvia. "We're going to need your cars."

Sylvia nodded. "This way."

***

Marla flipped on the lights as we entered the long garage. In the three-car space, there stood a silver Mercedes, Sylvia's car, and a nondescript SUV, the family's spare car. Sylvia crossed to the closed fourth garage and pushed a button on a separating column in between. A steel partition opened. Instead of Marla's small import, a big, black Land Rover waited silently.

Sylvia turned to me with a wan smile. "I was saving it for Christmas."

"I don't know what to say." In a few strides, I crossed to her and hugged the taller woman close. "Thank you."

"At least I got a chance to show it to you." Sylvia sniffed into my hair. "A-Alexa wanted to be the one to give you the keys."

Grey slipped the keys from Sylvia's fingers and tossed them in a wide arc to Matt. "You can take it or the SUV. We'll go in the Mercedes."

A brief wind dropped the keys into Matt's hands.

"Cheater," Grey muttered under his breath.

"Ryan is coming with me," said Matt. "She's also a candidate."

Grey balked. "What?"

"What?" Sylvia echoed.

Matt opened the garage doors. Outside stood a line of six black SUVs. In front of the cars, a group of about twenty or so men had gathered. Half of them looked to be boys ranging between sixteen to twenty years old. The other half of the group was older.

"The other candidates." Matt waved at them. "And their wizard guardians."

Matt turned to a craggy-faced older man. "Where are the other three cars?"

"The ones from the South were... found," he said grimly. "No doubt it'll be a blip in a local news report. The gargoyles have gotten clever at hiding their tracks."

Thinking of the shadow-dragon's destruction, I muttered, "Sometimes."

"I am Oliver." A cute boy wearing a wristband stepped forward with an easy smile. "And this is my guardian, Clarence."

The older craggy-faced man nodded at us. "I'm afraid we may have been followed."

"I know. I had a vision," Matt replied grimly. "We don't have much time. Split the candidates up between the two Jeeps in the garage and the first three of our cars. I want two guardians in each. The remaining guardians will take our other Jeeps and try to lead the gargoyles away. Save space for me in the Land Rover." He glanced at me and Grey. "As well as two others."

Grey opened his mouth to protest.

"Paul's father asked that you call him after we reached here," another guardian said.

"All of the parents have asked for you specifically," Clarence interjected.

Matt nodded. "Of course. I'll call them from the road—"

"The animals tell me there is a disturbance in the woods," one of the guardians shouted.

Suddenly, everything seemed to happen at once.

"Get everyone in the cars," Matt shouted.

The guardians scrambled, pushing the candidates. One

guardian with tears in his eyes gave his candidate a quick hearty pat on the back before shuffling him into a car.

"I see four big Hummers at the top of the lane," a boy shouted.

Upon the heels of his warning, a bomb seemed to explode upstairs in the manor. The manor shook down to its foundations. Boxes and sports equipment from the racks on the garage ceiling came crashing down. A box almost hit Marla on the head. A large crack tore through the ceiling, snapping the steel track of the bigger garage door as easily as a ribbon. The door started to plunge down. Matt stuck his hand up. The garage door magically stopped mid-fall.

Grey pulled me away from Matt. "You don't have to go, Ryan. This isn't our fight. No matter what Emrys says."

The whole garage shook again as another explosion sounded outside. The acrid smell of smoke indicated who knew what kind of havoc inside the manor. Our home.

"I have to get upstairs," Sylvia cried.

"No," Matt commanded. "You don't have time to get anything. We have to go now."

I looked at him. He stood in the middle of the chaos, yelling directions at the guardians while holding up the garage ceiling. Yet despite it all, he never flinched. His expression seemed almost cold. As if managing every task at once left no room for emotion. Then, sensing my gaze, Matt turned his head to look straight at me. Heat swirled in the faraway depths of his eyes.

I sucked in a breath. I forced myself to turn away.

He walked to me. "Do you want to find out why this is happening to you, Ryan?"

I stilled, a chill falling over me. "What do you mean?"

Matt's gaze became solemn. "Think, Ryan. Your life hasn't been normal for a long time and from what I can surmise, your life hasn't been normal ever. It's because of this. Come with me and you'll see why. You'll see why you're a candidate."

I stared at him. It was a lure. One I wanted very much to swallow. But how could I believe him?

A rumble of noise came from outside. Matt cursed. "We have to go now, Ryan. You need to decide."

Slowly, I found myself taking a step toward the Land Rover.

"Ryan?" Grey said.

Words stuck in my throat. How could I leave them? But I had to do this. I was tired of accepting fate. "I have to go, Grey. They killed Alexa. I can't let them win—"

Grey blanched. "You're right. I'm being gutless. I'm coming too."

"No," I said vehemently. "That's not what I meant. You don't need to go because I am—"

He gave me a crooked smile. "What better reason could I have? We're family, Ry."

Matt pointed me to the open back door of the Land Rover. "Ryan, now!"

I opened my mouth to protest, but the garage shook with such noise I wouldn't have been heard.

Sylvia ran up to us. Grey looked at her. She saw the decision in his eyes before said he could say a word. Tears sprang in her eyes as she pulled us all into a tight farewell embrace.

"Take care of your brother, Ryan," she whispered in my ear.

***

Matt and the other cars pulled out of the driveway just as the four Hummers arrived. More fireballs whizzed by them. There seemed to be shields on the candidates' SUVs since the fireballs kept bouncing off them. Some of the guardians shot fireballs back.

Stray fireballs bombarded the manor. It burned as we sped around to the back of the house. It might have resembled a scene out of a bad movie, except that my heart felt broken. We drove straight into a thicket of trees. At Matt's command, they parted to reveal a hidden lane.

"The Ragnars have been prepared," Matt said.

The group of cars thundered into the thicket. I sat in the passenger seat of the Land Rover. I looked behind to see the Hummers following as we raced along the lane. A few minutes later, we emerged onto a two-lane road that ran behind the manor. Matt stopped the car.

He turned around in his seat and stuck his hand out of the window. "*Pidadhatte.*"

Blue light shot out of his hand. The entire forest seemed to rise up. Trees and vines closed around the hidden lane, swallowing the four Hummers. Oliver, who'd ridden along with us, whooped in the backseat.

"The spell wouldn't have worked if the path had been built differently," Matt said to me. "The Ragnars know how to build an escape route." He pulled out his cell phone and started punching at the screen. The cell phone refused to connect.

"I hate these things," he muttered. He tried again. This time it connected. "Take the long way out of town. The gargoyles will send more. We want them to see you. And I want one of you to lead the Mercedes to safe ground. Good luck."

Matt switched off the phone. He started down the road.

I turned to watch the group of decoy cars lead away the Mercedes.

"We'll take care of them," Matt said. Matt opened and closed his fist. "*Anukrta.*"

Blue light surrounded the troop of cars. A set of phantom cars appeared behind us, looking completely identical. They turned at a split in the road.

"That should confuse them," Matt said with a tired grin.

"You'll tire yourself out," Clarence observed from the backseat. "We need you alert, Master Matt."

"Master Matt?" I muttered.

To my surprise, Matt blushed. "It's a title."

I didn't reply. Down the disappearing length of road, I saw the flames consuming Ragnar Manor. Tears streamed down my face as my home burned. I tried to wipe them away, but wasn't fast enough.

Matt halted the car. Behind us, the caravan screeched to a halt.

"Matt?" I said.

Matt blew out a breath. Gray clouds swirled above us.

"No," Clarence said urgently. "You don't have much left."

Matt closed his eyes. His right hand fisted. "*Varasati.*"

A faint blue glow surrounded his fist. Above us, the clouds turned darker.

With a muttered curse, Clarence dialed his cell. "*Varasati,*" he yelled when it connected.

The diameter of the clouds became bigger and bigger until it reached the manor. The sky thundered in warning. Then, it started raining. On the edge of the horizon, I saw the red outline of flames above the manor dissolve quickly under the watery onslaught.

I grabbed Matt's hand and squeezed it tight.

With a tired smile, Matt slumped in his seat. He blinked as if he were fighting sleep. "I think you're going to need to drive, Ryan." He pointed to a sign on the road for the highway. Underneath it was a direction marker for Boston Logan Airport. "We're booked on a flight in a few hours."

"We're going to London?" Oliver said, clearly excited.

"No, we're going to my home. To England, but not to the sword as of yet. The Council has a stronghold in the countryside." Matt yawned. His eyes shut. "We will be safe there."

***

We arrived at Logan at different terminals. Clarence drove. The group split up into three partitions of about eight people each. One team was going through New York to Manchester.

One had gotten stuck with a stopover in Philadelphia, then to Edinburg, Scotland. I somehow got on the direct flight to London. I actually don't know how we had tickets because the flights were all oversold. A man offered me an outrageous amount for my ticket as soon as he saw where I was headed. Matt, and the few remaining guardians traveling with us, hurried us through the reservations desk to security.

Later, I stood behind Grey in line at the front of the airplane as we boarded.

"Want to trade seats with me?" Grey asked.

"I guess," I said, glancing at my ticket. I was on the aisle. 21C. Then I noticed the number on Grey's ticket. "You have a middle seat!"

"Your legs are shorter than mine," he defended.

I scowled at him. We moved up into the first class cabin. Matt lounged in a window seat a few rows down.

"Comfy?" Grey asked, his voice heavy with sarcasm.

Matt waved his hand. Grey's ticket fluttered in his hand. "Don't say I never did anything for you, Ragnar."

Grey looked down at his ticket. "I'm in 21C."

"Hey!" I looked at my ticket. 3B. It was the empty seat next to Matt. Pushing past Grey, I dropped into the spacious seat. "Nice. We have our own TVs."

Grey gaped at me. The people behind him grumbled as he was blocking the line. With a grimace, he walked into Coach.

I turned to Matt. "You just can't stop yourself from needling him, can you?"

"He thinks he knows everything," Matt said.

"I don't know anyone else like that."

Matt didn't respond. He started rifling through his seat pouch.

"What are you doing?" I settled into my cushy seat.

He pulled out a sick bag. "Looking for this. Prepare yourself. I've gotten sick on every takeoff."

The stewardess came up to us. She smiled at Matt, completely ignoring me. "Do you need anything?"

"Is it too early for a drink?" He smiled. "I'm afraid I'm a bit of nervous flyer."

The stewardess made a sympathetic noise, but shook her head. "We're not supposed to before the flight—"

Matt held out his jacket. Their hands brushed as he handed it to the stewardess. I saw a small spark of blue fire. The stewardess's pupils dilated. Matt said, "Even the smallest pint of ale would be a great help."

She let out a high-pitch giggle. "I'll bring it right away."

I thrust my jacket under her nose. She took it with a happy smile. "Anything else for you, sweetie?"

"No." I elbowed Matt after she hurried away. "What did you do to her?"

"A small energy spark. It acts like an adrenaline boost. She'll be really happy for a few hours."

"Use that trick on girls often?" I said.

"She's not my sort," Matt replied.

I couldn't resist asking, "What is your sort?"

His eyes traveled over my face. "Someone with a little

mystery."

I was saved from answering when the stewardess appeared with Matt's beer. He gulped it down in two swallows and held the can back out to the stewardess. She blinked in surprise, but hurried off when the pilot's warning for takeoff came on.

Matt tugged on the collar of his tight white T-shirt. "This thing is a steel beast and we're trapped inside its belly—"

"It's going to be okay."

His face twisted into a scowl. "Do you have any idea how little control we have up here? Anything goes wrong and we've got no recourse. This mode of travel is complete insanity."

I bit the inside of my cheek to keep from laughing. "Does the big bad magician not like planes?"

"I am a wizard," he muttered. "Magicians do parlor tricks."

"Wasn't Merlin a magician?" I watched the plane roll down the runway.

"Arthur never could get it straight. He used the word magician and it stuck. It's completely insulting."

I raised a brow. "Feel strongly about it?"

He grunted and glanced out the window—which was a mistake. The plane taxied down the runway and jerked to a stop as it reached the takeoff line. Matt's shoulders tensed so much I thought his bones would crack. I laid a hand on his bicep. He jumped, clearly startled. I moved to pull it back, but he laid his other hand over mine. Syrupy warmth spread over me.

"Merlin the Magician sounds better." I tried not to wince when Matt's grip on my hand tightened. "Tell me more about

Merlin."

He shrugged. "Not much more to tell than what you already know."

"Most of what I thought I knew about all this seems to be wrong," I retorted. "What's the real story? I mean, Merlin was supposed to be King Arthur's mentor. Practically handed him the throne, but then, let Arthur screw it all up."

"He didn't let Arthur *screw it all up,* as you put it. Camelot just wasn't filled with all that ridiculous romance and idealism they have in the movies. They were real people. Arthur made mistakes."

"Because Merlin abandoned him."

I was half-amused, half-startled when Matt actually huffed.

"You don't understand at all. Merlin and Arthur thought they were doing all the right things. The ruling structure back then held the king at the top. Below him, the nobles ran their fiefdoms. Merlin and Arthur thought more checks and balances were needed, so they put the Round Table knights in the middle. The knights were Arthur's emissaries. They went where trouble was and kept an eye on the nobles. It's how Arthur held the kingdom together."

"Checks and balances," I said. "It's a good idea, but it didn't really work, did it? All that Guinevere and Lancelot stuff divided everyone's loyalties."

"Camelot fell apart at the end because Arthur couldn't keep order among the knights. Not because of some supposed love triangle."

The plane jerked again as we started the run to take off.

"I thought the knights of Camelot were the best and brightest."

"They were, but you have to understand how the wizards fit in. Every knight had a wizard, sometimes two, traveling with him. A healer and a jack usually."

"Jack?"

"Jack of all trades. An everything wizard. Not very powerful in any one thing, but knows a little about everything."

The plane rose. Gravity pressed down on us. Matt paled, his face turning a sickly, almost green color.

"So Merlin and the wizards caused Camelot to implode?"

Matt made a noise of dissent. "Merlin didn't see it coming. During Arthur's time, the wizards lived among the Regulars in peace. They weren't in hiding, but they also weren't treated as equals. They petitioned Arthur for a seat at the Round Table. Arthur stalled them because it would have made the nobles, who were all Regulars, unhappy. It was unfair. They should have been given as much recognition as the knights they served. They lived in the path of danger, but they weren't given a vote on the Round Table."

"No taxation without representation. I've heard that before," I said.

"Anger built up for years. The wizards began to segregate themselves. Merlin tried to warn Arthur. But another wizard, a very powerful one, rallied everyone against Merlin and Arthur. He turned Arthur's son, Mordred, who was incidentally a half-wizard, against his father. With Mordred at his side, he pulled together the other wizards to strike back at Camelot."

I prompted, "Really? He sounds interesting."

Matt's fingers curled around the armrest. "He wasn't *interesting*. He was completely reckless. If Camelot was teetering on a cliff, he was the one who pushed it over the edge."

I arched my brow. "Pretty heavy accusation, isn't it?"

Matt gave me a look. "No, it's not. You weren't there."

"Neither were you," I said.

Matt paled as the plane picked up speed. The plane shuddered from turbulence.

"What did you see in your vision about me?" I asked.

Matt didn't reply.

"Did you notice how fast the pilots are pushing the plane? I've heard the faster the plane goes, the more turbulence. I wonder if they're having trouble keeping the nose up—"

"Be quiet, Ryan," Matt said, through clenched teeth.

"Tell me what you saw."

"Gods, you can be frustrating!"

"Tenacious," I corrected.

"Annoying."

I narrowed my eyes. I said mildly, "When the plane shakes, it seems like it's going to tear itself apart—"

Matt growled in frustration. "I saw you and Vane. My brother. You and he were... kissing."

My jaw dropped.

The plane made one final push and leveled out.

"We're up," I said.

Matt sat back with a sigh. "Yes."

I extracted my hand from his grip and took the sick bag from him. I put it back into the pouch. "You didn't need this."

His eyes widened in surprise. "No."

With a grin, I pulled my green iPod out of my bag and popped matching buds into my ears. I closed my eyes, ready to shut out the world for a little bit.

Matt exhaled loudly. "Not you, too. What is with everyone and their gadgets?"

If I'd been chewing gum, I would have smacked it—loudly. I cracked open an eye. "Are you really eighteen?"

Matt's cheeks flushed. "Quite."

"Quite," I mimicked.

With a half-smile, Matt settled back into his seat and looked out the window. I followed his gaze. Outside, the bright sky had changed quickly to dark.

Matt's brow furrowed and a faraway expression took over his chiseled face. I checked the impulse to touch him again. To make sure he was really real. Really there. Really beside me.

I still had the feeling I was going to wake up any second back in bed, back at the manor. That things would be back to what they had been before yesterday. That Alexa would be sleeping just down the hall.

I shook my head as if I could shake straight my fragmented mind. I looked at the singular Matt Emrys.

"Wait, you *do* have a brother?"

THE COUNCIL

Except for Matt, whose pallor resembled that of a ghost, the flight went smoothly for everyone. We landed in the midmorning at Gatwick Airport. I had no idea where we were going. The guardians took care of everything. An hour-long train ride took us into town. We got off at Victoria Station inside the London Underground, a cavernous maze of subways that the locals called the Tube. After a dizzying number of escalators and several train changes, we somehow made it out of the Underground and I found myself staring out at the English countryside as we sat on a long-distance train. A full sun shone down on the Castle Cary train station when we finally stopped. The signs told us we were somewhere near Bristol. Most of us were ready to collapse. I figured it was somewhere around ten a.m. in Boston.

Several cars were waiting for us outside the station.

At the sight of them, Grey let out a groan. "How much longer?"

"It's another ten miles to Glastonbury. The place we're

going is on the far side, so another few miles after that," Matt reassured. "Don't worry. This ordeal is almost over."

Matt energetically grabbed his bag and walked to the first van in the line of five.

We trudged after him.

I murmured, "Think we'll get a shower today?"

Excitement gleamed in Billie's eyes. Billie was a candidate from Virginia. "This is so amazing. Matt told me we're going someplace where they do nothing but magic."

"Except we can't do magic." Grey reminded him.

"Yeah, exactly how is that going to work out?" I said. "Do they know we're coming?"

Billie replied, "The Council sent Matt to recruit candidates. We're here with him. He's all we need."

Matt's cheeks flushed red.

I recognized the look. He was keeping something back. A curl of unease tightened inside me. "Matt, what's going on?"

"Not to worry. You're all candidates." He ushered us into the first van.

I would have pestered him more, but I was too tired. I let him hustle me into the van. The van itself was tiny—not exactly the giant SUVs we had driven back home—but from what I'd observed in my short time in England, I doubted the cars got much bigger than this.

Matt sat beside me, looking out the window. The white-knuckled flyer had vanished the instant we'd landed. The farther out into the country we got, the more relaxed he seemed. My head bobbed as the van ambled over seemingly endless rolling hills. The one-lane road we drove on seemed the only sign of civilization.

I yawned. I wanted nothing more than to rest my head against Matt's shoulder, but it seemed weird after what he'd told me about his brother. Not that I'd done anything, but I still felt somehow guilty. I yawned again.

"We're almost there, Ryan," he said without turning his head.

My cheeks heated. We passed a sign for Glastonbury. "Why here?" I asked. We went up a small hill. In the distance, a small town lay nestled in a valley. Above the town on a triangular terraced hill, a tall tower sat like a beacon that could be seen for miles.

Matt answered, "Glastonbury Tor. It's a ruined church. Two thousand years ago, the sea washed right up to the hills, making the hill an island. The tower is called St. Michael's tower, the warrior saint who beat back the darkness. Some say that Glastonbury is where sea met the land and became the meeting place of the dead, the ancient Isle of Avalon."

"Is this place protected? Do the gargoyles know about it?"

"The wizard Council has kept it hidden for centuries. At one time, the Keltoi controlled this land. Then, it passed to a rather famous king you know." Matt gazed out over the town. "They say he and Guinevere are buried at Glastonbury Abbey. The ruins of the abbey still remain inside the town."

"How is it protected?" Grey asked. I could hear the apprehension in his tone.

"There is a shield over the stronghold. Any supernatural creature not specifically invited is restricted from entering. An ordinary passerby would just see humdrum little buildings."

We never went into town. Somewhere off in the outskirts, a dilapidated brick estate stood in the middle of grey fields. A stone wall surrounded it. We stopped at iron gates, but the buildings inside were hardly impressive. Two manor houses, two stories tall and not very wide. The houses connected by a small archway. It was... quaint. And didn't look as if it could house more than twenty people.

Our driver got out of the van and went up to the gate. He shouted something. A harsh wind burst through the air, and *open sesame*, the gates opened.

Our driver jumped back in the van. As we crossed the archway, I noticed a small wooden plaque next to the gate. It declared, "Avalon Preparatory Academy."

The van followed the driveway up to the closer of the twin buildings. The driver stopped the van just before large double doors.

"Everyone out," Matt said.

We all emerged hesitantly. All of the candidates wore befuddled looks on their faces as they took in the nondescript manor. Matt and one of the guardians went up to the double doors. Spanning the center of the wood doors was a seal, an intricate carving of a lion with wings.

"The lion symbolizes the Keltoi," Matt explained. "The wizards."

The doors opened.

A svelte woman with straight, dark hair and long legs stepped out. Her gauzy, moss-colored dress flowed around her like a soft cloud. Her eyes passed over us in a single sweep before coming to rest on Matt. She smiled—a luminous smile that made her whole face glow and made its recipient want to bask in its glory.

The sweetness of it made my teeth hurt.

She held out her hands to Matt. "We are so glad you are back. It has been too long."

Matt clasped her hand briefly. "Marilynn, it is good to be back. Is the Council ready?"

The smile on her face dimmed just a bit at Matt's perfunctory greeting, but she cheerfully said, "We are ready. When you sent the list of all who were coming, I was stunned. I can't believe you have found so many. We searched for years and only identified three or four families."

"I am known for having a certain knack," Matt said dryly.

Marilynn giggled as if he'd made some hilarious comment.

Matt glanced at me. "Even I had a bit of a surprise. I found one more than expected."

Marilynn frowned at his intent expression. She followed his gaze to me. Her smile faltered. "Please, candidates, follow me."

She disappeared back into the manor. Matt took a step after her.

"Matt." I stopped him. "Where are we?"

Matt flashed his white teeth. He made a sweeping gesture to usher us into the manor. "Welcome to Avalon Prep, candidates. We are what remains of Camelot. Welcome to wizard school."

***

We entered into a huge foyer. At the end, I could see a set of stairs, but most of the dark hardwood space was empty. A glass door stood near the stairs, yet light didn't reach far inside. Marilynn led us to a small bar, the only other piece of furniture in the foyer. Behind the bar, rows of cubbies held papers like some old-fashioned hotel.

So this was wizard school. It seemed so ordinary—not exactly an impressive castle fortress. Not quite Camelot.

"Welcome to our admissions area. This building holds the administration. It used to be an inn," Marilynn said. "The second building holds more offices. The school is actually past the glass doors." She pointed to end of the foyer.

Marilynn pushed a button on the bar and a flat-panel computer screen rose out of the counter. "Now let us confirm that I have your names in the system. We need to ensure your records are in order so you are properly enrolled into school."

She took out a large cardboard box from behind the bar. "But before we begin, I must ask you to turn over any electronic devices you may have brought. No cell phones, no music players, nothing from the outside will be allowed. You will be provided with everything you need."

"The guardians already took our cells," Oliver said.

Matt had already taken mine. My fingers still itched for it. There were a few grumbles while everyone pulled out watches and music players and put them in the box.

"Good." Marilynn nodded. "Let us begin." She started rattling off our names. Everyone confirmed that they were present. When she came to the end of list, she nodded again. "Good. Nothing is out of order. Most of you have led fairly ordinary lives."

Paul stepped forward. "What about me?"

Marilynn raised a brow and clicked a few buttons on the keyboard. "Paul Mason. You've an interesting history."

"A life that is now in the past. Here and now is what matters. The future hinges on you, candidates. The past no longer applies," Matt interrupted.

A clapping sound came from the other end of the lobby.

"Nice speech, brother. Shall we test whether you really mean it?" a voice drawled.

A man walked down the stairs into the foyer. I did a double take. It was the history professor from the news, Dr. Northe.

"Vane," Matt muttered.

Vane hooked his thumbs in tight jeans. His face was eerily similar to Matt's. His hair was slicked back. He was lean, but well built. His hazel-brown eyes sparkled with brilliance. I didn't have time to notice anything else.

A blue fireball shot through the air at Vane.

The fireball had come from Matt. Vane laughed and threw it back at its owner. Matt volleyed the ball back again and added a second one. Then, he added a third and a fourth, creating a barrage of fireballs. Matt's double halted them in the air, one by one. He pulled them into one big fireball and shot it back at Matt.

A candidate let out a small yelp as the blue fireball whizzed by him, catching a few strands of loose hair. The bitter smell of burnt hair filled the room. It was enough of a warning shot to make us all step out of range of the firefight.

Matt halted the giant ball before it reached him. He hurled it back across the room with enough force to make the room shudder.

"Enough," a loud voice shouted.

A group of white-robed men and women entered through a side door. A wizard with a short, white beard glared at Matt and Vane. The giant fireball stilled at the center of the room and shrank into nothing.

Matt immediately created another one. He didn't hurl it, but held it ready. Vane copied him.

"Councilmember Aurelius, why is my brother here?" Matt demanded.

"*Second Member* Aurelius," the white-robed wizard corrected. "Vivane is here for the same reason as you. He has brought candidates."

"Please, do call me Vane. Vivane is so…"

"Girly?" Grey snickered quietly behind me.

Vane's sharp eyes went straight to us. He blinked in surprise and… recognition when he saw me. For some reason, I tensed. His gaze passed over me and I relaxed. Vane turned back to the men and women in white robes. They had moved to stand a semicircle. No doubt, the infamous Council.

"Do you know who he is?" Matt demanded. "He's a murderer."

"Is that any way to talk about family? I know you are a mite upset with me—"

Matt exploded. "You tried to kill me!"

"Yet you are not dead." Vane shrugged carelessly. "Hence, no murder."

"No thanks to you," Matt said. "You entombed us in a cave!"

Vane crossed his arms across his chest. "And when *you* got out, you left me trapped."

Matt ground his teeth. "How did you get out?"

"I managed, as I always do... by myself. But that is all in the past, as you said." Vane's eyes roved over the candidates standing behind Matt. A slight sneer curled his lips. "But what do we have here? *These* are your mighty set of Regular candidates?" He eyed some of the kids in the group in ratty jeans and travel-worn T-shirts. "Wherever did you pull together this ragtag pack? I say we send them all back home—for their own safety. My wizard candidates are the only ones we need."

As if on cue, seven or so kids came downstairs to gather behind Vane in pack formation. Boys in tough street wear and one girl with dyed red hair and a dragon tattoo looked on with impassive expressions. A large brutish boy—obviously the leader—stood in front of the rest. The girl stood beside him, in girlfriend position.

Vane's boots clicked on the wood floors. He strode in front of Aurelius and faced the Council. "Merlin trained Arthur to take the sword. Like you are proposing to do with these candidates. With the wizards on his side, Arthur enjoyed every advantage. But what did he do with such a gift? He used it to betray us."

"Then what happened? Did he thank us? No. Instead, he blamed us." Vane ranted. "When Arthur's knights couldn't hold the kingdom together, they cursed us. They blamed magic for their problems. They drove us out of our homes, and when I woke, I learned after Mt. Camlan they had driven us into hiding. We've been cowering in the shadows for over a thousand years. But no longer. Our time is now."

He turned to look at us. "We should learn from the past. A wizard candidate is far superior than any Regular."

Matt snorted. "You were never tolerant."

"And you are too tolerant. Even after all they've done, I wager you'd still rather talk to the gargoyles—"

Matt protested. "I know we're past that—"

"What happens when *the one* gets the sword? No Regular can resist the temptation to use its power. What happens when they turn the sword back on us? Regulars are too easy to corrupt. At least we can trust our own kind—"

"Please." Aurelius raised a hand. Quiet fell over the room. "Vane, we realize you have a point."

"What?" Matt exclaimed.

"That is why we have devised an admissions test. *All* of the candidates—the wizard and the Regular ones—will prove to us and to themselves that they are truly candidates. We have gathered water from the Lake of the Lady."

Matt made a sound of disgruntlement. "My candidates do not need to take a test. I have *seen* them. Or are you questioning my visions now?"

Some of the councilmembers demurred. Aurelius held up his hand. "No, indeed."

"My candidates will happily take the tests," Vane said. "We are not afraid."

"Neither are we," said Billie, who was standing beside Grey.

Vane smiled in satisfaction.

"Let me talk with them," Matt told Aurelius abruptly.

Aurelius nodded.

Matt drew us to a corner of the room.

"What is the test?" someone said.

"I'm not ready to take any test," Oliver said anxiously.

"I thought we came here to get ready," I said.

"I wouldn't mind a second confirmation that I really am a candidate," Paul said.

Matt looked over the group. "You *are* candidates."

"What are we supposed to do with this water?" I asked.

"You've no doubt heard of the Lady of the Lake. In Arthur's time, she alerted Merlin that the sword had appeared in the lake. Merlin moved it to the center of town. We later found out that the lake had special properties. If you take a drink, you will see. That is all you will have to do. Take a drink. Tell us what you see."

Oliver nodded earnestly. "That's it?"

Matt reassured, "I have no doubt that you can do this. All of you. If you want to."

"What if we don't see anything?" I asked.

"That's the point. If you see anything, you are a candidate. The water only interacts with those to whom it has an affinity. Just like the sword."

Grey crossed his arms across his chest. "Let me understand clearly. You brought us here to train, but the Council wants us to prove that we actually are candidates in order to receive the training. If we don't, then... what?"

"I don't know," Matt admitted. "We need their help. We need their protection."

"Good to have choices," Grey muttered. "Am I the only one who has a bad feeling about this?"

"No," I said. "What aren't you telling us, Matt?"

AVALON PREPARATORY

"You are candidates," Matt repeated. "You will not have a problem. Believe me."

"The gargoyles came after my whole family," Billie said grimly. "They put my brother in a hospital. They didn't do that without reason. I believe Master Matt."

From the other side of the room, Vane let out a loud yawn. "Should we order a bite to eat while you dither?"

My eyes narrowed. I muttered, "I'll take the test just to shut him up."

The tension on the fourteen faces surrounding me broke.

"So will I," said Oliver with a laugh.

"Me too," Grey said.

The others echoed the agreement.

Matt looked at Aurelius and nodded.

"Councilmember Thornton, please bring out the water,"

Aurelius commanded.

A pedestal holding a plain glass bowl was brought forward. Thornton picked up an urn. He poured a bit of ordinary-looking water into the bowl. Light from an overhead sconce reflected off the water's surface. I thought I saw a faint blue shimmer.

Aurelius said, "Who will go first?"

"We will," Vane said. His candidates shadowed him. Vane nodded at the brutish boy who stood in front. "Mark, step up to the water."

Mark strode to the pedestal. He cupped his hands together. Thornton prompted him to move his hands over the bowl. Mark complied. Thornton poured water into his hands. He slurped up the water. Around me, everyone stilled in equal parts apprehension and anticipation. Nothing happened for the first few seconds. Then, Mark let out a small grunt. He sank to his knees and started dry heaving.

I found myself taking a step toward the pedestal.

"Do not disturb him," Aurelius warned me off. I stopped.

Matt moved to stand beside me. "Look at the bowl."

Water in the bowl on the pedestal shimmered brighter and brighter. Images flashed through the water—Mark dueled with Vane, Vane defeated him, and Mark fell to the ground.

"The water shifts through the past," Matt explained. "In this case, they've linked it to the one who drinks the water."

"How is that possible?" Oliver asked from behind us.

Vane gave him a sardonic look. "Magic."

I leaned closer to Matt and whispered, "Why these images?"

Matt's breath tickled my skin. "It must be the most significant event on his mind. It's different for everyone."

On the floor, Mark shuddered. Thornton set down the urn and helped him up.

"Well done, son," Aurelius told him. "Those who see the water are confirmed as candidates." He gestured Mark to go to Marilynn. "Please report to admissions. She will give you your schedule and room assignment. Welcome to the Avalon Preparatory Academy."

The brutish boy tried to retain a tough demeanor, but I saw how slowly he moved as he walked to Marilynn. The rest of Vane's candidates glanced at each other. Gone was the air of arrogance.

"No pain, no gain." Vane crooked his finger at the lone girl of the group. "You're next."

She chewed her lip, hesitating. Vane whispered in her ear. Whatever he said, she must not have liked because her short, red hair swung around her face like razors as she marched to the pedestal. Vane watched her go with an impassive expression.

Aurelius signaled the councilmember to proceed with the urn. The girl took the water in cupped hand. She swallowed it quickly. A moment later, she let out a loud scream and fell to her knees. Her whole body shook.

The water in the bowl shifted, showing brutal images. A woman, an older version of the girl, probably her mother, hit the young redhead over and over again. As she watched the beating, the girl started crying.

I had to look away. Grey let out a low growl.

"Matt," I said. "Stop this."

Matt raised his hand and the water in the pedestal sloshed, breaking the stream of images. He went to the girl and offered a hand up.

The girl got up angrily. "You shouldn't have interrupted the test." Her hands fisting, she looked at Aurelius. "Did I pass?"

Aurelius nodded. "Please see Miss Marilynn."

Vane signaled another candidate to come forward. A young boy, who couldn't have been more than fifteen, walked bravely to the pedestal. Thornton poured water into his waiting hands. The boy didn't move to swallow it. Instead, he just stared at it. Vane cleared his throat loudly. With a start, the boy swallowed the water.

Nothing happened. The bowl on the pedestal remained still.

"Give him more," Vane said.

Thornton looked at Aurelius. Aurelius inclined his head in agreement. Thornton complied. The boy drank a second helping. Still nothing.

"He is not a candidate," Aurelius declared

The boy went pale. "No. I can't go home. The gargoyles burned my house down. My grandmother is gone. I don't have any place to go back to." Beseeching eyes sought out Vane. "You said this is where I belonged."

Vane gave the boy an uninterested glance. "You are not a candidate. You will be fine."

"You do belong here," Matt said. "You are a wizard. You

can go to school."

Aurelius said, "Yes, he would be eligible. But we are not a charity. The school has tuition. He needs a sponsor."

"I have no doubt Vane has enough to help," Matt said. He looked at Vane. "Unless you want to turn the boy loose with his knowledge of the candidates."

"I have the perfect forgetfulness spell," Vane said.

Matt shook his head. "Unbelievable. You know, after how long the boy has been with you, the amount of memory you would have to modify, you risk turning him into a turnip."

Aurelius looked to Vane. "Vane, he is your responsibility."

Vane crossed his arms. "The Council rejected him. He is also your responsibility. I will sponsor him and pay for the admissions test. That is all. He can always work off the rest after graduation."

Aurelius sighed. "Marilynn, come take this boy for regular enrollment."

The boy gave Vane a grateful smile. "I knew you would be my savior."

Vane inclined his head at the accolade. He signaled the next candidate to step up to the pedestal.

Matt's words about his brother and me reverberated in my head. I whispered to Matt, "Your brother is a toad. I wouldn't kiss him even if I was a princess."

"He's more than that—he's dangerous," Matt replied without humor. "Vane is like a hurricane. He doesn't care what he wrecks in his path. He only cares about what he wants."

I raised my brow. "Dramatic much?"

"If only I was."

The last of Vane's candidates went to the pedestal. As I watched the bowl, I pondered on Matt and Vane. The brothers had issues with a capital 'I.' I'd never seen Matt so wound up.

Aurelius looked at us. "Is your group ready?"

My stomach knotted. Grey caught my gaze. The same fear was reflected in his eyes. What horrible thing would the water bring out from us?

I took a bracing breath. "Matt, will the water be the same for us Regulars as it was for the wizard candidates?"

"It should be," Matt said. "But I couldn't say for sure."

"That's really helpful," I said dryly.

Grey took a step forward.

I stepped in front of him. "I'll go first."

"You're sure?" Matt said, his face tight with worry.

Discreetly, I squeezed his hand before heading to the pedestal. My gaze collided with Vane's. He watched Matt and me with interest. I glanced away.

Thornton poured a few drops of water into my cupped hands and I hoped no one noticed how hard they shook. I inhaled the scent of earth mixed with calming lavender. The liquid tasted cool and sweet. I drank it in one swallow.

The next thing I knew, I was on the floor as my stomach tried to climb out of my mouth. Black spots danced in my vision. The urge to collapse overwhelmed me. Heaving, I fought it.

Like a crowbar to a damaged lock, the water tore down the

barriers in my mind, exposing its dark, hidden corners to harsh light. Memories crashed over me.

On the floor, I choked out, "M-Mom."

***

Mom yelled at me as we readied to leave the house, complaining about how I'd woken up late even though I knew we had a flight to catch. As she squirted perfume on herself— lavender, my mother's preferred scent—I rolled my eyes. So what if we were two and a half hours early instead of three?

Getting to the airport three hours early for a domestic flight was ludicrous. Especially for a trip I didn't even want to go on. I didn't want to spend Christmas with some boring family I didn't even know. Plus, I liked Christmas in Texas where decoration and lights mixed with the warm air. What could be better?

Being cooped up in a house, due to the inevitable blizzard, in Boston with strangers didn't sound thrilling. Snow was overrated. I had griped the whole month about how we should be going to our neighbor's, like we did every year. I didn't want to miss the tree hunt and our neighbor's breakfast. The holidays were about tradition. Not to mention, I wouldn't be seeing my boyfriend Morgan—tall, dark, and delicious—for a whole week. Did she know she was ruining Christmas?

"If you're not ready in five, I'm throwing you in the car. You can get on the plane in those ridiculous men's boxers," she yelled from downstairs.

"They're comfortable to sleep in," I reiterated as I pulled my suitcase out of my room. "Anyway, I'm already dressed."

"You're a girl. I wish you'd behave like one once in a while. Did you pack a nice dress like I told you? The Ragnars go all out on Christmas Eve. There's a black tie party. Last time they had entire scenes out of *The Nutcracker* carved in beautiful ice sculptures. You'll love it."

"Ballet is boring."

"You didn't used to think so. I know you gave it up for fencing—"

"Because you made me," I retorted.

"It will be better for you in the long run," she said.

I rolled my eyes again. I was pretty sure no one had used a rapier in a real fight since the 1700s.

Mom grabbed the car keys from the hook and gave the house a quick onceover. We'd be gone for over a week. It was the first vacation we'd taken in two years.

I slowly dragged my suitcase downstairs. I left it at the foot of the stairs to take one last look at the tiny Christmas tree in the living room. It was nothing like the giant eight-footer we usually splurged on.

I tried one last time. "Christmas should be at home."

Mom's face softened at this declaration. "I know it's hard, Ry. We've always made Christmas about being home, but as long as we're together, we'll be fine. You'll have fun with the Ragnars, I promise. I loved my Christmases with them when I was a little girl." She wrapped me up in a tight hug. "It'll be good for you to make new friends. I've loved having you to myself for so long, but you're going to be graduating before you know it and you'll need those connections—"

The muted sound of the doorbell cut her off.

"Don't forget your purse. You need ID," she commanded.

With a grumble, I went upstairs.

Mom went into the living room. I heard her fling open the front door. The walls of the townhouse were paper thin.

"Morgan, I'm sorry," I heard her say, impatiently. "We don't have much time."

Grabbing my purse, I hurried back down. Mom didn't like Morgan, and I was pretty sure she would slam the door in his face without even letting me talk to him.

"Morning, Mrs. D." Morgan asked, "Is Ryan here?"

Mom said, "Of course, but we're in a rush—"

I stopped just before the living room. Another hulk-sized man in a black trench coat came up out of nowhere behind Morgan. Between the two of them, they covered every inch of the doorway.

The man's face... changed. It turned from normal to the face of a monster in less than a second. I halted just outside the door to the living room. Long fangs emerged from his mouth.

"Ryan," Mom screamed. "RUN!"

A set of Katana swords—my mother's favorite—hung on the wall. I grabbed one.

His forehead went Neanderthal, becoming wider until it protruded out of his face. In a scene straight out of a vampire flick, the man-monster grabbed Mom by the neck.

"Wait," Morgan rasped, his voice very different from the one I'd spent hours listening to on the phone.

I'll never forget the horrible sound of my mother's head cracking as the boy I loved threw her against the wall. Although it was as innocuous as the soft creak of the door, the sound reverberated through me. I backed into the hallway. I tried to scream, but nothing came out of my throat. It probably saved my life.

"We have to find the daughter," Morgan said in a frustrated tone.

"She smells good. Powerful." The other man knelt down to pick up my mother's wrist. I watched, frozen, as he sunk his teeth into her flesh.

A whimper escaped my mouth.

Morgan crossed the living room to the hall in the blink of an eye.

"Ryan," he crooned. "Come here, baby."

I backed away. He lunged at me, but somehow I was faster than him. I ran out of the hallway into the kitchen and slammed the door shut. Morgan tore through it like it was tissue paper. What happened next was a blur.

I held the Katana in front of me. Shaking from head to toe, I asked, "What are you?"

Morgan put up his hands. He started to walk slowly toward me. "Don't worry, baby. Everything will be fine. Don't you see? I've done this for us. Now, we can be together... always."

"Stay away," I said, taking a step back. My body hit the kitchen wall.

I was trapped.

Morgan smiled. He walked up to stand just before the tip

of the unsteady sword in my hand. "Ah, baby. You can't hurt me."

In a blink, he grabbed the sword from my hands and turned it against me. The razor-sharp edge caressed my skin with deadly intent.

"One last kiss?" His lips twisting into a sadistic smile, he reached out to caress my cheek. His cold hand slid further down past my neck. He tore open the button of my shirt and reached inside. He squeezed a breast with force.

I thought I would throw up.

He never saw my mother come up behind him. She held the other Katana. She tried to chop off his head. Morgan caught the blade with his hand. With an angry smile, he turned around. Blood covered his hand, but he didn't seem to be bothered.

"I'm going to enjoy killing you, Mrs. D." With one hand, Morgan clawed my mother across the chest with talon-like fingers. With his other hand, he drove the Katana into her stomach.

My mother fell back onto hard, marble tile. I screamed.

The backdoor of the kitchen burst open. A man entered wearing the dark blue uniform of a paramedic. Morgan ran at him with a yell. The paramedic extended a hand and blasted Morgan back against the kitchen wall. Pictures hanging on the wall crashed to the floor. Morgan grunted.

The paramedic moved quickly. He picked up the sword from the floor, where Morgan had dropped it. Morgan got up from the wall with a snarl. His face extended into beast-like proportions. He moved with speed, despite his bulk. In the blink of an eye, he stood inches from the paramedic. Morgan's eyes blazed triumphantly.

The paramedic swung the sword. Morgan's head fell to the floor.

Blood spurted all over the walls. It spurted all over me. It seeped across my mother's pristine floor. Morgan's body slumped and rolled. Covered in sticky red, I met the paramedic's impassive eyes. I fainted.

The next thing I knew, the paramedic's face hovered over me as he shook me awake. Piercing hazel eyes bore into mine.

"What did he say to you?" he asked.

I could do no more than stare at him. Moonlight from the bay window highlighted the cold cut of his high cheekbones.

"What did he say to you?" This time his voice sounded oddly distorted, as if were speaking through a filter. The voice washed over me with velvety softness. A sense of calm filled me.

"Nothing. He was m-my boyfriend," I whispered hoarsely. "Morgan."

"Yes, the boyfriend," he said. "They did spend an unusually long time on you."

Another boy came in through the hallway. Despite his brutish size, he grimaced as he came up behind the paramedic. "What a mess. Do we take her with us?"

The handsome paramedic shook his head. "Mother and daughter obviously fought off the gargoyle without magic."

"They had swords," the boy pointed out. "There's another one in the living room. Dead. No head. They knew what they were doing."

"The mother did. Unusual, but still they are quite obviously Regulars. And Regulars are not our concern." The paramedic drew together my torn shirt and started to get up.

"Come, the hunt continues," he said. "We must follow."

I grabbed his wrist with the last bit of remaining strength. "W-wait. Y-you can't leave. You need to help my mother—"

The paramedic looked at me for a long moment. "Yes, I will help. But you must let go."

I released him.

He stretched his wrist. "Surprisingly strong grip for such a delicate girl."

"H-help," I said.

"I will." He put a hand to my head and muttered, "Time to rest... and forget."

As my eyes fluttered closed, I noticed the nametag on his uniform. *Vane.*

***

On the floor, in the foyer of Avalon Prep, I did throw up.

Matt rushed to me. "It's all right, Ryan. You're done. It's all done."

"I'd forgotten. How could I forget how my mother died? Sylvia said the police told her it was intruders. She said they told her Morgan had been killed defending us. She lied." I sat back on the floor.

Matt put a hand on my back. "I'm sure to protect you."

"She shouldn't have lied." I shivered, suddenly cold, as

anger coursed through me. I didn't need to be protected. *Why did they all think otherwise?* My eyes snapped to Vane. "You made me forget."

"Indeed, I did," said Vane, without apology.

He'd also saved me. But he didn't want me to remember. I stared at him. "Why?"

"Yes, Vivane," Aurelius commanded. "Why were you at the girl's house?"

"Isn't it obvious?" Matt said. "He doesn't have the sight. How do you think he rounded up his candidates? He's been following the gargoyles about."

"He's rescuing candidates?" someone said.

"Hardly," Matt scoffed. "The gargoyles don't discriminate between Regulars and wizards, but Vane does."

I looked at Vane with dawning horror. "You didn't tell the kids they were being targeted?"

He gave an unemotional shrug. "You survived—"

"My mother didn't!" I jumped up. I tried to lunge at Vane.

Matt caught me and held me still. "He's not worth it."

Vane continued without acknowledging my outburst. "The others may have also. I don't know."

"Or care," Matt added.

Aurelius cleared his throat. "What is done is done. We must look to the present."

"Master Aurelius, look at the water," Thornton interrupted in an awed tone.

The other councilmembers circled the pedestal.

"I've never seen anything like this," a woman councilmember declared. There was a chorus of agreement throughout the group.

"How is it possible?" another member said.

Reluctantly tearing my gaze from Vane's, I looked at the pedestal.

The water was red with blood.

"Matt?" I said uncertainly.

He tucked a strand of hair behind my ear. The simple gesture calmed me.

"Where did you get the water?" Matt said to Aurelius.

Aurelius's gaze didn't move from the water. "We found it in your cave, of course. We've been monitoring it for almost a thousand years. How do think we knew when you woke?"

"Woke?" I said.

"Well, this has taken a most interesting turn, *Matt*," Vane drawled.

"Don't speak to me," Matt snapped.

"We don't have time for this," Aurelius said. "Let us proceed with the test. Who is next?"

After a moment of hesitant silence, Grey stepped forward. "I'll go."

***

It took another hour to get through the candidates. Unsurprisingly, Grey's visions had been about the shadow-dragon and Alexa. I was still holding his hand—or he was holding mine—when Aurelius confirmed the last candidate. I ran my tongue across my teeth. Matt had magically cleaned my mouth and now it felt fresher than before I had thrown up.

Marilynn had cleaned up the floor while Matt was taking care of me. From the glare she gave me, I was pretty sure she and I were not going to be friends anytime soon.

After the pedestal had been taken away and the Council dispersed as mysteriously as they had appeared, Aurelius gathered the candidates.

"Congratulations and welcome," he intoned. "Your guardians and mentors have briefed me about you, but you do not know me. I am Aurelius Ambrose. As well as holding the title of Second Member of the Wizard's Council, I also serve as the head of this school."

"Today, you are in a remarkable position. Some of you are wizards and some of you are not. However, all of you are beginners. Many students start at Avalon Prep at a very young age. You will be among the first to enroll as part of our special program. For those of you still in school, your time will count toward your secondary school education, and thus, allow you to graduate, if that is your wish."

Aurelius walked back and forth in front of us. "Dangerous times are upon us. Most of you have had encounters with the gargoyles already. If seeing them in your fellow candidates' visions was a first, I am here to tell you that the threat is very real. The gargoyles started hunting down candidates as soon as we did. They would see you dead to increase their chances of being the ones to pull the sword out of the stone."

"You have taken a great step today by coming here."

Aurelius's lips curved into a grandfatherly smile. His short beard moved back and forth. "In the upcoming days, you will be pushed beyond what you think you can handle. Although it may not feel like it now—you are where you belong. You are part of a new family. Not since King Arthur's time has the sword come back to the land—"

"Who cares about King Arthur?" Mark said. "He's like a million years old. What are we supposed to do now?"

Aurelius gave him a disgruntled look. He waved his hand and the glass doors opened behind him. "Now, Mr. Brown, I realize you are exhausted so I will excuse your outburst this once. Your objective is simple enough. You will train at Avalon Prep. For your survival as well as ours, we will prepare you for whatever trial the sword may throw at you. There have been deaths enough. It's time for a smarter approach." He paused to make sure he had everyone's attention. He did.

"Vivane has volunteered to train you on swords. He is the finest swordsman alive today."

"Vivane!" Matt burst out. "Aurelius, I would speak to you right now."

Aurelius sighed. With a nod, he looked at Marilynn. "Candidates, you will get your welcome kits from Ms. Marilynn. Then, please follow her on the tour of the school. It will be most enlightening for you to see what we do here."

The candidates shuffled off toward Marilynn.

I saw Vane trying to slink out of the room. I marched over to him and cut him off before he reached the glass doors leading outside.

"You could have saved my mother." I poked a finger at his unyielding chest and became annoyed when he didn't even blink.

Vane leaned down until his lips grazed my ear. "I debated coming in at all."

I pushed him away. "Why did you?"

"I had to know about you." His eyes slid over me. His gaze rested on the necklace Sylvia had given me. "You were hard to read. I should have realized it was purchased magic obscuring the truth."

"You are unbelievable," I said. "Matt was right about you."

"Was he?" he drawled. "But really, you shouldn't believe everything my brother says."

"Matt—"

Vane laughed. "Is that what you think his name is?"

I frowned. "What?"

"If you're going to make it as a candidate, you must figure out who you can trust," Vane said. "Let me help you out. What do you know about Arthur? He pulled the sword from the stone. He founded a great kingdom. He became a legend. But someone else besides Arthur became just as famous. If Arthur was the puppet, he was the puppet master."

"Yes," I said steadily. "I know who you mean."

Before I could blink, Vane grabbed me by the waist and turned me to face Matt. Matt pulled at his jacket in frustration as he argued with Aurelius. I noticed he wore skater-punk shoes.

Vane whispered, "*Vasana.*"

With a gimmicky zap, a costume appeared on Matt. He wore a blue felt robe with white stars. On his head sat a matching pointed hat. His face had aged to look about a hundred years old. A long, white beard extended from his jaw to his feet.

Against my ear, Vane said, "Now, let's put it together. One, he was a wizard. That is true. Two, he was old. That is *false*. Actually, he was about… oh, say, eighteen. During Arthur's time, he would have been considered a mature adult, but not so much now. Three, he always thought he knew best for everyone. Know anyone like that? Four, he was considered the most powerful wizard of all time because… he could see the future. What is his real name?"

Matt broke off talking to Aurelius. Looking down at himself, he cursed.

Matt said, "*Vasana-apte.*"

It must have been a counter-spell because the cartoon wizard disappeared. Matt returned to normal. Matt glared at Vane. "You're an ass."

"And you always make things hard for yourself." Vane let go of me with a chuckle. I barely noticed him leave. My eyes were glued on Matt.

"Tell me it's not possible," I said.

"Ryan—"

"Oh, G-God," I said. After the trauma of drinking the water, I didn't think I could possibly hurt more today, but this new betrayal hit hard.

"I'm sorry," Matt said beseechingly. The deep pools in his

eyes stretched into infinity... or a thousand years or so.

I made a mewling sound. Hearing my distress, Grey left the other candidates and crossed the room. He grabbed me by the waist.

"What's going on?" he demanded. "Matt?"

Bile bubbled inside me. It climbed up my throat and burnt through my nostrils. I had trusted Matt. We had all trusted Matt.

I turned to Grey. Somewhat hysterically, I said, "His name is not Matt. His name is Merlin."

THE MOST FAMOUS WIZARD

The candidates, including Vane's, realized something was going on and came over.

My voice rose high. "He lied to us."

Aurelius walked to us.

"It is past time I introduce myself properly," Matt announced. "Things have been hard enough to explain, so I did not bother with this information. However, I do hope after what you have seen today, you will believe me when I tell you the truth about myself."

His eyes met those of the candidates without wavering.

"My true name *is* Emrys. Throughout history, though, the name has been known by a slightly different translation used by Arthur and his knights. I was known to them as Merlin."

The red-haired girl asked, "Are you a vampire or something? Like an—" Her voice dropped to a whisper. "— *immortal?*"

"No, I'm not a vampire or immortal," Matt—no, Merlin—

said. "Vane and I fought a long time ago. We happened to be near the Lake of the Lady. Our fighting caused an explosion. We both became trapped. Entombed in a cave. Frozen in time. Until a disturbance woke us a few years ago."

"A disturbance?" Oliver said.

"I'm not sure what it was. I have a feeling the Lake knew it was time. That the sword would appear again."

"So you're not a vampire?" the red-haired girl repeated. She sounded disappointed.

"Not at all," Matt quipped.

"Shouldn't you be talking in medieval English or something?" Grey said skeptically.

I looked at him in surprise.

"I did pick up a few things from you," Grey explained.

Matt smiled with good humor. "Good question. But you forget I am a wizard. I have an ability to learn at an accelerated speed. Also, I'm quite good at mimicking."

"But—" another candidate began.

Aurelius held up a hand. "I can confirm Master Merlin's tale. We have protected the tomb for over a thousand years." He glanced at the candidates. "No matter how it came about— I think we can all agree that having Merlin on our side is a good thing."

I glanced around at the crowd behind me. Pretty much all of the candidates were murmuring with awe. Even Grey was looking at Matt with new respect.

"Candidates, please follow me," Marilynn called us to attention. She marched to the converted hotel check-in desk and turned on a computer monitor. The candidates dutifully gathered around her.

Matt tried to get my attention. I shook my head. There wasn't much left to say.

I walked to the crowd of candidates. Marilynn rattled on about the history of the school. Apparently, it had been around for a long time. She went through a list of people who had graduated from the school, several politicians and celebrities. I would have cared, but there was only one famous person spinning around in my mind.

He had gone from badass boy on a bike, to ultra-powerful wizard, to someone completely out of my comprehension… someone completely out of my league. My hands fisted. Why did I even care?

Grey sensed my melancholy and threw an arm over my shoulder. I leaned into him. Marilynn gave me a sardonic look as she passed out black cases to everyone. I opened mine to find an iPad inside. Several candidates whistled. Despite my agitated state, it impressed me, too. Maybe wizard school wasn't going to be as lame as I had thought.

"All of your schedules and assignments will be done on these," Marilynn explained. "The whole school is on these. We've had them for a while now."

"Niiice." Oliver whistled. "I thought magic didn't work with electronics."

Marilynn let out a laugh. "You've been watching too many movies. Magic doesn't work on them, but it doesn't mean we can't use them. I don't know about you, but how these techs work seems like magic to me."

"Yeah." Several candidates laughed.

"Your class schedule and other various apps you will need have been downloaded into these. You will all have the same schedule, since you are in what we call a special training program, separate from the rest of the school."

"Does it have a name?" Oliver asked.

"The Excalibur program," Marilynn said with cheek. "When students start here, they are given titles. They are called apprentices. You will be addressed as pages."

"A page?" I asked. "You mean as in the page to a knight?"

Marilynn nodded. "You *are* training to be a knight after all."

"I thought I was training to be king," Oliver muttered.

"Arthur didn't become king because of the sword. That's a myth. He used it to maintain his kingdom. There's a big difference." Marilynn held up an iPad. "Back to the here and now. This also has your sleep assignments—"

"When do we get sorted into houses?" a Regular candidate piped.

"No houses," Marilynn said briskly. "We have a simple system. Girls are in Morgan Hall. Boys in Monmouth House."

There was a sound of disappointment from a few of the guys. "No girls in the showers?"

"Sorry, you're not here for that kind of learning." Marilynn walked to the glass doors. "Now, if you will follow me, we will do a quick tour of the school grounds. Class starts tomorrow."

As soon as we stepped outside, I gasped.

PRIYA ARDIS

Soft sun shone down on a misty cathedral at the opposite end of a football field-length courtyard. The cathedral had a long, pointed tower with beautiful rose and ivory stained glass windows. Pink-petal flowers and deep green ivy climbed the stones from the ground to the cathedral's roof. A large fountain stood in the middle of the courtyard with water falling from several lion heads. Between the misty air and rolling slope of the earth, the grounds reminded me of a long lost fairy tale.

More buildings made up the rest of the rectangular courtyard. The huge garage, which we'd seen from outside, stood to the right. Buildings had been spaced up and down the rectangle, all connected by a ten-foot-high wall of grey stone. No one would be wandering into the school by accident—or wandering out.

Marilynn walked us along a covered veranda that curved all the way around the courtyard. She pointed out several buildings that consisted of classrooms. Students sat around on the grass. Most were busy punching things on their iPads. Some played soccer on the grass. It would have looked like an ordinary school, but then I saw someone float the soccer ball toward the goal. From the groans of the other team, this seemed to be an acceptable way to score.

"The cathedral holds the Great Hall. It is where we hold all of our gatherings. It is also the gymnasium. You will spend a great deal of time in there for your physical training." Marilynn pointed to a plain-looking building next to the cathedral. It had a huge clock high up on its face. "That is the Council building. It houses all the members, as well as your teachers."

The clock chimed loudly when the hour turned. It

* 100 *

reverberated through the long courtyard. A sea of students spilled out of the buildings. We stopped to stare at them.

"There are so many," Grey muttered.

"The school is much larger than it first appears," Marilynn replied.

Grey watched the students playing with the floating soccer ball.

"Alexa would have loved this," I said to Grey. He nodded.

We had almost completed the circle around the courtyard when Marilynn signaled for us to stop again. She pointed at twin stone buildings. "Morgan Hall and Monmouth House are right next to each other. The dining hall connects them, so you will be eating together."

The dormitories were not as ornate as the cathedral, but they had a lot of windows. Lion-shaped, stone rainspouts stuck out of the corners as a marker for each floor. I counted five.

"Before I leave you to get settled in, there is one more thing." Marilynn handed us badges. They were small cloth discs containing a stitching of a dragon. "This marks you as part of the Excalibur program. You will notice all of the other students with similar badges. These mark what your skill area is. For those of you who are wizard candidates, you will receive other badges as your powers become defined."

"What are the different badges?" Oliver asked.

Marilynn shook her head. "You will find out more when you have your first class tomorrow. Boys, please follow me into Monmouth House. Girls, remain here until I return."

She and the boys walked off. Which left me alone with the

sole other girl. It seemed odd just to stand around without speaking, but I struggled to find something to say to her. I didn't really want to ask about her vision. I felt bad enough for just watching the brutal beating. No wonder the girl looked like she'd gotten out of rehab just a few weeks ago.

I asked what I hoped was a simple question. "How did you meet Vane?"

"I was doing cage fighting for some lowlifes. He got me out. I thought he was trying to buy a good time, you know, but then he showed me what he could do. Magic. Said I could do it, too." Her hair swung like spiky icicles as she shook her head. "How wild is that?"

"Wild," I repeated. "So you don't want to get the sword?"

Slouching against a veranda column, she frowned at me like I'd asked something dumb. "Of course, I do. Why wouldn't I? It's the ultimate power. Whoever gets it will be famous."

It took a minute for me to digest what she said. "Do you really think everyone will know you pulled the sword?"

"After the Total Tremor, they can't very well hide it, can they? Everyone in the world knows about it." She kicked her foot. "Whoever gets it will never get put down again."

For a second, she dropped her tough persona and vulnerability shone clearly on her face. It was obvious Vane had made some grand promises to his candidates.

At least Matt hadn't done that. I chewed my lip. Matt hadn't talked at all about what would happen after someone pulled the sword. Becoming famous didn't sound like a good idea to me. More questions Matt—*no, Merlin*—had conveniently skipped answering.

I looked at the girl. A pang of pity filled me. She reminded me of a lost puppy at the pound. "You're risking your life just to be famous?"

The girl straightened away from the column. "Aren't you?"

I shook my head. "The gargoyles were after us. We had no choice."

A red eyebrow lifted. "If you say so." She grinned and her gaze turned to the courtyard. The soccer match had become a semi-wrestling match between a group of guys. "You have to admit, though, it's not so bad here."

I smiled. It was the kind of statement Alexa would have made.

Marilynn came out of the building. She pointed us to the other building. "Miss DuLac. Miss Cornwall. Let's go. I will introduce you to the head of the residence hall. She will explain the details of the arrangement."

Turning on her heel, she strode into Morgan Hall. I hurried after her. The other girl followed slowly. The minute I stepped inside Morgan Hall, I felt at home—maybe because the country chic décor matched Sylvia's study in Boston almost perfectly. I wondered what Sylvia would say if she saw it. I had a feeling she had no idea how deep the Ragnars' ties to the wizard world went.

Marilynn led us past a spacious living area with huge couches and an enormous plasma screen TV. She stopped at a small office tucked into a far corner of the first level. "Ms. Joseph, I have new students for you. Arriane DuLac and

Georgiana Cornwall."

A stout woman with round glasses and rosy cheeks sat behind a desk. She was watching news coverage of the sword on her flat-screen LCD. She reluctantly turned away from it when we entered the office. She gave us a brisk onceover.

"My name is Ryan—"

"I'm Gia—"

We both burst out at the same time. I smiled at the red-haired girl. She grimaced.

"That's all well and good." Ms. Joseph held out two keycards. "Ms. Fay didn't inform us that we needed a room until this morning, but everything is ready. You will share. We have four to a room here, but since you are joining late in the semester there will be only two of you. The card has the room number. You may show yourselves upstairs. You'll find a welcome package on your bed with some essentials. Other than that, please show up promptly to meal times. Food will not be kept waiting for you if you miss it." She finished with a shooing motion. "That is all. Go on now."

"Aren't you going to show them the common areas?" Marilynn asked.

"I'm sure they'll figure it out," Ms. Joseph said. "The girls are old enough. We don't need to coddle them, Ms. Fay."

Marilynn's face twisted into a mask of frustration. "Fine, I suppose I can show them."

"Uh hum," Ms. Joseph said, turning back to the TV. We'd taken a few steps outside when she stopped us. "Wait. Is *he* back, Ms. Fay?"

Marilynn turned back. "Who?"

"Don't be coy, Ms. Fay," Ms. Joseph said. "You attended his lectures before he left, just like the rest of us… and it wasn't to hear him speak."

Marilynn turned red. "I don't know what you're talking about—"

"Merlin, of course." Ms. Joseph sighed like a little girl. "I never imagined someone like him being so handsome. Do you know when he'll start his lecture series again? I get asked about it every day, you know. There is a list of witches eager to sign up. It's not just the student witches either. I've been talking to Sir Calvin over at the teachers' residence—"

"Ah, yes," Marilynn cut her off. She glanced at me, then away. "I will ask him, but I don't know if the lectures will happen. He is quite busy." She nodded at Ms. Joseph's monitor. "You can understand why."

"Yes, of course." Ms. Joseph sighed in disappointment.

"Merlin taught here?" I asked.

"Oh, yes," Ms. Joseph replied. "When he first woke, the Council brought him here right away. He taught for a little bit—" She lowered her voice. "—before he had the visions. Then he set off on the hunt." She let out a girlish sigh of longing. "It was the best lecture series we've ever had. He's so young for being so wise. I could listen to him for hours. Of course, I don't remember exactly what he said. It was *how* he said it. You must remember, Ms. Fay. You always sat right in the front row."

"Ah, yes. Quite enlightening." Marilynn didn't look at me.

Gia interjected, "Ryan knows him quite well. Maybe he told her."

For the first time, Ms. Joseph looked at me skeptically. "Really? You know him well."

"Er, yes," I said.

Marilynn snorted. "I'd say so."

When three sets of eyes looked at her in surprise, she colored, muttering, "They're candidates. Part of the Excalibur program."

Ms. Joseph's large eyes turned on me with bunny-like plea. "Oh, do tell. How well did you know him? Have you actually had a whole conversation? What is he like? Does he eat?"

Although the barrage of questions was overwhelming, the last one made me pause.

"Does he eat?" I repeated cautiously.

Ms. Joseph nodded earnestly. "He's so powerful. Who knows? Maybe he's advanced past eating."

Wow. I stared at her slack-jawed for a second. *Advanced past eating.* I had a vision of Matt scarfing down pizza on our first date. "No, he definitely eats."

"How do you know?" she demanded.

"Uh, he likes pepperoni."

"That's so American," Marilynn scoffed.

"I like pizza," Ms. Joseph exclaimed. "I'll talk to the dining staff. I wager they'd love to make him some. Do you think he would like that?"

I was starting to feel like I'd fallen into an alternate

universe. I'd never been interrogated about someone so closely before. It was like he was a celebrity. "Um, sure."

Ms. Joseph clapped her hands with glee. "Wonderful."

I glanced at Gia. She snickered.

Ms. Joseph touched her hair as she looked at the wall with dreamy eyes. "What I wouldn't give to be a candidate. You'll be getting to spend so much time with him."

Gia cleared her throat. "Ryan doesn't need to be a candidate for that."

Ms. Joseph's eyes widened. "Her and *him*? Together?"

"Of course not," Marilynn scoffed. "She is too young for him." Her brow furrowed. She looked at me and asked point blank, "You and he have never… dated?"

"W-well," I stammered. "Not *never*."

BASIC ELEMENTS

Ms. Joseph gave me an awed look.

Marilynn made a small sound of distress.

"Are you alright?" Gia asked her.

Marilynn huffed and took a deep breath. "I'm fine." She pointed us out of the office. "However, you two need to get going. The lift is that way. Your room is on the fifth level. I'll leave you to find it."

Before we could say anything else, she'd pushed past us and hurried away.

"Poor girl," Ms. Joseph sighed, looking after Marilynn. "I know just how she feels."

With a forced smile on my face, I backed out of the office. Gia followed. I scowled at her. "Matt and I are not dating."

Gia laughed. "That was hilarious."

I halted midstride. "You told them that to get a rise out of them?"

"Sure. It was too funny," she said. "And I really don't like that Marilynn. She's kinda stuck-up."

I couldn't disagree with that. Still, I groused. "Why did you have to bring me into it?"

Gia laughed sardonically. "Because whether or not you admit it, it's true. You two were hanging all over each other."

"We went on a date. Possibly two. Depends on how you look at it." I felt my cheeks turn red. I was babbling. I stalked into the elevator and punched the button for our room. "Anyway, it's finished. Over. I mean you wouldn't date a guy who keeps lying to you, right?"

Gia gave me a look that said I was the world's biggest idiot. "He is Merlin. And it's obvious why he lied—"

"What? Why?"

"Hellooo." Gia leaned against the mirrored wall of the miniscule elevator and checked out her teeth. "He's the most powerful wizard of all time. And he likes you. He probably didn't want you to freak."

But I was freaking. And I didn't like Merlin. I liked Matt.

***

Early the next morning, a mass of students filled the courtyard and veranda as they rushed to classes. Grey and I walked together. Grey wore khakis, a long-sleeved T-shirt, and a jacket. He looked at my jeans, rumpled shirt, and barely-made hair with amusement.

"Tough night?" he asked. The school map application on the iPad directed us into an imposing stone building.

I yawned. "Gia is not the quietest sleeper."

"Who?"

"My new roommate. The girl with red hair. One of Vane's candidates."

He nodded. "Hot girl. The brute's girlfriend."

We walked down a long hallway with classrooms to the left and right.

I rolled my eyes. "She may be someone's girlfriend, but she kept mumbling about Merlin all night."

"Oh, that's why," he deadpanned.

I punched him in the shoulder.

Grey yelped. "Watch it, bruiser. Why is it that every time *The One* is even mentioned you turn violent?"

With a little growl, I punched him in the shoulder again.

His eyes flickered over me. "You look soft, but you pack a mean punch."

I opened my mouth, but didn't get a chance to retort. We reached the end of the hallway and entered a corner classroom. It was a huge room. At the front stood three blank black chalkboards side by side. The sterile smell of forced learning didn't seem to be present. High open windows and the scent of wild flowers seemed far from the dungeon-like atmosphere of the classrooms I was used to. Grey and I sat on one long bench attached to a mahogany bench table, nothing like the flimsy individual metal desk and chair combo that were the norm back home.

Dinner last night had been odd. Round tables with fine white tablecloths and sit-down service felt more suitable for a wedding than a school cafeteria. The heavy silverware we used might have even been real silver. Everything about the wizard school, from its immaculate landscape, to the iPads, to the gourmet food, screamed money. Of course, if every wizard family was as rich as the Ragnars, I guess the opulence shouldn't have surprised me.

It was a far cry from the life my mother's teacher salary could have afforded. I smoothed down my jeans nervously. I hadn't felt this out of place in Boston, mostly because there had been enough normal kids in school to make up for the crazy rich ones. But here even the superfine, softer-than-silk cotton sheets on my bed last night had brought to my attention how completely out of my element I was.

To distract myself, I glanced at the kids in the room. There were around forty or so. The Regulars made up about half. Vane's candidates sat in the back. A row of about fifteen kids sat in the front. I didn't recognize them at all. They hadn't been at the admissions test.

Outside, the clock tower chimed. I tapped my iPad. The calendar told me that I was scheduled for Basic Elements in the morning, then a break for lunch, and then Physical Training in the afternoon.

The classroom door swung open.

Matt strode into the room. He crossed to the teacher's desk and set down a leather satchel. "Welcome. For those of you who don't know me, I'm Merlin. But I go by Matt Emrys. A modern name for a modern time."

He held up his iPad. "Many of you have these. I'm here to tell you—they're useless." Matt snapped his fingers and copies of a heavy tome appeared out of nowhere onto our desks.

Groans filled the room. It was one impressively thick book.

"Part of learning magic is to feel it. To touch it. To smell it. You can't get that sense from one of these." He pointed to the iPad.

"Why do we care about magic? We don't have any," Grey asked.

"Precisely. You will be learning how to defend yourself against magic." Matt came around the teacher's desk and leaned against the edge casually. It irked me that I noticed how hot he looked. He glanced at me as if he'd heard my thought. I looked away.

"Let us start with why you're here. These things do have one use." Matt picked up the iPad from where he'd tossed it. A flat-screen TV lowered in front of the black board. With a few taps, a news broadcast started streaming.

A news anchor said, "…five days have passed since the infamous stone fell in Trafalgar Square. Reports of damage and casualties are still being reported from the effects of the Total Tremor. However, no one has been able to give a satisfactory answer to the question on the world's mind—*why?*"

"But that hasn't stopped more and more visitors from coming. They have flocked from around the world to try their hand at pulling the sword from the stone—" The broadcast showed a line of people curving more than a mile around the narrow London streets. "There seems to be no end in sight. While more and more have come away empty handed, some have not left at all."

Portraits of five people filled the screen.

"Some would dismiss it as a game. But the game can be deadly. These five young men have tried their luck at the sword. All five have died. All from the same cause—a heart attack. Is it curse or coincidence?"

The shot panned back to the square. A line of soldiers in body armor and carrying what looked like Uzis formed a circle around the sword. Police officers facilitated the movement of people in line.

"What does it all mean?" the news anchor said. "We do not know, but this reporter knows one thing—good or bad, the sword is undoubtedly the stuff of legend."

Matt paused the broadcast.

"One gargoyle. Four Regulars. All dead. What does it tell you?"

"That the Regulars should go home," said a thin boy with black geek-chic glasses sitting at the very front of the class.

A girl sitting beside him giggled. Vane's candidates laughed. Oliver made an angry sound and started to get up.

Matt signaled him to sit down. Oliver reluctantly complied. Matt stared at the boy with glasses. "Blake Emerson. If I may ask, when did you first arrive at Avalon Preparatory?"

Blake folded thin arms in front of him. "When I turned thirteen."

"How many defensive spells do you know?"

"Over one hundred thirty," Blake answered. Kids near him murmured in appreciation. Blake nodded with cool composure.

Matt leaned back on the teacher's desk with equal

composure. "How many have you used?"

Blake straightened. "Practical training doesn't start until after graduation—"

"The answer is zero," Grey said.

Matt nodded. "All practical magic is held off until a wizard has passed the wizard trial and becomes an apprentice. Then, they are put under the mentorship of an older wizard and taught how to use magic in real life."

"And you?" Matt asked the girl sitting next to Blake. "When did you arrive?"

She replied, "Thirteen."

"Twelve," said the boy next to her.

The next boy over said, "Sixteen."

Another girl said, "Twelve."

Matt gave Blake a bland look. "Mr. Emerson, today you will begin practical training. By the time you leave here, you will have performed every spell you know. Is that acceptable to you?"

Blake touched his glasses. His body alive with a sudden surge of energy, he nodded eagerly. "Yes, sir."

"And for those of us who don't have magic?" I asked.

Matt gave me an enigmatic smile. "You will soon learn how wrong that question is. While Regulars don't have magic, they can be taught how to fight against it. It is not something that is advertised, certainly, but it is possible. If you have a good teacher, you will learn that magic doesn't guarantee someone the upper hand."

Blake made an awed sound. "I had heard that Merlin could teach even the Regulars, but I thought that was myth. You must be even more powerful than legend says."

Matt shook his head. "It is more important to be knowledgeable than powerful."

I tapped a fingernail on the solid walnut table. "But you are... more powerful?"

Matt's eyes flickered. "Yes, I am."

There was a pause as we absorbed this.

"Let us proceed with today's lesson. Open to the first chapter." Matt waved a hand and all of our books flipped open. Pictures of men in different color robes performing magic appeared. "We have found that a wizard tends to have strengths in certain areas. These areas are defined by the four elements—water, air, fire, and earth. For example, a water wizard generally tends to make a great healer. Air wizards have telekinesis. Fire tends to control energy. Earth has a close connection to growing things—shape shifting even."

"Let us go to the next page," Matt said. This time he let us flip the page. I sucked in a breath at the picture of a two-faced monster. One face looked normal. The other was the head of a beast—a furrowed Cro-Magnon brow and a mouth with protruding fangs.

My heart beat faster. *Morgan.*

The boyfriend who I had safely forgotten until yesterday. Memories of Morgan as my boyfriend had started fading after my first few months in Concord.

Morgan the monster filled me with violent repugnance.

The musty smell of the book only sharpened the memories. I forced myself to breathe. Matt watched me from the front of the room. He took a step away from his desk and halted.

With his gaze fixed on me, he continued. "This is a depiction of a gargoyle. The most significant obstacle you will be facing in the quest for the sword. The two faces indicate how they look before and after they turn. A gargoyle can appear like any other person. When they turn, however, you see the beast inside. In addition to owning teeth that can rip your throat out, gargoyles have super strength, super speed, and great healing powers."

"How are we supposed to fight something like that?" Grey asked.

"Knowledge." Matt looked down and flipped our books to the next page. It showed a picture of the moon. "Gargoyles are at their most powerful at night. Catch them during the day and your chances of beating them go up significantly. There is a basic theory behind elements. While the types of our powers are defined by physical elements, the strengths of those same powers are tied to time. In the gargoyle's case, it is the moon."

I swallowed. "Can you get turned into a gargoyle?"

Matt looked at me for a moment before he shook his head. "They have been around as long as wizards… or the Regulars. They have always stayed together—their society is rigidly hierarchical—which I believe kept their numbers small during Arthur's time. I don't think that's true any longer. But no… I have never heard of anyone being turned into a gargoyle. As far as I know, they are born that way."

Matt flipped the page again.

It showed a picture of a silver sword. "And this is how you kill them."

I sat up straight.

"Stab them with silver?" Oliver asked.

"No." He glanced at me.

"Vane took its head off with a sword," I said.

Several kids—except the wizard school candidates who hadn't seen my memories—shifted in their seat uncomfortably.

Matt looked at me with a worried frown. "Yes, the best way is to sever the head. Almost everything else, and they will regenerate. You can bury them, but they will dig themselves out. Or if you were a powerful enough magician, you could blow them up. Disintegration may work."

Blake scoffed. "Not even a Master has that much power."

The girl wizard said, "You could supplement your power."

"There is a high probability you would die," said Blake.

Matt laid his hands flat on top of the desk. "Wizards are most likely to die from exhaustion."

"We call it 'flame out,'" Blake said.

Matt raised his brow. Blake's cheeks turned red.

"Flame out," Matt said. "A most appropriate phrase."

Blake preened at the compliment.

I eyed Matt. I remembered him in the woods, battling the giant dragon. I asked, "How do you know how powerful a wizard is?"

In a know-it-all tone, Blake answered, "The more powerful the wizard, the more magic they can do. Most wizards only have one specialization. A powerful wizard can have many."

"How do you kill a wizard?" Grey asked.

"A Regular can't," said Mark from behind.

"They can indeed," Matt corrected. "Without our magic, wizards are quite fragile. Take a shot from a gun. A stabbing. If there is no healer present, any wound can be quite fatal. Even with a healer." Matt didn't look at Grey or me. "Things can get out of control."

"But you can probably turn them into a toad or something before they get close enough, right?" said Billie, one of the bashful Regulars.

The classroom laughed, breaking the tension.

"Brute force magic is expensive—hard to conjure and tiring to execute. Using the element of surprise is by far the best option," Matt said.

Blake asked, "I still don't understand why we're talking about this. The wizards are all on the same side."

"Expect the unexpected," Matt said. "The gargoyles have been amassing magic for decades. And you never know if they have turned a magician. There are always rogues. Not everyone agrees with the way the Council has decided to keep magic hidden all these years."

A few gasps came from the front row.

"It is not possible," Blake said. "The Council binds anyone's power that is considered dangerous."

Matt smiled. "A valid point, Blake. However, you have forgotten that the sword itself is a magical object. Its powers cannot be bound."

I watched the wistful look on his face with interest. "You talk about it as if it were a person."

"It's tempting to think of it as such. But it is not. It does not have emotion. It is worse than facing a person. The sword feels no compassion. It will not stop if you cry foul or if you try to surrender. It is extremely dangerous, and it will test you. This training is to make sure you have the skills to pass that trial."

I said, "What happens if you don't pass the trial?"

"You have seen the news broadcasts."

Silence fell across the room. A picture of the Italian kid, Gianni, went through my mind. He could have been one of us sitting in this class.

"They were unprepared," Matt said. "You will not be."

"As I said, the element of surprise is the best. There are also shields that can be acquired—either magical or charmed objects. Gargoyles, because of their innate abilities, can avoid many spells. So all of you, Regulars and wizards alike, will need something extra."

Matt pulled forward the leather satchel he'd carried into the classroom. From inside the bag, he brought out a handful of silver necklaces and several silver rings. Each piece of jewelry held a large gemstone pendant. "Charms. Wizard or Regular, please come and get one. The charm resonates with its owner. Pick the one that *feels* right. But remember, this will be the single most powerful weapon I will hand you. So choose wisely."

The candidates at the front scrambled to get up and get to

Matt's desk. I watched as the Regulars and Vane's candidates crowded behind them. Mark muscled through the others. Another wizard boy next to Blake got shoved aside as Mark snatched the ring he had started to pick up. The rest of Vane's candidates followed his lead. A few of the unwanted rings went tumbling to the ground.

Gia picked up a plain silver chain with a big ruby gemstone. Something about it struck me as oddly familiar. I stared at it, wanting it. Needing it with an intensity that came out of nowhere.

Gia moved to put it around her neck. I nearly leapt from my desk to snatch it from her. Gia put it back down. I let out a breath.

The Regulars stood around trying to catch a glimpse of the charms while Vane's candidates picked through the bunch.

"They're going to rip apart everything before we can even take a look," Grey said

Inspiration struck me. Taking out my iPad, I typed up a quick email. In the back of the room, fifteen or so iPads started beeping.

Gia marched back to her desk. She picked up her iPad. "Who sent me an event request to 'Get In A Line?'"

I grinned as I stood up to go to the desk. Matt raised a brow when I reached him.

I shrugged. "Sometimes you have to do what you have to do."

"Yes, you do," he said.

"Why am I surprised you agree?" I said in a snarky tone.

He picked up the silver necklace and held it out like a carrot. I reached for it.

Matt's hand tightened on it. The red gemstone seemed to heat under our combined touch. I tugged it. My hand grazed his. The friction between our hands sparked a fluttery sensation deep in the pit of my stomach.

Matt said, "The *Dragon's Eye*. Nice choice. This belonged to a queen once."

"Which one?" I asked.

Matt didn't answer. "Let me put it on you."

Since he still held onto the amulet, I had no choice. I inclined my head and slipped off Sylvia's necklace. Matt pulled me away from the desk, making space for the other candidates to continue picking out their charms. His breath caressed my neck as he put the charm on me. Warm fingers skimmed my skin.

I prompted, "Done, Merlin?"

He snapped close the clasp. "My name is Matt."

"That's just a cover."

He leaned closer. "I am Matt."

"Why?" My whole body tightened. My spine became rigid. I took a bracing breath. "Why would you not want to be known as the most powerful wizard in the world? Why wouldn't you want to be Merlin?"

Even though we stood in the middle of a classroom surrounded by students, it seemed as if there were only two of us present.

"I am Matt," he said in a low tone. "Because I can't even

remember who Merlin is. Matt is real."

He let the amulet drop. The gemstone fell on my bare skin. I gasped at the heat emanating from it. It sat on me as if I'd always worn it.

Matt stepped back with an enigmatic smile. "Perfect. It's been waiting a long time for you."

***

"Now that you are more or less on the same footing, I will be sorting you into groups," he announced. "Each group will contain at least one wizard."

Everyone rose. With a wave of his hand, he cleared the tables and benches. They slid to the edges of the room up against the walls. Matt assigned me to Blake, Oliver, Gia, and Paul.

"Now, one wizard from each group will come to me. I will give you an attack spell. The rest of your group will be defending against you. Those of you defending, use the amulet to see through the spell and reach the wizard. If you can touch him, you can disable him."

"I'll go," Blake volunteered. I glanced at Gia. She shrugged.

Blake scuttled over to Matt. Matt huddled together with the 'attack' wizards. Blake returned, trying to hold a serious expression on his naturally cheerful face.

"Ready?" he asked.

"Sure," I said, lining up to be first.

Gia stopped me. "I'll go first. Try it on me."

Across the room, I saw everyone else doing the same. Grey was going first in his group. I turned back to Gia and Blake.

Blake raised his hand and shouted out a spell.

"*Prazaanta.*"

I could barely make out the word as it grazed past my ear, the syllables warbled and warped sounding. It hurt to hear the word, but then it faded. Blake's palm punched out at Gia as if to direct the flow of the spell toward her.

Gia froze in place. For a second, I saw her skin turn a pale blue. I glanced over at Grey. He, too, had a slight sheen of blue. All across the room, every single candidate stood paralyzed. No one had stopped the spell.

"Merlin," Grey said. "This is bogus. You need to give us better instructions."

"See the spell coming. Don't let the flow hit you directly. Step away. Move. Don't stand and take it." Matt folded his arms across his chest and leaned back comfortably against the front of the teacher's desk. "Let's keep going. Next person, step up."

Oliver moved forward. I held up my hand and shook my head. Oliver let me go again. Blake sent the same spell. I heard the word almost as if I could see it. The air in the room seemed to thicken. I felt a breeze from where the spell originated. I saw the air move as the spell snaked toward me. The amulet on my chest felt cold... and dead.

My hand reached up to touch the gemstone even while my feet moved me out of the way of the blast. The spell moved as I moved. It repositioned and headed straight for me.

Matt was full of crap. The amulet had no special affinity for me. It didn't even work.

TRAINING

The spell blast hit me like a wallop of wind. All of a sudden, the amulet glowed, just as it had done when light hit it before. Red fire rose around me, creating a barrier. The spell glanced off me and dissolved. Red fire faded. I wiggled my fingers and toes just to make sure I could.

"Nicely done." Matt clapped. He walked over to our group.

"What was that?" Blake demanded, his cherub face turning purple. "You said to move. That had nothing to do with moving."

"By moving, she activated the amulet. It sensed her heightened state and responded."

I looked down at the quiet gemstone. Red winked back at me. "I woke it up."

"My turn." Oliver gestured at Blake. Blake shot the spell to him. Oliver stepped out of the way as I had done. I saw the spell follow him. Oliver's soft-blue amulet glowed. It didn't create a barrier like mine, but somehow the spell dissolved.

"Well done," Matt said.

I opened my mouth to ask him about the lack of barrier, but Matt had already gone on to another group. I saw across the room the same defensive move being used. Some succeeded. Some didn't.

Three hours after the class had begun, Matt called it to an end. Everyone ran out toward the dining hall. We only had half an hour for our lunch break and we were all starving. I took my time putting Matt's heavy tome into the school shoulder bag we'd all been given and securing the iPad. I traced the detailed stitching on the front flap of the bag. It had the same lion emblem on it that had been on the front door of the school.

When the last person had left the classroom, I marched up to Matt. My stomach let out a lion-like roar.

"The amulet uses up your strength," he said mildly. "That's why you're so hungry. You should get to lunch."

I laid my palms on his desk. "Do you want to come with me?"

Matt stopped in the middle of closing his bag. "I can't... I mean... I could. Teachers are allowed, but I... can't."

I fiddled with my new amulet. "I see."

Matt watched my movements. Self-consciously, I stopped.

"Which queen did the amulet belong to?"

Matt closed his bag. "Why do you ask?"

"I want to know."

"Do you want to give it back?"

"No!" I said. And stopped. I rubbed my eyes. "I don't know why I said that. This thing is doing something to me." I tugged at the amulet.

Matt moved swiftly to stop me. He put his hands on mine to still them. "Don't take it off."

"Why?"

Matt didn't answer.

"If you don't tell me, *Merlin*," I said, "I'm tossing this right now."

Matt took a step back. His gaze lowered to the floor. "I made it."

I stilled. "What? What does that mean?"

"Charms are as powerful as the wizard who makes them. I've only ever made one in my life." He confessed. "And you're wearing it."

"You wanted me to have it. You brought it out for me," I said sharply.

"It is the most powerful charm in existence. I want to keep you safe, Ryan."

I raised a brow. "Then why are you acting so strange?"

"Why are *you* acting so strange? So attached? *You* feel a strong connection to it—"

Matt's dark gaze locked on mine. My heart skipped several beats.

"—because you feel a strong connection to me."

He meant he knew I liked him. I felt the tips of my ears turn red.

Matt came around to stand directly in front of me. His heart thumped against his chest. It seemed to beat so loudly it echoed around the room. I laid my hand against it and took a breath. For a long second, we just stood there.

I didn't want to move. Ever. Yet, I still asked, "Which queen did it belong to?"

There was a pause. Matt said, "Does it matter?"

Like cold water, his words washed over me. After all the things he'd held back from me, I don't know why it kept surprising me that he wasn't finished. Anger renewed itself inside me. His name was not *Matt*. He was *Merlin*.

I broke away from him. "Yes, it matters. How am I supposed to trust you when you're never honest with me?"

"You can't trust me?" Matt gave me a measured look. "It seems like you don't trust anyone."

"What?" I said with a frown.

"The vision you saw in the Lake water. You never said a word to me about your mother back in Boston."

"You knew she had died. I didn't even remember the rest until yesterday!"

"And Vane? I saw the way you looked at him when you first saw him—"

"I recognized him from TV—" My eyes narrowed. "Wait, is this about your stupid vision? After what he's done, how can you even think that I'd k—" I grimaced in disgust. "Kiss him?"

"Have you heard of a term called '*Silvertongue*?' It is a person who has a certain way with words. There is a power in words. Some can lift you up high. Some can shatter you." Matt turned. With his back to me, he picked up his bag and slowly said, "I have no doubt '*Silvertongue*' originated from the rare wizards who have the same gift as Vane. What my brother says, whatever he says, you want to believe him. You might hate him now, but he has a way of slipping through your defenses."

Matt turned around. He reached out to touch the ruby gemstone. His fingers skimmed the edge.

"Matt." I said the name with a wealth of longing that kept threatening to spill over and consume me.

Matt let go of the amulet. "I thought you decided to call me Merlin."

***

After a quick lunch with Grey and a few of the other Regular candidates, we hurried toward the cathedral where the next class was scheduled. I had peeked at the schedule of a wizard student sitting next to us. She had six classes—just like the curriculum back home—except besides math, all of her advanced classes bore labels like Fire Elements, Water Elements, Air Elements, etc. Types of magic, she explained to us.

Although I wouldn't have been able to do anything in such classes, I still felt a bit envious of her. It sounded much more fun than a whole afternoon of something called Physical Training. I translated physical training to gym. I was looking forward to it about as much as a three-hour dental cleaning.

My *Friday Night Lights* Mom had often wondered how I could possibly be her daughter. While I hadn't done that badly in fencing, I hadn't loved it. As for basketball, volleyball, tennis, and whatever sport of the day my mother signed me up for, I had been a disaster since day one. And yet, my mother had insisted I try, year after year, since preschool.

Grey, on the other hand, wore an expression of rabid anticipation. Sometimes his whole master-jock persona could be really irritating. We paused just inside the cathedral and stared around in awe. Stained-glass windows shimmered bright rainbow lights onto the white stone floors inside. More white stone formed the walls and curved into the high ceiling. A stage rose up in the middle of the room. Only a few chairs surrounded it, but the space was certainly big enough to fit hundreds of students.

Blake strode by us.

Snapping out of our trance, Grey and I rushed after him. My boots echoed as we crossed to a corner of the cathedral. It was then that I noticed several curved archways leading off from the main area. We followed Blake into one and discovered a turret with a winding staircase. We climbed up to the second floor. It led out into a smaller, but still quite large, gym-like room with gleaming wood floors. Intricate moldings stood out on the door and windows. Rustic racks of weapons hung along the walls. The room reminded me of a medieval training room, except that a very modern gel mat outlined a workout space in the middle.

Vane stood in the middle of the mat. He wore a black martial arts uniform made up of a short kimono and matching loose cotton pants. Except for his shorter hair, it was eerie how much he looked like Matt. The disparaging expression on his face when he spotted me was one I'd never seen on Matt, though. So much for the infamous charm Matt had warned me about… not that I cared. From the way he'd treated the poor kid who hadn't turned out to be a candidate, Vane wasn't someone I really wanted to try to charm me.

Grey nudged me toward the dressing rooms after Blake. They stood off to the back of the room inside another arched doorway. We split up as he went into the men's. Inside the women's dressing room, a wall-to-wall mirror covered one side completely. Several stalls took up the opposite wall. Ducking into one, I pulled a cloth curtain and tugged on a white uniform. It had been placed in my school bag among a few other supplies—including a hair tie. I saw no place to store my bag, so I lugged it out with me.

"Not bad." Gia emerged from an adjoining stall in uniform and posed in front of the mirror.

I agreed. The mirror showed that the uniform fit well on me. I even had shape, despite the loose fit of the top and pants. I twisted the flyaway strands of my wavy hair into a ponytail. Gia did the same. Somehow, while Gia projected fierce Amazon warrior, I looked like a twelve-year-old cheerleader.

"I don't think anyone will notice," she said.

"Notice what?"

She smirked at me. "If you sneak out of here. You look like you're about to throw up."

"I'm fine."

"Forget something?" Gia pointed to my feet where my gym bag lay. "You should really label it. They all look the same."

She took a pen out of her bag and tossed it to me.

I bent down to get my bag as she went around me. The

dressing room door slammed shut. I quickly labeled my bag and went to the door.

It was locked. Gia had locked me inside.

I pounded the door for several minutes. No sound came from the other side. Cursing, I stared at myself in the mirror. My face was flushed. Wide eyes shone bright. Dark blond hair escaped in droves from the tight ponytail I'd tried to stuff it into. I looked helpless.

My cheeks huffed in and out like a puffer fish. For a second, I just wanted to give up. It had already been a long morning. Every time I talked with Matt, he ground me down into a mass of lumpy mashed potatoes.

But was I really going to let *Gia* defeat me this easily?

I marched to my bag and pulled out my iPad. All of the candidates reported offline. That only left one person. I bit my lip, debating it for a second. Then, I took a bracing breath and punched in the message. The reply came back swiftly.

You'll owe me one. Vane texted.

Forget it. I texted back.

No show today = No show, period.

I made a sound of extreme frustration. I punched in my reply. *I owe you one.*

Two minutes later, Grey unlocked the door. "Vane sent me."

"I'm going to kill Gia." I stomped out of the room and into the hallway. "I just traded my soul to the devil."

The clock chimed, warning us that we were about to be late. Out in the gym, all of the candidates stood at attention on the exercise mat. Gia and Mark snickered as Grey and I approached the group.

"Ms. DuLac and Mr. Ragnar, thank you for honoring us with your presence. If it pleases you, shall we begin?"

Vane stared at me. No one spoke for long seconds.

"S-sure," I mumbled.

"How kind of you to condescend," Vane replied mockingly. More of the candidates snickered.

Vane stopped the noise by raising one steely eyebrow. "I am Vane. You may address me as such. In this training class, I will make sure you are as fit as you can be. You will also be learning how to win a fight. How to properly defend and attack. We will start with the basics—hand-to-hand combat—before working up to sticks, swords, and guns."

A few murmurs of surprise went through the room.

"Yes, even guns," Vane said. "Although guns are fairly useless against those well trained in magic, the Council has instructed me to include every threat in the curriculum. However, we have a short amount of time for you to become experts in this area—so I will be spending the least amount of time on this part."

"Is that because Regulars are the ones who most have to worry about guns?" I asked.

"No, DuLac," Vane said in a measured tone. "It is because we don't have much time. Period. Don't worry, though. I'm sure the Council will see fit to provide you with some body armor if you are so troubled."

Vane turned back to address the class. "Our main objective

is to become proficient at all of the sword forms. The sword is the most effective way to kill a Gargoyle or a wizard—"

"Why is it the most effective?" I interrupted.

Vane took another long breath. "Swords resist magic. Surely, you knew that. Any other questions?"

I opened my mouth.

"Not from you, DuLac," Vane said. "Let us give someone else a chance."

No one said a word.

"I will start by putting you through a simple series of tests. This will determine your ranking. Every other week, we will retest and rank again. Every week, I will be the only and absolute judge of where you stand—and, thus, what you will learn."

The message in his little speech was clear. Toe the line, take what he dishes out, or suffer the consequences.

Vane gave us a minute to absorb this. He barked, "Ready?"

"Ready, sir," chorused the class.

"Good." With that one word, Vane set to torturing us.

For the next hour, we did an exhausting set of aerobic exercises and karate kicks. I was used to working out so I was tired, but not winded. The other Regulars—all in good athletic shape—seemed at the same level. Blake and another one of the wizard girls looked as if they were about to pass out. Vane's candidates glanced around with bored expressions.

"Next I will be showing you kendo forms," Vane said. He handed out arm-length wooden sticks. "Watch as I demonstrate. I will only do each form once. Then you will repeat. Your ranking will depend on the correctness of the form as well as your ability to replicate it. If you think you can look at your neighbor to remind you, just remember that they probably don't know it any better than you."

We did that for another hour. At the end, I thought I would drop where I stood. I was mentally and physically exhausted. Even Vane's candidates had been challenged by the mental alertness it took to remember each step when your muscles were on fire.

"You will pair off into groups," Vane instructed. "Each of you will pick one form that you have learned. One person will stand in the middle. The others will form a circle around him and attack with their one form. The defender may respond with any form. You will do this for five minutes each. You will not stop until time has been called. This will be your last test."

As soon as we started, I knew I was going to fail. We paired off into loose groups of five. Blake insisted on going first. He stood in the middle as we charged him.

It was a massacre. No thanks to me.

I dropped my stick twice, but Mark the Brute and another one of Vane's candidates hammered at Blake until he fell to the ground.

"Enough." I stepped in the middle and held up my hands.

In two strides, Vane reached our group. "There is no enough. You either win or lose. Since Emerson has not voiced his surrender, why, I wonder, do you feel the need to step in?"

I stood my ground. "He would if he could."

Vane peered down at the fallen boy. "His mouth looks

uninjured to me. Emerson, are you able to speak?"

Blake squeaked, "Y-yes."

"Is that all you have to say?" Vane said. "Hesitation will not work against a gargoyle. If you do not have the confidence to stand up in practice, then you do not belong in training. There will be no mercy out in the real world. Do you understand?"

"Y-yes," Blake repeated.

"Stand up," Vane commanded him. "Learn. Don't cower." He turned back to me. "Are you going to be his shield in battle, too? We do not have time for showboating, DuLac. Your turn will come soon enough."

I gaped at him. *Showboating?* "I was trying to help—"

"Helping when you're not needed doesn't help anyone but you," Vane said. "However, since you have so much enthusiasm, let us tack Emerson's remaining time onto yours."

"But—"

Vane raised a brow. "Can't handle it?"

"What—" I could feel everyone, not just in my group, but throughout the room, staring at me. I wasn't about to let Vane win. I marched into the middle of our circle. Blake was still on the ground. I extended my hand to help him up, but he shook his head and rose on his own. He gave me a wary look as he took his place and closed the gap I'd left in the circle.

Vane stood just outside the circle. "Emerson had three minutes left. So you will do a total of eight."

"Fine," I bit out.

The next eight minutes were a disaster. I managed to stay on my feet, but I was going to have bruises up and down my body for days. Finally, Vane whistled for everyone to stop. The circle broke and he stepped through to me.

"Interesting technique." He picked up my stick that had fallen after being knocked out of my hand near the beginning of my time. "It works better when it's in your hand."

"Maybe you should teach me first," I replied.

"Really? I had thought that you didn't need teaching, since you seem to be under the impression that you know everything."

My jaw tightened. "If I knew everything, why would I be here?"

Gia cleared her throat. "Should we continue, sir?"

"By all means…" Bowing his head, Vane stepped out of the circle.

Forty-five minutes later, I hurried out of the training room. I'd never been so happy to leave a class. Before dismissal, Vane had us line up in order. I was not in last place, much to my surprise. Blake, several of his friends, and some Regulars had been ranked below me.

Unsurprisingly, all of Vane's candidates made up most of the top ranks. Mark was first. Gia was second. Grey had performed so flawlessly Vane had no choice but to place him third. Oliver and Paul fell in positions below Grey. I was surprised Vane had allowed *any* Regulars in the top ranks. I wondered if the Council had imposed a quota requirement on him.

In the dressing room, I yanked off my sweat-drenched uniform before I got into the stall still in a heightened state of agitation. A stitch tore on the shirt. I cursed.

Gia smirked at me. "You should have listened to me earlier and snuck out."

Another girl, one of Blake's friends, came in behind us. "This is ridiculous. He's punishing all the candidates he didn't bring in."

"No." To my surprise, Gia looked at the younger girl protectively. "He wants you to succeed. You're a trained wizard. Unfortunately, you're just that bad." She glanced at me. "You, on the other hand, if he didn't have it in for you before, he does now."

"As if you care," I muttered.

Gia laughed. "Make your life easier, DuLac. When he says jump, just ask how high. Or better yet, don't—all the better for me. While you're butting heads with him, I'll be learning."

My shoulders curled inward.

"Don't look so defeated." Gia ducked into her stall. "You surprised me, DuLac. I didn't expect you to stand up to him. Vane scares the crap out of me."

I turned to leave the dressing room, mulling over Gia's words.

"Hey, where are my boots?" Gia yelled from the stall.

I smiled in satisfaction. It was short-lived. Almost immediately, the weight of guilt bore down on me. Even though she totally deserved it, tossing her boots into the boys' dressing room seemed petty.

I rushed out of the arched door, back into the gym, and straight into Vane.

Strong arms caught me before I fell backwards. "DuLac, is your mind ever on this earth?"

I jerked away from him.

His expression shuttered. "Never mind."

He gestured me toward another small opening on the opposite wall from the exit. "Let's have a quick word in my office."

"Er—" It was all I could think of saying. Gia was right. After that class, I didn't feel like conversing with him any more than absolutely necessary. "Grey is waiting for me."

He pointed to my bag. "Text him that you'll meet him later."

Damn the digital age. Matt would have never thought to text—he only did it when he couldn't avoid it—which should have clued me in to the fact that he had grown up in the fifth century. It seemed Vane was different.

"Uh, I'm really hungry. I don't want to miss dinner. How about later?" I tried.

Vane arched a gold-tipped brow. "How about now? You owe me."

Calling that in already? Reluctantly, I shot off a text to Grey.

I followed behind Vane. He topped me by almost a foot. Between his height and broad shoulders, he took up most of my field of vision. Although I knew he and Matt were close in age, the purposeful way he walked made him seem much older.

Inside the small opening, another set of stairs spiraled downward. I took the narrow steps two at a time to keep up with Vane. When we reached the bottom, he opened a door that led to the most awesome office I'd ever seen. The room had little furniture, yet every inch of wall space had been covered either by a weapon or flat-screen TV. An RPG showed two knights paused in the middle of a joust.

"You're playing video games down here?"

"Role-playing games. They are excellent for improving hand-eye coordination." Vane crossed over to a cushy leather chair, a video game nerd's must-have accessory. "Something you could improve upon."

I eyed the giant TV screen with skepticism. "You asked me here to play games?"

"No, but you'll know when I do," Vane said with a slight leer.

I felt my cheeks heat.

Vane leaned back in the chair and pulled out an attached keyboard like he was in a Western drawing out his gun. He punched a few keys. The TV screen flickered on with video footage of Matt and me at the food court at the mall back home.

I demanded, "What is this? How did you get this?"

Vane smirked. "Modern magic. Shall we watch? This is my favorite part."

On the screen, Matt leaned over to wipe a dollop of mustard from my lips. I hadn't noticed before, but in the middle of a wipe, his face changed. His eyes became glazed and he froze.

I turned my face up—I hadn't noticed anything wrong—

and our lips met. Tentatively, at first. Then, the kiss became hard and heavy. It went on for an excruciating long minute. Matt broke off the kiss first. He wore an odd expression of pleasure and pain. I opened my eyes on the video. My heart twisted as I watched myself smile shyly at Matt.

Matt jerked backwards.

Vane paused the video. "Did you see it?"

No. My heart was breaking a second time. Matt had not kissed me. I had kissed him.

Hoarsely, I said, "See that you're a perv? Yes, I do."

"He had a vision," Vane said impatiently. "But when you kissed him, it stopped. That's why he backed away. You blocked it."

I said, "What?"

"Do you understand anything, little girl? I've figured out what's wrong with you," said Vane. "The gargoyles are stronger. They are just as capable as any candidate we have. But we've got an advantage. Merlin's visions... unless you cock it up."

I blinked at him with incomprehension. "I haven't done anything."

"You don't have to. I saw him with you. He's not doing a good job of resisting you."

I stared at Vane. After a pause, I turned to leave. "You've been down here in the creepy clubhouse too long, Vane. You don't know what you're talking about."

Vane raised his hand. A breeze came out of nowhere. It tightened around me like an invisible hand. I couldn't move.

"Let me go," I gritted out.

"Stop being so difficult." Vane stood up, a hulking form with broad shoulders and a solid chest. He strode up to me. He walked past me to go to a wall filled with various swords, scimitars, and bows. He took down an antique wooden bow and arrow. He notched the arrow.

He said, "Let me connect the dots. Merlin has visions. It's what he does. If he doesn't have visions, we can kiss this little contest for the sword good-bye."

I eyed the weapon in his hand. The arrow pointed straight at me. And I couldn't move.

"What are you doing, Vane?" I said.

His lips curved into a devastating smile.

ROUND TABLE

Vane flicked his hand and I was jerked around to look at the giant TV again. The video of Matt and me at the food court switched to show a painting with a girl wearing a toga. She held her hands over her eyes.

"Did you know the Lady of the Lake also hung out with the Greeks? Her people went by different names in different cultures, but they were the same beings. Most of our powers come from them."

"So…?" I drew out.

Vane pointed to toga-girl. "Her name was Cassandra. She was a daughter of Troy. She was cursed by Apollo to see the future—"

"But no one would believe her. Yes, I know."

"The curse is not just a story." Vane stood up. "Cassandra survived the fall of Troy. She passed down the curse."

"You think I'm cursed like Cassandra?"

Vane laughed. "No. I think you're a descendant of Apollo.

You render the curse neutral. In my life, I've only ever known one other who was a descendant of the sun god."

"Apollo wasn't real," I scoffed.

Vane raised a brow. "I wouldn't insult them. They may not be visible, but reality is in the mind."

I rolled my eyes.

"Apollo isn't real. Arthur isn't real. Merlin isn't real," he mimicked. "How many times have you said that?"

I shut up.

Vane lifted the bow.

"What are you doing?" I asked.

"Relax." He walked up behind me.

I felt the heat of his body on my back as he reached around me to put the bow in my left hand.

"Take it." His voice tickled the curve of my ear.

My fingers closed around the roughly textured wood bow. "How did you know I'm left-handed?"

"I know a great deal about you." Taking my right hand, he positioned my fingers on the string. I clenched my teeth when he turned me to face a target on the wall behind his desk.

"Now, shoot," he demanded.

My teeth clenched, I imagined his smug face in front of the target. I shot. The arrow flew off the bow, slicing a bit of skin off the inside of my elbow as it went. I yelped. The arrow went wild and bounced off one of Vane's ultra-thin monitors.

Vane made a sound of impatience. "Stop thinking. Just shoot."

Blood dripped from my arm. My eyes stung with tears from the sudden pain. I blinked rapidly to clear them.

"Stop crying, DuLac," Vane snapped. "Are you a candidate or not?"

My lips thinning, I focused on the target. This time, when I pulled back on the arrow, an odd out-of-body feeling came over me. They say you never forget how to ride a bike. This felt the same. My hand moved as if the muscles remembered how to shoot. Before I knew it, the arrow zinged past my cheek straight toward the target.

It hit the small dartboard with a loud punch. The dartboard flew off the wall and smashed onto the floor.

"Not bad," Vane said, taking the bow from my hands.

"Not bad?" I turned around. I realized I could move. I gave Vane a gloating smile. "I killed it." I frowned. "I'm not sure why, but it felt as if I'd done it before. I've never shot a bow and arrow before."

"Apollo's twin sister Artemis was the Huntress. Their symbol was the bow and arrow. This isn't a coincidence."

"Or you just magicked it."

Vane smiled. His eyes lightened with the genuineness of it. "I didn't, but you'll have to trust me."

And oddly enough, I believed him. Vane was a jerk, but he hadn't lied so far.

Vane grabbed my arm and pulled me toward him

Before I could protest, he put his hand over the cut I'd gotten from the bow. He mumbled a magic word that made my ears ring. The cut closed. He slid a thumb over the healed skin.

I bit my lip as he teased the sensitive area.

I pulled away from him. "Why did you tell me all this? Why not tell Matt?"

"He already knows." Vane reached out to touch my amulet. "As I said, he's not doing a good job of resisting you."

My heart leapt into my throat. I forced it back down. "What do you want me to do? I can't just stop seeing him."

"You can see him. You just can't... kiss him." His eyes roved up and down my body. "Proximity is a factor, I think, but you haven't crossed the line. I want to make sure you don't."

I'm sure my face must have turned a scorching scarlet. Did I have a letter on my shirt declaring 'H' for ho? I crossed my arms over my chest.

Vane looked at me from under hooded eyelids. "Merlin must think you're special if he gave you the *Dragon's Eye* amulet. Only one other has ever worn it."

"Who?" I asked, though I wasn't sure I wanted to know.

Vane hit a button on the TV and the RPG switched back onto the screen. Vane clicked 'Save' on the menu. A closing scene played of a beautiful maiden handing a ribbon to a knight in shining armor, riding a white horse.

My heart twisted a little as I watched the romantic scene. "Is that how it really was?"

"For a handful of insanely fortunate nobles. However, the majority of people were poor and hungry. Life back then could be harsh on the best of days and perfectly brutal at other times." He hit a key on the keyboard again—to a porn shot of a woman in a leather mask and little else, gyrating against a guy in a business suit. He gave me an arch look. "I prefer this time period."

The sad thing was that porn shot wasn't even porn. It was on broadcast TV. That didn't shock me, but watching the seedy scene with Vane made me squirm—just as he'd intended, I was sure. I made a sound of disgust. "Do you even have a soul?"

"I'm sure my brother would say I don't, but then, there can only be one hero. And one heroine."

"Who?" I repeated.

"Can't you guess?" Vane switched the TV back to the RPG. He paused the picture on screen. The maiden sat next to a king, but she watched the knight. She wore a crown.

"Guinevere," I said.

***

That evening, I chewed on a fry—no, a chip. I made a face. It tasted too salty… and too soggy. Yet, it was still the only good thing about the traditional meal of fish and chips I had ordered. It had looked better on the crystal-crisp iPad screen. *Blech.* Food in England had yet to impress.

The menu itself was genius. The online school app let you order your meal before you walked into the dining hall, and it would be ready as soon as the perky greeter showed you to a table. I sat with Grey, Oliver, and a few other Regulars. The dining hall was busy. Students crowded the other tables. I noticed that many of them would look over at us and then turn away giggling and whispering.

"Haven't they seen a bunch of Regulars before?" I asked after the tenth time it happened in the span of five minutes.

Oliver coughed. "It's not the Regulars, Ryan. It's you."

"Huh?" I said, in between chews of a limp chip.

Gia sauntered over to our table. "DuLac, seems as if it's gotten out that you're dating the most legendary wizard in the whole world."

I choked on the chip. Coughing, I spit it out. "What?"

Gia plopped down in an empty chair. "I'm pretty sure Ms. Joseph is the center of all gossip around here. I've made you super popular."

I glared at her. "Find your shoes yet?"

"I knew it was you." She scowled, then turned to smile at Grey. "But don't worry, DuLac, your brother retrieved them for me."

Grey gave her a very male look. "Glad to help."

She winked at him. "Nice training session. You should have been placed in front of Mark. You clearly did better than him."

"Thanks," Grey said, surprised.

"I was a Regular until Vane found me, and if he hadn't, I would be still. But Vane is wrong. With Merlin on your side, the Regulars have as much of a shot as the rest of us."

I sniffed. "Does this mean you're not going to tank us anymore?"

"That was genius with the door, wasn't it, Goldilocks?" Gia chuckled.

My cheeks puffed at the nickname.

Blake and a friend of his came up to our table. He adjusted his glasses and cleared his throat. "May we join you?"

"Are you sure you won't be contaminated by sitting with us lowly Regulars?" Grey said.

Gia rolled her eyes. "Sit down, wizard boy. Can you conjure up some pumpkin tea? I hear it's a must-have at English schools."

Blake groaned in response. Oliver and I let out a laugh.

"Pumpkin tea?" Grey made a face. "Sounds gross."

Everyone at the table laughed again.

Mark the Brute and the rest of Vane's candidates came into the dining room. They elbowed out the other wizards waiting politely in line to get a table. Mark frowned when he noticed Gia with us.

"Later, kids," Gia mumbled to the table.

She went to talk to Mark. Within a minute, they were arguing. Gia stomped out of the dining room. Mark went over to his friend at a nearby dining table.

"Trouble in paradise." Grey whistled. He shoved a large forkful of rice in his mouth, took a hurried swallow of water, and got up. "I'll see you later."

"Where are you going?" I asked.

"I saw her looking up the way to the library earlier." Grey slung his school bag over his shoulder. "Think I suddenly feel the need to study."

Oliver leaned forward. "The brute won't like it."

"I can handle it." With a cocky smile, Grey ambled away.

Blake tapped his fingers nervously on the table. "I've been thinking... after the training today... there's something not right. Why go through this training with us? Why not have us take our chances with the sword right now? Why wait when we're in a 'race' with the gargoyles?"

Oliver took a loud bite of a chip. "Why?"

Suddenly, I felt very aware that everyone else at the table was watching me as they waited for an answer. I took a breath.

"I don't know," Blake answered. "But she can find out... from Merlin. I heard that you and he are shagging—er—I mean, you and he are close."

I sputtered. "W-we are not shag—doing that."

"Nice one." Blake's friend elbowed him.

"It's a good idea." Oliver stepped in. His gaze fixed on me. "The point is, you're the only one who can get him to talk."

I touched my amulet. Realizing what I was doing, I forced my hand back to the table. I sighed. "Fine."

I met Blake's gaze. "Are we friends now?"

"There can be only one winner, but the sword will decide who. We can work together to make sure we all get a chance." He started to get up.

"I like you, too." I turned my megawatt smile full on.

Blake stumbled. The back of his knees knocked against the heavy chairs. He straightened, self-consciously raking his hand through his jet-black hair.

"And thanks for trying to help me today," he mumbled.

He and his friend walked away.

PRIYA ARDIS

"Forget it, Emerson." I heard his friend hiss at him. "You have no chance with her. She's got Merlin."

My smile dimmed. I looked around the dining hall. A girl from a few tables over gave me a semi-awed look before she turned back to her friend. They all figured I had Merlin in my pocket. Except it was a pocket with a black hole and it kept drawing me in deeper.

**

Two weeks later, the trees in the courtyard had adorned themselves in a bright array of fall leaves. More and more they sought rest on the ground as winter closed in on us. The occasional wind scattered the leaves, creating eddies of earthy colors.

The sweet October morning filled my senses as I stood in Matt's class defending myself against a pain spell. Bench tables and seats had been moved out of the way and stacked up high against the sides of the rectangular room.

We continued to practice defending against spells. The amulets neutralized some types of magic automatically, but the trick was in knowing which ones. All of it came down to recognizing the magic thrown at you. Who knew there was such thing as a confusion spell to make you believe you'd turned into a toad (aura color: purple) and one that could actually turn you into a toad (aura color: green)? Only the most powerful wizards could perform the whole range.

I glanced at Matt from across the room. He smiled as he talked to a girl, one of Blake's witch friends. He glanced over at our group and my heart leaped. His eyes went straight past me.

My mind on Matt, I didn't quite hear when Blake shouted

* 150 *

something to me.

Before I knew it, the pain spell we'd been practicing hit me from the side. I screamed and fell to the floor writhing. Pain shot through my body in sharp steel ribbons.

Matt rushed over. "Ryan, use the charm. Fight it."

I closed my eyes. I could hear my teeth chattering. Pain threatened to overwhelm me. "H-help," I said.

"You can do this, Ryan." Matt's hand soothed my hair.

It only increased the sensation of pinpricks driving into my skin and burrowing through my muscles. I shut it out and instead, thought only of the amulet. Warmth spread out bit by bit, like a slow unfurling of an umbrella. Seconds felt like hours, but slowly the pain receded. I opened my eyes.

"I'm so sorry," Blake said, his face ashen. "I meant to shoot that to Oliver. I don't know what happened. It went wide—"

Oliver anxiously said, "It bounced off my shield."

"The amulet can act as a deflector as well as a neutralizer." Matt helped me up. He took me over to his desk and sat me down in the teacher's chair. I leaned back into the smooth wood. "Remember this the next time you think you can't break free, class. You can. I think that's enough for today." Matt inclined his head at the wide-eyed students. "You're dismissed."

The class dispersed. Students grabbed their bags from the side of the room as they headed out.

"So sorry, Ryan." Blake lingered over me.

"It's alright. I'll be fine," I said hoarsely. My throat felt sore, as if I'd been screaming for hours.

His face ashen, Blake nodded and walked over to his bag.

Grey handed it to him with a quick pat on the back.

"I don't know who looks worse." Matt stood over me, beside the chair. The last student left the classroom. "You or him."

I looked up at Matt with a dry look. "Thanks."

"No matter. This was good for everyone to see," he said. "We haven't gotten to it yet, but you can turn your shield into a weapon."

I stared at him in disbelief. Not only had he not bothered to ask if I was okay, he was actually going to dismiss the whole thing as a great demonstration. I rubbed my arms and winced; my skin still stung with pain.

"That's more words than you've said to me in two weeks," I grouched.

Matt's face tightened.

"Were you in love with Guinevere?" I burst out.

He raised a brow. "I see you've been talking to Vane."

"You made the amulet for her."

"What? No. Is that what Vane told you? She was Arthur's wife. Let me be clear. I was not in love with her. Arthur asked me to make the amulet for her."

"How can I believe you?" I said.

Matt knelt down next to the chair. He turned it until I was facing him. "Do you want to believe me?"

I sighed. "Why are we still training, Matt? Why are we sitting here while the gargoyles are trying to get the sword as we speak?"

"It's safer for you and your little followers if you don't know."

I colored. "I don't have followers."

"I can't tell you," he repeated

I scooted back in the chair. "You don't want to tell me. There's a difference."

Matt cursed. His fist clenched. A bench beside us exploded with a loud wham.

I jumped up.

My legs weak, I stumbled.

Matt caught me by the waist.

A small tendril of hope uncurled inside me as his gaze searched my face.

He sighed with reluctance. "Ryan—"

I grabbed his shoulders. "I thought a wizard couldn't make something explode without getting drained."

A brow lifted with arrogant confidence. "I'm not just any wizard. And it's a bench. Not very complex."

My fingers dug into tight biceps. I knew I shouldn't. There was too much at stake, but I couldn't help it. I wanted Matt. In my head, I whispered, "*Matt.*"

Something of what I was thinking must have shown on my face because Matt's fingers on my waist tightened. Before I knew it I stood smashed up against him. I could smell nothing but his scent—of time and earth and desire all mixed up in one.

He muttered against my mouth. "Ryan, please—"

GARGOYLES

"Ryan." Grey and Gia ran into the classroom.

Matt broke away. I leaned on the desk.

Gia mumbled, "We heard an explosion."

Grey noticed the splintered bench. "Ryan, are you all right?" He moved to cross the room toward me.

I shook my head. "I just need a few minutes."

Gia grabbed Grey. "Right. You heard her." She marched Grey to the door. She tossed a wink over her shoulder. "We'll see you at lunch."

She closed the classroom door as they left. I heard Grey mumble an ineffective protest.

Matt moved to stand on the other side of the desk. "We can't do this, Ryan. I haven't told you the consequences."

The clock tower chimed outside. Seconds passed in infinite increments on an undefined scale.

"Because I'm marked by Apollo?" I said.

Matt cursed. "Is there anything Vane didn't tell you? There is no proof the curse actually exists. But how can I risk it? There's too much at stake."

"Fine, I understand." I walked slowly to get my bag. I opened the classroom door to leave and paused at the threshold. I turned to face him. "Just because we're not going out doesn't mean you have to do this alone. I am your friend."

Matt stuffed fisted hands into his trouser pockets. The grooves on his face deepened with grim regret. "I failed Camelot once before. I trusted too much. Look where it got us. Look where it got Arthur. I won't allow the same thing to happen again. Not this time."

"I see." My fingers tightened on the strap of my gym bag. "You want me to call you Matt, but it's you who won't let go of Merlin."

***

I slipped into my training spot, still fuming over my encounter with Matt. Every time we had a real conversation, I ended up with nothing. I wanted to smash something. My insides churned all the way through the first forty-five minutes of forms, until I was too exhausted to think anymore.

Vane walked past me with a snide expression. "Looks as if you have a bit of excess energy today. Wonder what could have caused it?"

Gia had obviously ratted me out to him. We bent down into a lunge. My hamstrings and thighs burned, but I held them perfectly perpendicular to the floor. I didn't reply.

"Not speaking today?" Vane continued. "You do look a bit,

shall we say, disheveled."

A boy in front of me snorted. To my relief, Vane rounded on him and started taunting him instead. A few minutes later, we broke for weapons training. Vane assigned me to do figure eights with long staffs along with the rest of the lower ranks while the higher ranks picked out practice swords.

I marched over to Vane and threw my staff at his chest. "I want to talk to you."

Vane caught it easily with one hand. "About what?" He tossed the staff back at me.

I caught it, surprising myself.

Vane gave a nod of approval. "I see you are learning something, despite all the time my brother is wasting teaching you magical defense. Any competent wizard will beat you despite your trinket."

I touched the amulet. "We're doing just as well as the trained wizards."

"They should be destroying you. It's pathetic how lacking in practical experience the students at this school are." Vane looked down his nose at me. "What do you want, DuLac?"

"I want to learn swords." I tossed the long staff back at him. Vane knocked down the staff without touching it. It clattered to the floor.

Someone in the room gasped.

Vane just gave me a steady look. "What makes you think sword training will make any difference?"

My jaw jutted out. "If it doesn't make a difference, then why can't I learn it?"

Vane extended his hand. The staff flew straight at me like a javelin. The tip rammed hard into my shoulder before I caught it. Tears stung my eyes as I huffed to catch my breath.

"You may learn it after you master the staff," Vane said.

"It's not like those doing sword training have mastered the staff either." I jabbed my finger at his candidates. "*They've* never even handled a staff."

Vane's eyes narrowed. "Are you questioning my methods?"

Internally, I grimaced. Maybe it hadn't been such a good idea to confront him in front of everyone. Maybe I should have waited until after class. But now that I had, I couldn't back down. I maintained, "I can handle a sword."

Vane towered over me. "My training. My rules."

I stuck my chin out. "You're afraid that I'm right."

Vane flicked his hand at the weapons rack. A sword flew out at me. For a second I thought he was going to let it skewer me. I ducked. Vane halted the blade right in front of me.

Mildly, he said, "All right, then?"

I wasn't, but I wasn't about to admit it either. I straightened. "I'm fine."

He crooked a finger at Gia to come forward.

"Let's see if you're as advanced as you think you are," Vane said.

I inclined my head at the others who were still on the staff. "If I win, I want *everyone* to be trained."

Vane raised a brow. "You're pushing your luck."

"If I can do it, so can they. They're candidates, too. We

should all have the chance to find out." I looked at Blake and Paul. "Do you agree?"

Blake nodded. So did Paul. One by one, everyone dropped their staff.

I faced off with Vane. "Well?"

For a second, I thought I saw a smile cross his face, but it was with a sober expression that he clapped. "Well done. I've been waiting for someone to show some initiative." He nodded at the Regulars. "If she can prove herself, all of you will be trained." He turned back to me with a sadistic gleam in his eye. "All you had to do was ask."

My stomach churned as I grabbed the sword floating in front of me—and almost dropped it. I hadn't realized how heavy steel could be. Vane smirked at me. Ignoring him, I heaved the sword up into the beginning form position I'd seen him demonstrate in class. I faced off with Gia. "No magic."

Vane shrugged. "No promises."

Gia advanced first. I parried her. We went back and forth. I could tell she was holding back. She let me think through the steps. After a few minutes, Vane made a noise of disgust.

"Enough," he said. A strong wind shoved at me. I looked up to see him separating his hands. He pulled us apart. He glared at Gia. "If I'd wanted to watch a training exercise, I would have told you." He beckoned Mark the Brute forward. "I want a real duel. She thinks she can handle it. Let's give her the chance."

Mark took Gia's place. Gia gave me a silent look that said, 'Good Luck.' The more time Grey spent with her, the nicer she got toward me. As Mark's hawk-like focus settled on me, I had a feeling I would need all the luck I could get. Mark didn't hesitate to come at me in a fury. Very aware of the sharpness of the blade, I barely deflected the first few blows. One nearly cut off my nose. Another swing. In slow motion, I saw the arc of the blade reflect off the light from the windows.

I stopped thinking. My heartbeat seemed to slow and a hum started in my ears. I swung up the heavy sword in my hand. My biceps screamed at the effort, but I managed to stop the blow. Our swords met with a clang. I kept his sword above me.

His eyes widened in surprise. Time caught up. My hands shook.

Mark smiled. Our next few sequences sped by in a blur. Every time he moved, I countered. I don't know how long we went back and forth. But then, he started throwing moves I had no idea how to respond to. He almost took my head off.

Finally, Vane said, "Stop."

Mark moved to swing again. A strong wind knocked the sword out of Mark's hand. It threw me backwards. It pinned Mark across the room. I slammed down on the gel mat. I heaved, struggling to breath. When oxygen returned to my brain, I could feel every eye in the entire room on me.

I made myself stand up. "I'd do better with training."

Vane tossed the sword back at me. I jumped out of its way. The edge barely missed me as the sword fell flat onto the mat.

"Clearly," he sneered, "you're ready."

***

"All you had to do is ask," I mimicked. "What bullshit."

I followed Vane out of the classroom. Instead of going to his office, he headed down the narrow confine of a turret-style circular stairwell that led out of the cathedral. I'd already apologized to the Regulars for getting their hopes up and failing. They'd actually been surprisingly sweet about it. Most had been awed that I'd even tried to stand up to Vane the Terrible.

"Vane," I called.

Vane came to an abrupt halt. We faced off midway down the stairs on a small landing. Although we were the last ones out of class, a few students milled around on the bottom steps.

With a flick of his hand, he slammed me high up against the circular wall. I gurgled as what felt like compressed air threatened to choke me. Someone below us gasped. I was pretty sure he wasn't going to kill me with witnesses present. *Still…*

A bland expression on his face, Vane regarded me with dispassionate eyes. "Let's be clear on one thing—I am not your friend, DuLac."

"Good to know," I rasped.

"Leave," Vane commanded the students lingering belowstairs. They scattered.

Great. We were alone. I closed my eyes and felt Guinevere's amulet warm. It broke Vane's hold and I fell… right on top of him.

He caught me easily. I must have surprised him. I was pretty sure if he'd been expecting the fall, he would have let me drop to the floor.

"You're heavier than you look," he grunted.

I dug my fingernails into his biceps. Unfortunately, the muscles were too hard to make much of an indention. "Matt and I weren't kissing."

"By the way your eyes are always eating me up, you can hardly expect the rest of us to believe in your restraint."

"I do not eat you up!" My whole face heated. Okay, that did not come out right. "I mean," I mumbled. "You know what I mean."

Vane set me down with a leer. "The lady doth protest greatly."

I glared at him. "Why are you such a barbarian?"

"*Sir* Barbarian," he corrected.

I wrinkled my brow. "Is that a joke? Did Vane make a funny?"

"*Sir* Vane," he corrected again.

"That explains why Camelot fell," I muttered.

Vane sighed. "What do you want, DuLac?"

I looked at him curiously. First, he'd tried to choke me. Now he was trying to play with me. I was starting to form a hypothesis that guys from the medieval time period suffered from bipolar disorder. "There is no need to tell the Council about Matt and me. You were right. Matt thinks I'm interfering with his visions. He doesn't w-want—" I broke off as the last word wobbled.

Vane gave me a look of disgust mixed with pity. "You're not going to cry, are you?"

"N-no," I stammered.

"Good." He turned to walk away.

I hurried to grab his arm. "You won't say anything?"

Vane looked down at my unpainted nails, then, followed along the length of my arm, up past the curve of my neck to my face. Conversationally, he said, "I could break you easily."

I tried to yank my hand away. He grabbed it before I could.

"But oddly enough, I don't seem to want to," he whispered. His fingers tightened on my hand until I winced. His hold eased, but he didn't release me. In a louder voice, he said, "My brother gave you the amulet he made for Guinevere. He must think you're special. You could be. Just be careful you don't end up the same way as she."

"And which way is that?" I asked.

He let go of my hand. "Burned at the stake."

***

The kiss consumed me, heating my body from inside out. I hung on for dear life and allowed my mouth to be devoured. The acrid smell of fire broke through the fog of pleasure dulling my mind. I pulled away. I lay in a field under the protective branches of a tree. Stars twinkled in the dark night. They shone down on the one I still had my legs wrapped around—Morgan. His face twisted. Fangs shot out of his mouth. His forehead enlarged to become swollen and hard.

"Time to have some real fun, babe," he said.

Fire blazed on the eaves of the tree above me.

I screamed. I grabbed a rock and hit him in the face. He snarled in pain. I wrestled out of his grip and started running.

But all of a sudden, a thick fog of smoke filled the field. I stopped.

From out of nowhere, Morgan jumped in front of me. His beautiful face twisted into a snarl. I cried as he grabbed me by the neck. We fell backwards to the ground.

He squeezed my throat.

I couldn't breathe. I was going to die.

"Wake up, Ryan," Matt's voice commanded from somewhere far away.

I jerked up in bed. My eyes stung with acid-like tears. My neck throbbed in pain. I coughed as smoke clogged my lungs. Flames engulfed our room. Fire alarms rang in ear-piercing screeches.

I stumbled out of bed.

"Gia," I cried out and wished I hadn't. Choking on smoke fumes, I ran to her bed. She lay deathly still. I grabbed her wrist. To my relief, her heartbeat felt normal. I scrambled to get her iPad out of her school bag to call for help. She'd stowed it under the bed. I didn't have to open the bag. The contents lay scattered under her bed. My lips thinned when I saw the iPad. Someone had smashed it. I had no doubt mine was in the same condition.

I looked at the door. A wall of snapping fire blocked the way.

The window. I hooked my arms under Gia's shoulders and dragged her to the lone window at the center of the outer wall. I put her down and touched the wall. The exterior stonewalls remained cold, but most of the interior burned as if it were made of tinderbox wood. I pushed the window shutters open. Iron bars covered the lower portion the window. The fire alarms should have disabled them, but Gia had told me that the bars also had a layer of magic on them. I had to neutralize it somehow.

I reached around my neck for my amulet and touched the iron bars. *Please*, I told it, *I need you.* An image of Matt flew in my mind. *"Kavas,"* a voice said in my head.

Heat filled the ruby gemstone. The iron bars swung outward.

With a cry of relief, I hung Gia half out the window and peered out... to the ground five stories below. Getting a room on the top level had seemed like a good thing. The entire residence hall had already evacuated to the courtyard in front of the building. Our room was on the side so I could only see them by craning my neck and looking to the right. Despite the alarms and burning inferno, I could hear various teachers taking roll count.

"Help," I yelled. No one heard me.

Floating balls of water exploded around us like grenades. I saw a white-robed wizard at the front directing fire hoses. I waved to him, but he was busy shouting instructions to the other wizards and he didn't notice.

I eyed the curtains around the window, but they weren't long enough. We could possibly make it down two floors, but I wouldn't be able to jump the rest. Not with Gia unconscious.

Leaning out of the window again, I spotted a narrow ledge that ran around the building. It was just wide enough for one person to inch along if I balanced just right. The ledge ran across several other rooms. Fire occasionally burst out through the iron bars like octopus arms. Once fire engulfed the whole floor, the ledge wouldn't even be an option. It was my best chance… if I was willing to leave Gia behind. Except I wasn't.

Flames licked my heels. I took the curtains from the window and used a technique I learned babysitting some of the neighborhood children back when my life had been normal. I wrapped the cloth around me and then used the ends to tie Gia to my side. I must have resembled a lopsided kangaroo. I cinched the curtain tight around my waist. I don't know how I found the strength, but with one hand on Gia and one hand against the wall, I edged out onto the ledge.

I'd only made it a few feet when it started raining.

I had a feeling the wizard firefighters had a hand in the sudden downpour. Inch by inch, I made it to the first window. Even a small spark of fire would set my highly combustible outfit aflame as soon as I tried to cross. I glanced at the corner of the building—only three more windows to go after this.

I took a breath and took another step.

I landed awkwardly and slid on the wet ledge. Gia and I fell. My side hit a protruding rainspout one floor down and I screamed. My rib cracked as it slammed against stone. Luckily for me, the part of the curtain that was wrapped around me also caught on the long snout of the beast-shaped spout. I grabbed at the stone edifice to hang on. My jostling caused the curtain to start unraveling. I let go of the rainspout with one hand and caught the loose cloth. Gia hung in the curtain sack like a baby.

I don't know how long I hung, holding the double weight of Gia and myself with one hand. I just knew I couldn't let go.

Seconds passed like hours. The adrenaline thumping inside me started to ebb. My arm numb and stiff, I felt my grip slip. Ash and rain clogged my nose. The night had become pitch dark. I blinked, trying to stay conscious.

"There they are," a voice called from below.

"Ryan, let go," someone else ordered.

I couldn't have resisted the command if I'd wanted to. My grip broke. Gia and I plunged down. Compressed air caught us before we hit the ground. We hung a few feet in the air while someone lowered us slowly to the grass. I lay on my back looking up into the starless night sky. Rain spit down on my face.

Vane peered down over me. "Enough lying down, DuLac. Get up."

I shut my eyes and giggled.

Vane roughly pulled me up into a sitting position.

"Better?" he said.

I opened my eyes.

Rain poured down his face. It followed in a line past wanton cheekbones over wicked lips, leaving his whole countenance clean and fresh. He smiled. All the harsh lines disappeared into something breathtakingly beautiful.

Wet mud covered most of my body. My clothes clung to soaked skin, exposing every secret, revealing every curve. I took a heaving breath.

I heard Vane's catch.

I squeezed my fingers. Thick, dirty goo squirted out from the spaces in between them. My hands fisted. I punched Vane in the face.

***

Hospital beds separated by thin wood partitions had been lined inside a barn-like structure. There were about twenty beds placed into two rows. Most of them were occupied. Many of the girls were suffering from smoke inhalation. Several healers dressed in robes over scrubs moved from bed to bed checking on patients.

Gia dozed peacefully on the bed next to mine.

A healer wearing a dull green robe walked up with a clipboard. He closed the partition, cutting off my view of Gia. I opened my mouth to protest.

"She'll be all right," he said. "And so will you, but I want to keep you here for the night. The fifth floor girls have the brunt of the injuries." The healer glanced up and noticed Aurelius in flowing white robes making his way directly to him. Hastily putting the clipboard on a hook on the hospital bed, the healer left to meet the head councilmember.

Aurelius glanced at me once or twice as he talked in whispered tones to the healer.

Matt entered the triage room and crossed through the long space straight to me. Vane stepped from around the partition curtain.

"I want him locked up for trying to kill me." I pointed at Vane.

Vane responded with a lazy onceover. "You look mostly alive."

Aurelius approached the bed without the healer in tow.

"I'm glad to see you well, Ms. Dulac. We've never had such a thing happen at the school before."

"It's his fault." I glared at Vane. "He threatened me, saying I would burn at the stake like Guinevere, and the next thing I know my room is on fire. Do you really expect us to believe it's a coincidence?"

"I think it would be best if we spoke more privately." Vane made a circle with his hand. A faint red light surrounded us, forming a nearly invisible bubble.

Aurelius frowned. "Ms. DuLac, are you saying the fire was not an accident?"

Matt made an impatient noise. "What have you done, Vane?"

Vane rounded on me. "I want to know the details. What happened in the room?"

"Why?" I demanded.

Vane smiled cryptically. "Tell me and I'll consider answering."

"Yes," Aurelius said. "I want a full account. Ms. DuLac, please tell us what you know."

I glanced at Matt. "This afternoon, Vane choked me in front of several students after class—"

"What?" Matt jumped up, hands fisted.

Vane snorted. "I held her up in the air. If I'd wanted to choke her, she wouldn't be here."

I leveled a disgusted look at him. "He compared me to Guinevere and said I would burn at the stake just like she did." I picked up the glass of water someone had placed on a steel nightstand next to the bed. I took a sip. My throat felt so swollen that it was painful to swallow. "Tonight, I woke with my room in flames. They covered the door."

"Completely covering the door? What about the walls near it?" Vane asked.

"I don't remember about the walls. I wasn't trying to get through them," I said dryly. "The window bars had some kind of locking spell on them."

Aurelius raised a brow. "Those have been spelled to open in emergencies. They should have opened automatically upon detecting fire."

"How did you open the window?" Vane asked.

I touched my neck. The amulet sat silent. "Somehow the amulet disabled the bars. I remember it heating. I thought I heard Matt—"

"It's not unexpected," Matt said abruptly. "The amulet has tied itself to you. It knew to defend you."

Vane's eyes fixed on Matt. He murmured, "Interesting."

I coughed. Matt handed me the water glass. I lifted it to my lips and took a long sip. Matt put a hand on my shoulder. Taking back the water glass, he touched my chin and gently angled my face to better see my neck. Without warning, he launched a fireball at Vane.

Vane barely caught it before it burned him. "What did I do now?"

Matt glared at Vane. "She's got bruises on her neck."

In a flash, Vane was out of the chair and at the head of the bed on the opposite side from Matt. I squirmed under their scrutiny.

"An air hold doesn't leave that kind of bruise. I didn't do this," Vane said. "Those bruises are deep. Someone tried to choke her. I'm surprised they didn't snap her neck."

"I dreamt Morgan was choking me," I said softly.

"The boyfriend?" Vane said.

Matt said, "Tell us about the dream."

I described it and ended with, "I woke up when—" I broke off abruptly. My eyes went to Matt.

"When?" Vane asked sharply.

I colored. "Matt called me in the dream."

"The amulet is protected," Matt said musingly. "They must have tried to take it from you, but it wouldn't come off."

Vane nodded. "When the alarms went off, he probably got out in the chaos. Only he was clever enough to lock the iron bars in her room."

"It could have been a girl," I said. "It would have been easy for one to blend in during the evacuation."

"A lot of wizards entered the dorm after the alarms went off." Vane pointed out.

Matt shouted, "You suspected a traitor. You used her as bait, didn't you? You risked the whole building!"

"I did not mean for my words to be taken literally." Vane's gaze locked on me. "I only said it to you."

"You said it loud enough for anyone near the stairwell to hear," I said acidly. "Don't pretend that this was an accident. You specifically said Matt gave me the amulet—"

In a blink, Matt was on top of Vane. He grabbed Vane by the collar and decked him hard on the jaw. Matt pulled back to throw another punch.

Vane barely managed to block him. He locked Matt's arms in a tight hold so Matt couldn't move. "Merlin attacking with his bare hands. Color me shocked. But I was right, wasn't I? You like—"

"I could easily kill you," Matt ground out, throwing Vane off him.

"Please," Aurelius asked. "Why did you do it, Vane?"

"Isn't it obvious?" Vane backed away from Matt. "There's a traitor among us."

The words hung in the air with subversive malice.

Aurelius tugged on his short beard. "The lead healer told me Ms. Cornwall had been put under a sleeping spell."

Matt sat down on a spindly wooden chair. It groaned a bit under his weight. He arched a brow at Aurelius. "Magic was used to lock the door. Magic was used to lock the iron bars. A sleeping spell was put on Gia. I'm sure they tried it on Ryan, but her amulet is strong enough to resist small spells."

"It was a wizard," I said.

"Maybe. Maybe not," said Matt. "These are the consequences in selling magic to anyone who pays for it."

"Now see here." Aurelius's face twisted into a scowl. "This is no reason to plug your platform. Selling magic is what keeps our world going. You can't blame magic. It is not the problem. The ones who use it incorrectly are the problem."

"Give someone a weapon and they will use it," Matt

retorted. "Selling magic sows the seeds of our own destruction. Why can't you see that?"

Aurelius and Matt glared daggers at each other.

Vane cleared his throat. "Could we get back to who tried to kill DuLac?"

"Like you care," I muttered.

Vane arched a brow. "I absolutely care about who gets the sword."

Matt and I both turned to give him identical looks of irritation.

"There is a traitor among us," Aurelius muttered. "I need to get the Council together. I will ask for an emergency session. Come up with a plan. If this is a strike against the candidates, more are sure to follow." He turned to Vane. "However, please, no more lures. The Council will not be happy that you initiated all this." He made a sweeping gesture at the healing room. "Even if it was not your intention, we cannot risk it."

To my surprise, Vane inclined his head in acknowledgement.

With a short nod at Matt, Aurelius withdrew from the bubble.

Matt looked at Vane. "What are you holding back now, Vane?"

"You know me too well, brother." Vane's lips curved up into a half-smile. He took out an iPad and pulled up headshots of four kids. "These are the latest candidates who have died. Three Regulars. One unknown wizard. Who is missing?"

"Gargoyles," Matt answered evenly. "They are not sending

candidates to the stone anymore."

"Because they know we have not sent ours. They suspect we have a reason. And how would they know even that much?" Vane came up to my bedside. He reached out to touch my neck.

I jerked away from him.

"Do you want to know who attacked you or not?" Vane said impatiently.

Jaw tight, I reluctantly swept aside my hair. Vane pushed down the potato sack of a hospital gown I wore.

"*Tapa.*"

The word caught the edges of my hearing. The skin on my shoulder burned excruciatingly. I yelped.

"There is an impression on your skin," Vane said. "My spell will extrapolate the remaining image."

My skin stinging with dull pain, I gave Vane a dirty look.

Matt handed me the hand mirror. "They must have been wearing something that dug into your skin when they tried to choke you. It's a gargoyle crest."

I stared at the dull burn. It was an emblem, a curvy V inside a circle.

The pit of my stomach sunk deeper. I gave the mirror back to Matt. "I've seen this before. On Morgan's notepad."

Matt put the mirror down. "The traitor is a gargoyle. They have infiltrated the school."

THE TRAP

"I caught Morgan doodling it. He acted really strange when I asked him what it was. He tore it out and threw it away." I looked at Vane. "B-but he's dead. You killed him, right?"

Vane nodded.

Matt squeezed my hand. "The gargoyle must be another member of the same clan. That would explain why they targeted you especially. Revenge."

Vane crossed his arms. "Whoever the gargoyle is, they will try again. We need to smoke the traitor out."

I sent him an angry glare. *Smoke. Seriously?* "For all I know, you set this up. You'd do anything to stop a Regular from succeeding."

Vane arched a brow. "I have little need to go that far. You Regulars are doing an excellent job of failing training all by yourselves."

"We'd be doing better if you'd train us properly. We should be learning swords."

Vane pinched the bridge of his nose. "Master the basics. Then, you will be able to advance. That is generally the way of things."

Matt asked, "What are you planning, Vane?"

"I'm going to find the gargoyle. Then, I'm going to put the beast down."

Matt nodded, seemingly unsurprised by his brother's matter-of-fact cold-bloodedness. "We have no idea who it is. How do you plan to get the gargoyle to expose himself?"

Vane's gaze flicked over the rows of injured girls. "I'll figure out a way."

"Meaning, as usual, you've only thought this halfway through," Matt ground out. "If a single strand of hair is harmed on any of these girls' heads, I will put *you* down."

"You can try." Vane crossed his arms over his chest and leaned languidly against the hospital partition. "Don't forget, little brother, I may not be as powerful of a wizard as you, but I defeated you once. I can do it again." He glanced at me. "Besides, you should thank me instead of getting in my way. Until we find the culprit, all of the candidates are in danger. She may be the first, but she won't be the last. He will try to take out all of them."

Matt's eyes flashed. "You will not use her as bait."

"What happened to sacrificing everything? You want me to sit back while the gargoyles exterminate us. We are talking about the fate of this world—"

"Nice try," said Matt. "We both know the only life you care about is your own."

High windows in the hospital let in moonlight. It highlighted the lighter strands of Vane's hair. He shrugged. "Yes, and I want to protect it. I am quite enjoying myself in this century. I'm not about to allow the gargoyles to ruin it all."

"We wouldn't even be in this situation if you hadn't trapped me in that cave. I could have helped Arthur. If the wizards hadn't defeated the gargoyles so handily back then, they wouldn't be so vengeful now. We used to be allies."

Vane yawned. "How long are you going to beat this to death? Arthur doesn't matter anymore. What matters is what happens next." Vane strode over to me and pushed back my hair to reveal the ugly bruises on my neck. "And what will happen next is death."

I made a face. "What do you want Matt to do?"

Vane raised a brow as if startled at my perception. "Just a small favor."

Matt ground his teeth loudly. "Which is?"

"The gargoyles know too much already. We must root out the traitor now before he can get any more information. Before he learns what Merlin's grand plan is."

"They won't find out. No one knows but me," Matt said with a tone of satisfaction.

"Feeling vindicated, are you?" Vane's voice lowered. "You see, he hasn't told them his grand plan yet."

Unwittingly, my mouth opened into an 'O.'

Matt's cheeks colored. "The sword is too important—"

"Trust no one but yourself," Vane said. "Tell me—how did that work out for Arthur?"

Matt let out a low growl. "I made mistakes with Arthur. I am not going to repeat them."

"Which gives you the excuse to self-righteously hoard what you know," Vane countered. He looked at me. "Tomorrow night is the All Saint's Festival in town. All upperclassmen are allowed to go. The Council wants to restrict the candidates from going. I want Merlin to convince them it's safe."

"Unbelievable," Matt cried. "You explicitly told Aurelius that you would not use anyone as bait. Are you pathological?"

"Unlike you, I'm a realist," Vane said. "She's been targeted. Are you going to sit back while they try again?"

"Now that I know, I'll be ready," I said. "I can take care of myself."

Vane pulled back the partition to show Gia. She was making whimpering noises as she slept. "You may be able to defend yourself, but what about those standing next to you?"

***

The next day, Ms. Joseph informed me that our floor had taken extensive damage and it would be weeks before anyone could move back in. However, we had been assigned new rooms—a flat—in the teachers' residence. I played her message on a hand-me-down iPad.

All of our things had been charred beyond recognition. Gia tried to keep a stoic front, but I could see she was distraught. Matt put in a call to Sylvia. I had been sure he'd know how to contact her and I was right. When we showed up at the teachers' residence and opened the door to our suite, Gia gasped in surprise. The spacious one-bedroom residence welcomed us with cheery bright décor. A cozy living area with a fireplace opened to an airy, well-lit eat-in kitchen. Beside the kitchen there looked to be a marbled bathroom and a door leading to a huge bedroom. Two trunks had been placed in front of it.

Gia cautiously opened her trunk and pulled out a gorgeous dress with matching shoes. "N-new clothes," she stammered. "All different styles. But how?"

"Grey's Mom got everything together. Matt arranged for it to be brought in."

Gia stared down at the trunk without moving.

"You don't like it," I said in disappointment.

Tough-girl Gia burst into tears. "No one's ever done anything like this for me before." She wiped her face with the sleeve of her shirt. "I don't know what to say." She mumbled, "T-thanks."

I smiled. I could almost see a glimmer of Alexa's grin from the corner of my eye. Before I could open my trunk, a knock sounded at the door. The door creaked open on its own. Both of us jumped.

"Sorry, it was unlocked." Matt stood in the doorway in jeans and a biker jacket. I flashed back to our last day in Boston. My heart skipped a small beat.

Gia let out an audible sigh of relief. She rushed up and punched him in the arm. "Thanks for the trunks."

"No worries." Matt grinned.

"I'm going to get some dinner with Grey," Gia said to me. "Do you want to join us?"

Matt's dark eyes settled on me. "Actually, I'd like to speak to Ryan."

Gia shrugged. "I'll see you later."

Matt waited to speak until the door closed after her. "The Council refused."

"On their own or did you tell them to?"

"Is there a difference?" he said, not denying it.

"You promised!" I'd asked him to bring Vane's request to the Council.

"I said I'd think about it. And I did. It's too dangerous—"

"Vane said I was the most likely target."

Matt's jaw tightened. "I don't trust anything he says and I'm not going to risk you—"

"It's my choice!"

"No," Matt said.

My cheeks puffed. "You can't just say no. I'm not a child."

Matt pinched the bridge of his nose. It took me back for a second. Vane had made the same gesture the exact same way at the infirmary. How could the brothers be so similar and so different at the same time? I wonder if Matt even saw it.

"We just can't trust him, Ryan," he said.

I made a sound of aggravation. "I'm getting so tired of this fight of yours."

"He tried to kill me!"

"You got trapped in a cave." I burst out. "Vane told me. You and he fought—"

"He attacked me!"

"Your spells got entangled and something happened and *boom,* you were trapped in the cave for a… really long time." I finished the last bit up lamely, because my math was just that bad.

"Over a thousand years!" Matt's mouth opened and closed. "How does he manage to do this every time? He manipulates everyone to suit him. Why should I be surprised he's gotten to you?"

I sank down on the sofa. "This isn't about him or you or me. *My family* is in danger and I'm not going to just sit back and do nothing."

"I know that—which is why I'm going to do everything I can to find out who the traitor is. There are certain tests I can try. It's a little tricky because gargoyles and Regulars come from the same genetic parent so it will take a bit of time, but I promise you I will not fail." Matt knelt down on the floor and took my hand. "Trust me."

"Do I have a choice?"

Matt squeezed my hand. "Trust me; we will be watching all the candidates very closely. No one will get to you again."

I arched a brow. "Why do I feel like my cage just got smaller?"

"It's for your protection." Matt pointed to the ceiling. "I'm in the flat above. Knock if you need anything."

"Why are we in the teachers' residence at all? The other girls are up at the manor house."

"I want you close."

I made a face. The statement would have thrilled me a few days ago. Today, it only served to tell me how tightly he held my leash. I held up my iPad to show the crack on the screen. Marilynn really did not like me. "Can you at least get me a *new* one? The Wi-Fi isn't working. It won't connect to anything. How am I supposed to get anything done?"

Matt took a miniature book out of his pocket. With a flick of his hand, he enlarged it. The heavy tome that was *Basic Elements* dropped on the coffee table with a thump. "Here you go. An extra copy. We're on chapter thirteen. I expect you to be caught up on the class you missed."

"You are too kind."

A few minutes later, I stood alone in the small living room, barely big enough for one sofa, one chair, and a coffee table. A TV hung on the wall. I stared at the flat's tiny but surprisingly well-stocked kitchen. Sometimes cooking relaxed me. Today, it looked more like a chore.

A knock pounded the door. I decided to ignore whoever it was.

"I know you're in there," Vane said through the closed door just before it flung open on its own.

"I know I locked that this time," I said.

"I am a wizard." Vane leaned against the doorjamb with tousled hair and a day's worth of stubble on his jaw. Even in plain black trousers and a simple grey V-neck sweater, he looked mouthwatering. Then he spoke and spoiled the image.

"I ask you to do a simple task and you fail," he chided. "Obviously, I grossly miscalculated your influence on my brother."

"Bite me." I strode to the door and swung it back on his smirking face.

He caught it before it could slam shut. "As delectable as that sounds, I need you to focus on the current situation. Our window is short."

I arched a brow. "What else can we do?"

"You can go to the festival. With me."

I gaped at him. "How? I can't even get out of this school."

"I have a plan," he said.

I crossed my arms and hugged myself. "How is the gargoyle going to know that I'm going to the festival when no one else is?"

"At lunch tomorrow, tell your little friends that you're going into town—"

"My friends are not traitors!"

"They might not be, but I wager whoever the gargoyles are using will be listening." Vane arched his brow. "This is your only chance to get to him first and you know it."

I arched my brow, mimicking him.

"If he is one of us, he won't be able to get out of the school either."

Vane's eyes went to the black bruises on my neck "Trust me. They won't waste this opportunity."

Morgan's face flashed in my head. I saw his head fall after Vane had decapitated it. The idea that another one of those wanted to kill me made me want to curl up into a ball.

"I don't know," I said, looking down.

Vane tucked a finger under my chin and pushed my face back up. "Don't you trust me?"

"Not at all," I answered.

Masculine lips curved into a wicked smile. "I think you're hungry."

I blinked. "W-what?"

"Come have dinner with me."

"No," I said.

Vane rolled his eyes. "Do you say yes to everyone else but me?"

"You make it so easy," I retorted.

"Fine, we'll eat here." Vane pushed past me and strode confidently into the kitchen.

"What are you doing?" I asked.

Vane pulled out various items from the mini fridge below the counter. He lined them up along with a few pots and pans. He grinned at me. "Watch this."

"*Pacika*," he commanded. A small breeze whistled through the kitchen. The food started to move and pretty soon was fixing itself. The salad chopped, the stove turned on, and butter poured itself on a pan. A pot filled itself up with water from a miniscule sink and noodles dropped into it. A few minutes later, two plates of shrimp pasta sprinkled with mozzarella sat on the bar just above the counter. A small salad lay beside them.

Vane handed me a glass of something dark. Out of

curiosity, I took a tentative sip. Then I took several gulps.

I sighed. "Real iced tea. How did you know?"

He took a bite from his plate. "I spent weeks watching you."

"I hadn't realized you watched so closely," I murmured.

He met my gaze with disconcerting directness. "I'm very thorough."

I took a long swallow of the iced tea. When I finished it, I couldn't resist another sigh of appreciation. I started on the pasta. It was scrumptious.

"I'm not going with you," I said between huge bites.

"Yes, you will. Do you know why?" Vane didn't wait for an answer. "Because you can't resist the chance to take care of this on your own. Because you care about the candidates."

His eyes raked over my jeans and plain T-shirt. "Wear something nice. I understand my brother bought you some beautiful clothes."

"That was Sylvia—"

"If he says so," Vane said. Like a typical male, he finished his dinner in less than five bites and headed for the door. "Come get me tomorrow when you're ready. I'm just across the hall."

"Y-you live across the hall?" I choked on a bite.

"Did my brother fail to mention it?"

"Why do I get the feeling he didn't know?" I said dryly.

Vane sent me an angelic smile. "Welcome to the building, neighbor."

***

He was Satan and I was following him straight to hell.

I tiptoed behind Vane as we went straight through the manor where we'd taken the candidate trial on the first day. At the admissions desk, Marilynn chatted away on the phone to someone. The hall was mostly empty. Just outside, students lined up to get into buses that were going into town.

"She's going to see us," I hissed behind him. "Why didn't we just get into a bus?"

"Because the monitors there are specifically checking for candidates," Vane said. "I'm extremely good at the chameleon glamour. How do you think I snuck around to see Guinevere without getting caught by the knights? Believe me, they were a lot more dangerous than a green like Marilynn." Vane strode confidently past Marilynn without bothering to lower his voice. He opened the front door.

Marilynn glanced up and stared hard at the door. I froze. After a minute, she shook her head, muttering, "Guess it was nothing." She went back to her call. "Listen, I ordered those replacements yesterday and you told me they would be here by today—"

Vane yanked me through the door. "Come on. At this pace, the festival will be over before we get to it."

"We're not walking into town, are we? Blake said it was fifteen minutes by car. He told me walking would be crazy."

"I've procured transportation," Vane said.

I tugged my hand away from his rough hold. "And I'm pretty sure everyone thinks I'm a 'ho. They all wanted to know who I was sneaking out with."

"I hope you didn't imply it was my brother. The idea is laughable—"

In the dark, my cheeks flamed. "I told them it was another student. I also told them not to mention it to Matt if they saw him."

The iron gates opened to let one of the school buses through. It wasn't one of the large yellow ones I was used to back home. The Avalon Prep buses looked more like black stretch limos. We slipped through the gates. As soon as we stepped past the school grounds, the road turned from paved stone to gravel—something my dress shoes did not appreciate.

I whined, "How long till we get to the car?"

Vane said, "Why did you wear heels? How are you supposed to fight a gargoyle in what you're wearing?"

"You told me to dress up!"

"I didn't say heels," he retorted.

I looked down at my black-and-silver lace dress with matching strappy silver shoes. Under the moonlight, the silver sparkled. "At least I'll be easy to spot."

"In that dress, the gargoyle won't be the only one targeting you," Vane muttered.

Before I could form a proper retort, we reached the end of the lane. Vane let out a loud whistle. A strong breeze blew back vines on a thicket of trees to reveal a black SUV.

I snickered. "Are you hiding a getaway vehicle?"

His face serious, Vane shrugged. "I like to be prepared."

I grabbed the handle and opened the door. Vane blocked me. In the dark, his face loomed above me. He leaned down so that his lips almost grazed my skin.

"I'll drive," he said.

"Oh." I let go of the door handle. "This is the driver's side. Wrong door. I'd forgotten."

I stopped babbling when he put his hand around my waist to lead me around the car and help me step up into the SUV. Even through the thick coat I wore, his touch felt oddly warm. I stared out at the road as he walked briskly back to the driver's side.

"Did you see anyone else leave?" I asked when he got in the car.

"No candidates, but the traitor will be there."

We drove along the dark road. There were no streetlights so we had to depend on the car's headlights to see. Trees swung in eerie rhythm as we crossed underneath.

Vane glanced at the stars. A full moon shone in the pregnant sky. "Tonight's a good night to be a gargoyle. They're at their most powerful at the end of the lunar cycle."

"What about wizards?" I asked.

"We like the sun," he answered.

I sat back into the plush seat of the SUV. The antique styling of the car's interior told me it was very expensive. Apparently, Vane was doing well. Realization dawned. I turned on him. "You sell magic!"

"It's the new way." He patted the dashboard lovingly. "A much better way."

I snorted. "A greedier way. Matt rides a bike."

"A Ducati is not just a *bike*," Vane corrected. "He may not be selling magic, but he's not above using it to get what he wants." He gave me a sidelong glance. "Merlin can't change what the wizards have evolved into. He just needs time to get his thousand-year-old ideas up to speed." The sky lightened as we approached town. Vane drove along the narrow streets. I took in the narrow brownstone buildings with their picturesque moldings. The whole town looked as if it had been around for a thousand years. Then again, maybe it had been. I was in England. Everything was old here.

In town, Vane found a place to park a few streets down from the square where the festival was taking palace. I got out and was immediately hit by an icy burst of wind. Shivering, I drew the coat I had thrown on at the last minute tightly around me, but it didn't do much to protect me. I stumbled along the rocky road in my heels. My teeth chattered. Tentacles of wind wrapped around my exposed legs.

Vane came around the car and grabbed me. He whispered into my ear. "*Tapa.*" Instantaneously, my skin warmed as if he'd thrown an electric blanket over me.

"Thanks." I sighed.

We walked toward the laughter coming from the town's center. Vane hurried in front of me. "I need you to be alert in case we get separated."

"What happened to being my shadow?" I scowled at his back. "Matt was right. I shouldn't have listened to you."

Vane's deep brown eyes glittered with flecks of gold under the streetlights. "We need to draw out the gargoyle. He's not going to do that if I'm at your side the whole night. Don't tell me you've lost your backbone, candidate. How do you expect to train for the sword if you can't face down a single gargoyle? Or were you hoping to hide behind my brother forever?"

"Fine," I bit out. "But if this goes bad and I don't make it—just remember you'll be facing the Council alone."

Vane tucked back a lock of hair that had escaped from the wool cap I wore. "If this goes bad and you lose even one golden strand, it won't be the Council I'll be worried about. My brother won't let me live long enough for that."

His words caused a warm flush. "You really think Matt would do that? For me?"

Vane stiffened. "Do I look like I want to be involved in your teen love saga? Ask someone who cares."

"Did you recently turn into a jerk or have you been one since birth?" I retorted.

"Since birth." With a quick twist of the boot heel, he turned back toward the festival. "But enough flirting. Let's get this started."

My mouth opened and closed like a startled guppy. I stalked after him. "I was *not* flirting. I don't know how I let you talk me into this."

"That was the easy part." Vane sneered. "All I had to do was imply that your little group might be in danger and you practically begged to come. You and my brother are perfect for each other. Both martyrs, the pair of you."

I wanted to stick out my tongue at him. Instead, I sniffed. "Nice try. You can't distract me, though. Why don't you tell me why you're really here, Vane? Why do you want to help us get the sword?"

"I thought Matt told you—why do I do anything? To save myself, of course."

"Yes, that is the reason." I huddled into the warmth of my coat, letting the heat spell warm me. I stared at his back as we walked. "I just hope that is *all* the reason."

At the town's square, people in glittering costumes milled around a running fountain. The Avalon Prep buses off-loaded to the side. Pockets of students in glittering party dresses filled the square. A long stone monument marked the center.

Every nook and cranny of the small square was occupied. Colorfully costumed people drank from old-fashioned goblets. Booths had been setup offering various food, drinks, and souvenirs. Near the monument, a high stage showcased a band. They alternately crooned and riffed their guitars in hard rhythm. A crowd gyrated to the beat.

"I'm going to find a spot up next to the stage. It'll be easiest to keep an eye on you from there," Vane said. "You mingle around." He took out a cell phone from his coat and held it up to me. "If you spot someone you know, call me. The number is already programmed in."

"That's your great plan," I said. "That's lousy."

"If someone is after you, they will find you."

"Fine. Whatever." A booth filled with feather masks caught my eye. I started to move toward it.

Vane grabbed my arm. "Don't get lured away."

I scowled at him. "I can take care of myself."

"Don't be foolish. This isn't a game. The gargoyle won't hesitate to kill you."

I rolled my eyes. "I am the bait, remember?"

"I see now why you aggravate my brother so much," he said, making a sound of frustration. He slapped the cell phone on my palm and tapped its screen. "Call. Don't think. Call."

Without waiting for a response, he took off.

I saw him head toward the stage. I went to the booth selling masks. I paid for a soft-looking one with silver owl feathers. I was putting it on when a hand touched my shoulder. My nerves were so jumpy, I almost shrieked.

Blake's face leaned into mine. "Don't freak. It's just us."

"Us?" I took a step back. Grey, Gia, Paul, Oliver, Blake and his friends, even Mark and the rest of Vane's candidates milled around the booth.

I gaped at the crowd. "All of you are here?"

"We weren't going to let you have all the fun," Gia said. "I figured if you could sneak out, so could we."

I crossed my arms. "And how did you?"

Gia grinned at Blake. "This one is not a bad wizard."

Blake's ears turned red. "My spell wouldn't have worked if you hadn't distracted the teachers. We snuck into one of the buses."

"Buses." Grey snorted. "Limos, you mean?"

I made a face. That's what I got for believing Vane. So much for protecting Grey from danger; now he was right smack dab in the middle. "Don't you think they're going to notice when so many candidates are gone? We're going to get caught."

"I am allowed to be here," Blake said.

"You're still a candidate," I reminded him.

"Don't be such a downer, DuLac. We won't get in the way of your date. Are you going to tell us who he is?" Gia glanced around the crowd. "Not that it's really necessary. I think we can be fairly sure it's a certain teacher we know."

Oliver said. "But I saw him going to the Council building as we were heading out."

Grey raised a brow. "So where is he?"

"He went to get drinks," I said, thinking quickly. "I'm going to meet him over by the band."

In an eager voice, Blake stated, "We'll come with you—"

"Uh." I quickly tried to think of an excuse to stall him.

Mark looked at us with a bored expression. "DuLac can get her date by herself. I'm going to see the band. This might be our last fun night. We shouldn't waste a minute." He looked at the other candidates. "Who else is coming with me?"

"I hear the band's sold out across the continent." Blake pointed to an open spot just before the stage on the other side of where Vane had gone. "If we go now, we can get a great view. Why don't we save a place for Ryan?"

"That's a great idea," I said quickly. "I'll meet you there with him."

Grey glanced at the spot before turning back to me with a skeptical expression. "You're not trying to lose us, are you?"

"No!" I let out a small laugh. "I'll be there soon." I started walking before they could come up with another probing question.

"You are so meeting Merlin, aren't you?" Gia called out as I hurried away.

I dialed Vane on the cell as I walked in the direction where he'd headed off. I had to convince him to call this off and force everyone to go back to school. The call still hadn't connected as I walked past several booths. I was glancing around trying to spot Vane when I saw a face that made my heart stop. Blond hair. Tall frame. Impossibly square jaw.

Morgan.

He was talking to someone under a street lamp. I couldn't see the other person very well—only a hooked-nose profile under the shadow of the streetlight. However, Morgan stood spotlighted by the streetlight, which had my mind reeling. I tried to move. To duck. I couldn't. It shouldn't have been possible. He looked up and spotted me.

Morgan broke off his conversation and slipped into a line in front of a closed tent booth. Without taking my eyes off the booth line, I hit redial on the cell.

Vane picked up the call. "What is it, DuLac?"

"My ex-boyfriend… is here." The Morgan lookalike paid an attendant and went into the booth.

"The dead one?"

"How many do you think I have?" I hissed. "Yes, the dead one. The gargoyle." I looked at the top of the tent. "He's gone into a booth called Mysterious Faces. There are a few people in line. I don't want to lose him. I'm going after him."

Vane cursed. "Wait, DuLac. It's a glamour. He's not real!"

I clicked off the cell. He was very real. He'd given me the same half-smile that had made me say yes to our first date. Two giggling preteens holding hands went into the booth ahead of me.

"Two tickets," the attendant said.

My hands shook as I tore off two tickets and handed them to him. The attendant opened the tent flap. I reached into the inner pocket of my coat and put my hand on the knife Vane had thoughtfully provided, and I entered. Inside, I saw immediately why the booth was called *Mysterious Faces*. It was pitch black with soft glowing strobe lights. Beast and ghoul faces had been painted onto mirrors. The couple in front of me was having a great time seeing their faces contorted into various beasts.

I walked through the narrow maze, heart pounding. Every twisted face seemed to jump out at me, and every face appeared to be Morgan's. I remembered only snatches of Morgan's beast face. Adrenaline had been running rampant in me the night he'd attacked my mother. I remembered the shock in his eyes before Vane had chopped his head off. I remembered the blood on the tile. My mother's blood.

I turned a corner. Another monster mirror jumped out at me. I turned to walk past it. The reflection reached out a hand. A knife gleamed in the dark as it swung down toward me. It took me a second to realize it was real. Using a technique I'd learned in Vane's class, I kicked at the knife. Thankfully my skirt had enough give so I didn't fall flat on my face.

The gargoyle's knife got knocked aside. I pulled out my

own knife. Morgan's face flashed in the dim, flickering light. I didn't hesitate to stab him. The knife went into his shoulder. He looked surprised. I felt Matt's amulet on my neck warm. It cast a shadow over the gargoyle. His face changed to a round cherub face that I'd never seen before.

"You're not Morgan," I said.

"No." The gargoyle grinned, his face twisting into beast form. He pulled the knife out of his shoulder. It fell at my feet. The wound—which should have been fatal—started healing rapidly.

I grabbed the knife and ran. Cursing my high heels, I stumbled out of the back of the tent and into a small alley. Away from the lights, the alley sat in dingy darkness. The gargoyle came after me. I ran down the alley. I almost made it out.

Another man blocked the way. He wore a red jacket.

He grinned. "You didn't think we'd come alone."

Hands closed around my waist from behind. I let out a small scream.

"It's me," Vane hissed. He pushed me behind him.

The Morgan lookalike caught up to us. The two gargoyles circled Vane.

"We've got protection amulets, wizard," the lookalike said. "Just give us the girl and we'll let you go."

Vane spat out a spell and let it loose at the gargoyle. The gargoyle's amulet glowed, but it didn't negate Vane's attack. Vane said his spell with more force. The gargoyle's amulet broke. Vane opened his palm and a lightning bolt hit the

Morgan lookalike in the chest. The gargoyle fell to the ground with a thud. His eyes rolled backward. He looked dead.

Vane leapt toward him. He took a knife out his pocket. "*Aayat,*" he said. The knife expanded into a sword. Vane chopped off the fallen gargoyle's head.

The other gargoyle made a surprised sound.

Vane turned to him with a cruel smile. "The amulet is only as powerful as the wizard who made it. He should have gotten a bargain on that one." Vane opened his palm and a fireball appeared. "Want to test yours?"

In the blink of an eye, the gargoyle came at me. He grabbed me around the neck and put me in front of him as a shield. "Try it, wizard, and I'll snap her neck."

Vane shrugged. "What makes you think I care about this one?"

"Don't underestimate us, wizard. Her name is Ryan. She is Merlin's. You know as well as I do that she is special." The gargoyle pulled me further into the alley. He pushed me down a short stairwell and kicked open a door. We stumbled through into some kind of basement. A dark, cavernous room where light only came in through a small rectangular window.

I saw no other openings. The basement might very well become my tomb. The gargoyle backed us up. He only stopped when we hit a column.

"Come out. Come out," Vane said from the doorway.

The gargoyle put his hand in his pocket and took out what looked like a grenade. He threw it in Vane's direction.

Fire erupted around us. I let out a startled yelp.

"Nice try, but do you really think a little fire will stop me?" Vane stepped into the basement.

"Do not come any further, wizard." The gargoyle's hold on me tightened. "I will kill her."

"Who do you have working for you at the school?" Vane demanded.

The gargoyle took us deeper into the basement. The fire still burned bright, blocking Vane off from us.

"Time is up, gargoyle." Vane stalked toward us. The fire fell away as he came forward. "Bad decision on the fire. It's only going to trap you."

The gargoyle laughed. "Then I'll open a new way."

Five gargoyles filed in through the basement door.

"Get the wizard," the gargoyle holding me said.

My time had run out. I kicked out with my foot and slipped out of the gargoyle's hold. He let out a growl of surprise. I ran to Vane. He pulled me to the lone window in the dank basement. He flicked a hand and the pane shattered.

Six gargoyles ran at us. Vane muttered a word. The fire expanded exponentially. The gargoyles coughed. I saw them grab their amulets for protection.

"Go first," he shouted. He started throwing fireballs at the gargoyles.

The gargoyles bunched together to use their amulets as a shield. I jumped up and caught the edge of the windowsill. I strained to lift myself out. I'd never been good at pull-ups.

Vane cursed. He ran to me and put down the sword. He grabbed my backside and tossed me up. I used the momentum to get myself out. My knees scraped on unforgiving concrete. Ignoring the sting of torn skin, I twisted back around to look in through the window.

"Run," Vane yelled, looking up at me.

I saw a gargoyle break through the wall of fire. He picked up Vane's sword.

"Vane!" I screamed in warning.

Vane turned to look. I moved to leap back in. Vane flicked his hand. I got blown back. The windowpane reformed. With a curse, I hit it with my feet, but the glass held strong. Vane had locked me out.

The gargoyle reached Vane with the sword held up high.

I pounded the window and let out a cry. Vane was going to die.

"I wouldna worry about him, lass," a gravely voice said from behind me.

A shiver went down my spine. I turned around. A man kneeled in the alley beside the gargoyle Vane had killed earlier. He shut the gargoyle's eyes. He looked up. Moonlight made his swollen forehead seem bigger. But even without the engorged gargoyle head, this man would have been a scary sight. He had a long scar running along his jaw and down his throat.

Fangs protruded past broad lips. "Time to have some real fun."

The gargoyle sounded just like Morgan. My whole body froze.

A SURPRISE

I touched my amulet and wished for Matt.

"You've given my cousins a lot of trouble." The gargoyle watched me with deadened eyes. "Instead of waiting for the wizards to show up, Morgan should have taken care of you right away."

I fell back against the window. "Morgan was your cousin?"

"Not of blood, but we're of a related clan. Yet our honor has been besmirched." He tilted his head, considering me. "Imagine our pleasure when we were told you would be slipping past the school's security."

"Someone at the school told you," I said.

The gargoyle made a tsking sound. "You cannot trust anyone these days, can you? That is why I always keep my word. Might be why I don't get called to help often. Most are too afraid to approach me." The gargoyle stood. He drew out a heavy sword that he'd been carrying on his back. He advanced on me, sword gleaming under the moonlight. "It is too bad that your family has been marked. I feel almost regretful killing such a fragile-looking creature."

I stumbled back. My hand caught on something sharp and sliced it open. I hissed in pain as blood flowed freely from it.

The gargoyle inhaled the scent of my blood. He stopped in his tracks.

"Interesting." His sword lowered. "I wonder if the king knows."

"Get him," Grey's voice said from behind the gargoyle.

All of the candidates stood beside him. Several beams of light hit the gargoyle at once. An amulet glowed on his neck. More beams of light hit him with the speed of a machine gun. The gargoyle fell.

Grey ran to the fallen gargoyle. "He's only knocked out. Tie him up."

Paul and Oliver rushed to the fallen gargoyle with a rope.

I cried, "Help me knock out this window. Vane needs help."

"Vane?" Gia said. "I thought you came here with Merlin."

I shook my head. "It's a long story."

Grey threw a rock at the window. The rock bounced back harmlessly. "It's magicked."

Gia tried to blast it. I saw a weak light, but nothing happened. "I'm drained from knocking out the gargoyle. Vane's magic is too powerful."

"Try again," I said.

"If we push too much, we'll use ourselves up," Mark said.

Gia said, "The only way we even have a shot is if we all try."

I marched up to Mark. "Try again."

He raised a brow. "How are you going to make me, DuLac?"

Before Mark could blink, I grabbed the sword that had fallen from the gargoyle. I held the sword out to him. "Think about this. We need Vane to train us. We won't have a chance at the trial."

Mark drew out a knife from his pocket and said, "*Aayat,*" the same spell Vane had used to elongate the knife into a sword. He grunted, "Keep your sword."

"Does everybody know this trick?" I muttered.

All of the wizard candidates except Mark blasted the window together. This time it shattered. Most of the candidates sank to the ground, completely exhausted.

"Stay here," I told them. "You can't help anymore."

"I'm coming," Grey said.

"We don't have time for this, Grey. Just stay here." Sword still in hand, I kicked off my heels and jumped through the opening. Inside, smoke filled the air, making everything hazy. A gargoyle lay on the floor. A silver sword stuck in his heart. I approached him slowly. He didn't move. I pulled out the sword. He still didn't move. With a relieved breath, I picked up the sword in the dead gargoyle's hand. I faced the basement. It looked like a war zone.

"I knew you'd find me a sword," Grey said, coming up behind me.

I was too glad to see him to give him more than a brief glare. I handed him the blade. We moved further into the basement, finally emerging from the dense smoke. We took cover behind a column and surveyed the scene.

The other five gargoyles surrounded Vane. He was barely holding them off, still firing fireballs.

"Separate the gargoyles," I told him. "Then Vane can take them."

Mark walked through the smoke to us. "I can take two."

He, Grey, and I ran at the gargoyles.

A red-haired gargoyle broke off to handle us. Grey reached him first. The gargoyle knocked the sword out of Grey's hand. The blow knocked Grey into a nearby column. He hit his head and fell to the floor.

Mark and I reached the gargoyle at the same time.

He parried with us both. With the sword in my hand, every move I made flowed smoothly. I didn't miss a beat. Even in a torn gown and no shoes, I moved with a speed that surprised myself. But I wasn't as skilled as Mark. Mark countered his gargoyle's attack better. The red-haired gargoyle knocked Mark's sword out first. The gargoyle lunged to finish Mark off when I stepped into the path of the blade. It sliced deep into my arm.

Startled, the gargoyle stumbled.

Mark kicked the sword out of the red-haired gargoyle's hand.

Another gargoyle attacked Mark.

I had the shot at the red-haired gargoyle's neck. My blade

went smoothly into a sickle-arc slice. The gargoyle's eyes widened. His face returned to normal. My sword faltered.

The gargoyle's face changed back into its beast form. He lunged at me.

Vane came out of nowhere, mirroring the gargoyle's leap. He had a sword in his hand. He didn't hesitate. The red-haired beast's head fell to the ground.

"He won't be getting up from that," Vane said.

The other gargoyles Vane had been fighting lay on the ground. He must have knocked them out.

"I thought I told you to leave." Vane took my shoulders and shoved me toward the window. "Go, before they get up."

A few feet away, Mark let out a cry. He was losing. A gargoyle hit Mark on the temple and he fell to the ground.

Vane hurried to help him. He stabbed the gargoyle, felling him. The knocked-out gargoyles started waking. Vane attacked them in a fury. I watched him with wide eyes. One by one the gargoyles got up. One by one, Vane killed all four.

When the last one fell, the thick smoke suffocating us dissipated and a strange quiet fell over the hollow basement.

The staked gargoyle I'd originally taken a sword from began to stir. Vane marched to him and severed his head before he could fully wake.

I sank to the floor.

A dead gargoyle head stared at me with blank, white eyes. Blood spilled out of his unattached body. I looked around. In the dim, flickering light, I could still see red sprayed all over the walls. It was exactly like the night my mother died. The sticky sweet scent of death clogged my nose.

My esophagus swelled, becoming bloated. I couldn't breathe. Couldn't swallow. I started hyperventilating. Vane grabbed my wounded arm. I felt a slight tingle as he healed me.

"DuLac, pull yourself together," he said, pushing his face right up to mine. To my ringing ears, however, his voice seemed to be coming from far away. My shoulders curled inward. My panting became harder. It felt as if every orifice I had was going to lose control.

Catching my chin, Vane kissed me. It was a hard kiss. His lips mashed against mine. It felt forced. Cold. I shook harder. He pulled back.

"DuLac, dammit." His nose touched mine gently. He kissed me again. His lips stroked mine. I let him. Slowly, I felt my body ease. I noticed that his fingers tangled around strands of my hair. My hands slid up hard arms. I squeezed muscled shoulders.

I pushed him away.

Vane swung me up. He began carrying me toward the door. "This time I'm going to make sure you leave here."

I dug my nails into his skin. "Grey. Mark."

"Are just knocked out. I checked. Once I get you out, I'll see to them. I've also sent the Council a text. They will send cleaners."

"Cleaners," I repeated.

"This mess will be gone within the hour." Vane continued slowly to the door.

Unwittingly, my head turned to the dark horror of the

basement.

"Don't," Vane said, squeezing me in warning. "You don't need to look again."

I nuzzled down, resting my head against his chest. "I saved your life."

"Don't get cocky."

I glanced up at Vane. Soft light from the window danced across his fair hair. His profile looked somber. I supposed so would mine after beheading seven gargoyles in one night.

Straight lips curved up. He said, "Your skill with the sword was quite impressive... and surprising. Holding out on us in class?"

"It's hard to explain," I said. "When I was fighting the gargoyle, I wasn't thinking. I wasn't trying to figure out the right step to counter with. I just moved. It's not the same as in class."

Vane let out a laugh. "Yes, very different—although the problem is usually the other way around. Students who do well in class freeze when it becomes real."

I tensed. "I'm not a killer."

"No, you don't want to be one," Vane said. "There's a difference."

Through the open door I could hear sounds of laughing and merriment coming from the square, completely oblivious to the mayhem just below the surface.

Vane's arms tightened around me. "You're a candidate. This is what it's about."

We reached the door.

Vane stopped. "DuLac, before we go up, about the kiss."

I looked up at him.

Hesitatingly, he said, "I was trying to shake you out of shock—"

"I get it." I cut him off.

"Good," he said quickly.

"Yes."

He glanced at me. "Not that it was horrible."

"Right," I said stiffly. "You were trying to help me. Nothing more. I get it. You really don't have to worry or explain. Don't worry. You're off the hook."

Vane leaned me against the basement door. With a quick twist, he turned me to face him.

"As long as I'm off the hook—" His lips swooped down to capture mine.

I let out a small squeak of surprise as he thrust me up against the door. His chest slammed up against mine. I found myself arching my back, wanting to get as close to him as possible, but I couldn't get close enough. Several hot seconds of tongue-delving action passed before I could form another coherent thought. While his left hand held me up, Vane's right hand traveled up my leg under my dress until his fingers found bare skin.

I pulled back. Quite eloquently, I garbled, "W-what?"

The door fell open behind me. I would have dropped straight to the ground if Vane hadn't grabbed me at the last second. I clung to him.

"Oh. Holy. Crap." Gia's voice penetrated my fogged brain.

A light shone down the stairwell, pinning me with Vane in its spotlight. I tried to jerk away from Vane, but he kept me in place. Gia and the other candidates stood at the door. They crowded in the small stairwell that led up to the street. Blake had a flabbergasted look on his face. So did the rest of them— except for Matt.

Matt.

It was my turn to be flabbergasted. My heart sank at the stony mask covering Matt's face.

"You came," I said to him.

"Yes." His eyes locked on mine. I couldn't read them, but I didn't have to.

He was pissed. Really, really pissed. His vision had come true. I finally understood why he'd been so upset on the plane. He'd seen it coming and he knew he wouldn't be able to do anything to stop it.

Vane's hold on me tightened. "Here to clean up after me as usual, Merlin? How is it that you always show after the real work is done?"

Out of the corner of my eye, I saw a shadowy figure watching us from the top of the stairwell. My throat went dry. The shadow fell just as it had under the streetlight when I'd spotted Morgan. The shadow's profile showed a distinctive hooked nose.

I leaned into Vane's neck and whispered in his ear. "It's him. At the top of the stairs."

In a flash, Vane's hand shot out. A single wave of magic

shot through the stairwell and hit the figure squarely in the chest. The boy flew backwards. Vane put me down and rushed up the stairs.

I followed behind slowly. Vane held the figure immobile on the gritty ground of the narrow alley with the same air hold he'd used to choke me in the cathedral.

"When did you start working for the gargoyles?" Vane interrogated him.

The boy made choking sounds.

"He can't talk, Vane," Matt observed mildly.

Vane loosened his fist a bit.

"It's Gordon!" Gia exclaimed.

Gordon stammered, "I d-don't know what you're talking about. I'm just here for the festival." He nodded at the other candidates sitting in the alley. "I saw them and wanted to see what they were doing."

I went to stand beside Vane. I looked at the kid closely. I said to Vane, "It's him—one of your candidates. The one who saw nothing in the Lake water. The one you wanted to abandon."

"I should have abandoned him." Vane tightened his grip again.

"P-please," Gordon pleaded. "I haven't done anything."

I glanced around and found Oliver and Paul. "Where's the gargoyle we caught? He knew I was sneaking out."

"You caught a gargoyle?" Vane said. "Where is he?"

Paul and Oliver exchanged glances. Paul had an angry

bruise on his head and Oliver cradled his arm as if he'd broken it.

Gia made an impatient noise. "The gargoyle got away."

Blake nodded at Gordon on the street. "I remember him in the dining room tonight. He sat at the table right next to us. He knew we were going out."

Vane turned a cruel smile on his former pupil. "I've heard enough."

Matt grabbed Vane's arm. "We need to take him to the Council. We need to question him properly."

Vane shrugged away from Matt. "If the bureaucracy gets hold of him, who knows how long before we get anything? I want to know if there's anyone else involved in this—now."

Vane put a boot on Gordon's hand. "What have you told the gargoyles? Who is your contact? Tell me now."

"I d-don't know anything!"

Vane squeezed his fist tighter. On the ground, Gordon's body shook. He made small mewling sounds.

"I'm not going to tell you anything!" Gordon let slip.

Vane smiled in satisfaction and loosened his hold. "Which means there is something to know."

Gordon jumped up and attacked Vane in a fury of flying fists. In a few quick moves, Vane subdued him and slammed Gordon back onto the ground.

"Who is your contact?" Vane repeated. "Do you want to make it to the Council, Gordon? Then, you'd better talk now."

"I thought you'd help me," the boy spat. "But you're all the same. Just like my grandmother. She wanted to have me locked up. But I took care of her, too."

Vane sighed. "What did you tell the gargoyles about the candidates?"

Gordon giggled. He looked at me.

"You mean about her?" he said. "Wouldn't you like to know?"

Vane's eyes narrowed. He stood over Gordon without a hint of mercy. "Which way is it going to be—easy or hard? Because either way, you're going to die tonight."

Vane's hand fisted. Gordon kicked his legs and tried to claw at the invisible force squeezing his throat. The boy's face started to turn blue.

I grabbed Vane's arm. "Vane, stop."

"*Visrajti,*" Matt barked.

"No," Vane shouted at Matt.

The magic choking Gordon fluctuated. I could see the faint red of Vane's magic battling with Matt's blue. The boy levitated up a few inches off the ground. There was an odd crunching sound. Gordon fell to the ground. His eyes wide open, but oddly still.

Matt hurried over to him. He knelt on the ground and put two fingers on the boy's neck, feeling for a pulse. Matt closed Gordon's eyes.

He turned back to Vane.

Vane scowled at Matt. "I had everything under control and then you had to interfere. He was starting to talk."

Matt shook his head. "So this is my fault?"

"No, you could never do your own dirty work, Merlin," Vane said softly.

"Matt, we've got company." I pointed to the end of the alley. A few curious onlookers were whispering among themselves. I could see a few of them working up the courage to come into the alley. A white van pulled up, scattering them.

It blocked the alley entrance.

"Cleaners," Matt said. He turned to the candidates. "Return to the school please. Right away. We've got a huge mess to sort out."

"I think I've had enough of this festival," Grey said.

There were murmurs of agreement. Grey led the candidates out of the alley.

Matt brushed by me. I caught his sleeve. "Matt, I'm sorry."

He stiffened. "I specifically told you *not* to do this. You went ahead anyway, and look at what you've accomplished. Your friends are barely standing. A boy is dead. Is that what you wanted, Ryan?"

"No." I watched the Cleaners put a white sheet on Gordon. I hugged myself. "I wanted to help."

"You did," Vane said. "We caught the spy."

"You put *every* single candidate in danger." Matt looked at us. "Do you two have any idea how much worse that would be than *not* capturing one collaborator? He may have been a traitor, but he was barely a threat."

I made a sound of protest. Matt cut me off. "Go home, Ryan. Next time, maybe you'll take a moment to think before acting."

My jaw clenched. "This may not have turned out as we wanted, but I know one thing, Matt. I'm not going to regret acting rather than sitting around waiting for my family or my friends to get attacked. *I've* already had that moment."

I read the faint flare of surprise in Matt's eyes, but he didn't say anything.

"But you're right. I think I should go home." I stalked out of the alley.

I stopped just around the corner. The nightmare of the entire evening threatened to crush me. I took a heaving breath. Vane came up behind me.

"Ready to go, Goldilocks?"

I scowled. "I am not Goldilocks."

"Yes," he said with utter seriousness. "You would never push around a pack of cuddly bears that way. I'd say you're more Dorothy."

I tilted my head to look at him. "If I'm Dorothy, what does that make you?"

Vane cocked his head. "Toto?"

Unable to help myself, I laughed. Vane put a hand under my elbow and guided me across the noisy square. The festival raged on around us. The frolicking had only increased as the night lengthened. I stopped just in front of Vane's SUV.

"Did you really have everything under control?" I asked.

"You heard the mighty wizard. What do you think?"

"I don't know," I said. "You don't seem very sorry."

Vane's jaw tightened. "I found him in Hong Kong. He told me the gargoyles burned down his house. That they'd killed his grandmother. I'm sure they did. But now I wonder if that was his price. I wonder if he had her murdered."

"Would you have killed him?" I asked.

Vane opened the door to the SUV. Resting one hand on the car, he leaned against it. "Absolutely. I would have done what was necessary."

Hazel eyes held my gaze. I could read the absolute certainty in those changeable depths. I believed him. He would do what it took. Whatever it took. Yet, instead of making me afraid, the knowledge somehow made me feel oddly safe... and treacherously breathless.

He extended a hand toward me, to help me inside the SUV. The intense way he watched me, the way his eyes lingered on my lips, told me he offered more than just a hand. If I dared to take it. Not looking at him, I did.

Warm fingers squeezed my cold ones as he helped me into the seat. He moved to close the door.

"Wait," I said.

I held out my left arm to show him a jagged scratch that extended from wrist to elbow. It had become swollen. "A gargoyle swiped me with his claw."

Vane traced the scratch with his thumb. The scratch disappeared. "That's the third time, DuLac. No more free services."

"Nothing with you is free," I said lightly.

"You have a cut here too." Vane traced my lips with his

thumb. Every hair on my body stood on end as if he'd stroked me with lightning.

Vane groaned.

I pulled away.

He let me go. "You and Matt can't be."

"I know," I said. Not that it mattered. Matt hated me.

Vane closed the car door and crossed to the driver's side. He slipped into the seat. His presence filled the space. Yet, it wasn't oppressive. The darkness invited me to be daring, and I decided to do the bravest thing I had yet to do this evening. I leaned over and put my hand on Vane's forearm. About to start the car, he paused. He looked at me.

"One more thing," I said. "Even you can't deny that I've proven myself tonight."

Vane startled for a second. "What?"

"I want to advance to swords."

Vane let out a laugh. "You're nothing if not surprising, DuLac."

Snowflakes started falling. One by one they splattered against the windshield. I stared out at the serene scene. The night looked deceptively peaceful. I wondered how long it would last. I tucked my hair behind my ear. Outside the windshield the stars winked like ice crystals.

"I can learn to do what is necessary," I said.

"Yes, I think you can." His fingers tightened on the steering wheel and he turned away to face the front. He stared off at some unknown point in the shrouded darkness of the road. He didn't say anything, and I started to feel the car close in on me.

I huddled in my coat.

As if sensing my slightest discomfort, Vane turned on the engine. Heat sprayed out through the vents. He pulled a knife out of his pocket. It was the one he'd used in the basement, the one that elongated into a sword. Without looking directly at me, he held it out. "Bring it to class."

I took the knife. "I also want the others moved up to swords."

"I know, DuLac."

He turned back to face me.

I asked, with unfortunate breathlessness, "What do you think you know?"

A smile broke out over his face. "Dorothy looked sweet, but underneath, she was all trouble. Just the way I like it."

I was afraid I liked it too.

***

"You're not even trying," Vane growled as he straddled me.

Sweat covered every inch of my body. I lay under him on the practice mat. The hard length of his thighs held down my hips. The training room had emptied hours ago. I stretched my hands as far as I could above my head. My fingertips brushed the hilt of my fallen sword. I couldn't reach it. I made a sound of frustration.

"You have to do better, DuLac," Vane said. His hand traced the line of my jaw, following it up past my ear. He caressed the thick strands of my hair. "Time is running out."

I arched my back. Vane sucked in a breath. His legs gave a bit. I had enough room to twist my hips. With an inelegant turn, I toppled him off me.

Vane fell on the mat. "Better," he said.

With a grin, I sat up. Moonlight beamed in through the windows. Weeks had passed since the night of the festival. Outside the cathedral, snow buried the courtyard, kissed the naked branches of trees, and generally consumed the school. Not much had happened as we rapidly approached Christmas.

"I'm missing dinner again," I said.

Vane rose up on one elbow. "It's your turn to cook."

I pushed myself up with effort. I went to the end of the room and got my bag. I didn't bother to change from uniform back into regular clothes; there weren't many students walking around outside at this hour. I thrust my legs into thick snow boots—the ones with the soft sherpa lining inside. Vane pulled on a black wool coat.

I texted Gia to get dinner started. I asked him, "Did you agree to extra training just to get free meals?"

"I made dinner yesterday."

"You fetched it from the dining hall. There was no iced tea."

Vane grunted and started down the spiral stairs. I followed him. The banisters of the stairwell twinkled with Christmas lights. The lights had been twined around a fresh pine garland. I inhaled the clean scent, letting it wash over me.

As soon as I stepped outside a blast of blizzard hit my face with bone-chilling force. Vane stepped in front of me, taking the brunt of the cold. The stone buildings seemed to glow in the dark, thanks to the blankets of snow covering them. White

Christmas lights and garland decorations had been tied around all the trees. Bright red bows adorned the tops of even the tallest of the buildings. For the first time, the school looked like a place of magic to me.

We fought our way to the teachers' residence as quickly as possible. Pine garlands decorated the lobby also, but here they had been unafraid to show off. Small, glowing sleigh bells danced and jingled merrily in the air.

Occasionally they would dance in sequence and play a familiar Christmas tune. I sang along to "Jingle Bells." I wasn't the only one. Vane hummed under his breath, too, although he got all the words wrong. He kept substituting odd words I'd never heard before... maybe from his time. I wondered if he realized what he was doing.

A few teachers in mage's robes hung around the glowing fireplace in the lobby. A hint of pumpkin spice filled the air as they drank from hot mugs and chatted.

They looked up as we entered.

A couple of them stared at Vane, but they didn't greet him. A few sent him leery glances. One sat in the center of the group. He wore a white councilmember's robe and played with an apple in one hand. It took me a moment to place him. He had held the jug at the admissions test. Thornton.

From the worshipful way the others were looking at him, he was obviously holding court.

"Banning the sale of magic is ridiculous," he said loudly. "What do they want us to do?" He floated the apple casually in the air. "Hold *regular* jobs?" He laughed at his own pun.

The others tittered.

Vane didn't bother to glance in their direction as we walked past. Councilmember Thornton nudged a much younger brown-robed mage. The young mage cleared his throat and straightened his shoulder. He ran after us.

"S-Sir," he said to Vane.

Vane didn't stop. The mage moved to stand in front of him. Vane halted. He harrumphed at the mage.

The mage swallowed several times before continuing, "We were told that you could create fireballs like Master Merlin."

"Yes," Vane said shortly.

"You must be very powerful." When Vane's eyes narrowed, the brown-robed mage laughed nervously. "They say you chopped off a gargoyle's head."

"Yes," Vane said in a measured tone.

"That's fantastic. Brilliant," the mage flustered. "I didn't know wizards battled with their hands. Was the blade magicked to strike true?"

Vane cocked his head. "No."

"Oh," the mage said nonplussed. "I guess we thought it might have been."

"You can do such things without magic," I stated the obvious.

The brown-robed mage sent me a quizzical look. "But why would I if I have magic?"

In one smooth movement, Vane drew out a knife from his coat and threw it across the room. It speared Thornton's apple and pinned it into the wood wall. Beside us, the young mage's mouth opened and closed.

Vane's voice boomed across the room. "Magic without work makes you sloppy." With a flick of his hand, he called the knife back. The apple dropped into the councilmember's hand, cut neatly in half. "Sloppy will get you killed."

The councilmember gave us a mock salute.

I followed Vane into the lift. I'd gotten out of habit of calling it an elevator. Vane punched the button to our floor.

As soon as the doors slid shut, I rounded on him. "Magic without work? Don't tell me you secretly like Regulars now."

"I don't dislike them... in this century. I just refuse to entrust my life to them."

"I'm a Regular."

Vane's lips curved up. "I don't dislike you either."

Something stirred in the recesses of his eyes. It beckoned me to look closer. I turned away before I could get drawn in. The old-fashioned lift jerked up. I quickly said, "You and Matt have more in common than either of you will admit. You obviously know the importance of not just depending on magic for everything or you wouldn't be such a good trainer."

Vane raised a brow. "Good?"

I cleared my throat. "Mostly good."

Vane smirked. "How is training going with my brother?"

My heart gave a little twist when I pictured Matt. He never spoke to me outside of what was absolutely necessary for class. I bit down on the inside of my cheek. "He can barely stand to look at me."

"My brother can hold a grudge."

I looked down at my snow boots. "You're happy about it, I'm sure."

"I'm not unhappy. We need Merlin's abilities to stay intact."

"It doesn't matter who gets in the way," I said dully. I shivered, cold despite the fact that it was a heated building.

Vane put a hand on my back. Warmth seeped back into my bones.

"I can't let him screw everything up again. He ruined it by allowing Arthur to rule Camelot even after it became obvious he couldn't."

I tilted my head up to meet his gaze. "Who should have been the ruler?"

"Merlin, of course."

The lift doors opened. Vane walked with me to my door.

I said, "The sword didn't pick Matt or you. It picked Arthur."

"Another piece of misinformation I see my brother didn't bother to correct—the Lady offered the sword to us first. To bring the land together. Merlin turned it down, saying it was too powerful in our hands. I never got the choice. The Lady loved his idea. She made the sword a bridge between all of our races."

We reached my door. I touched Vane's shoulder.

He stilled.

"You said time is running out. How do you know?"

Vane's eyes glittered. "My brother isn't the only smart one."

I bit my lip. "Are we ready?"

Vane touched my neck. The amulet warmed under his touch. I felt its heat spread across my chest. My pupils dilated.

"I'd say you're ready," he said silkily.

I shook his hand off the amulet. "Be serious."

"I'd rather stray off the yellow brick road into the poppy fields." Vane touched a hand to the knob and it turned on its own. It had been magicked to recognize only Gia and me. So, of course, Vane had found a way to grant himself access.

Gia banged dishes as she set the table inside.

"Alas." Vane sighed in mock regret.

With a shake of my head, I brushed past him. He caught my wrist.

"There is one requirement you should know. The sword can only be pulled my someone…"

I arched my brow expectantly.

Vane's lips twisted into a strangled smile. "Pure of heart."

***

An hour later, a knock sounded at the door. Gia let Grey in. A few minutes later, Blake entered. Vane, Grey, Blake, Gia and I regularly ate dinner together. But word was out and others would show up. Tonight, Paul and Oliver, were to join. The doorbell sounded again and six candidates instead of two came inside.

Evening meals at our place had turned into an event. Maybe because Vane brought beer—ale. We had no idea how he managed to get it every night, but nobody had gotten up the courage to ask.

I wasn't sure I wanted to know. I sat down in my usual chair.

"We need two more place settings," I told Blake.

He said a spell and the circular table expanded. Another kid pushed the couch into a corner. On the table, the food and a centerpiece of wreath wound around white candles remained intact.

Vane gripped the back of the chair next to me and leaned on it, waiting. He wouldn't sit until everyone else had—even though I could hear his stomach grumbling.

The etiquette continued to surprise me.

For someone who could be so blunt, he had really beautiful manners. I could picture him at the Royal Court of King Arthur. He would have loved the pomp and ceremony. I couldn't picture Matt enjoying it. He would have wanted to hide away in a remote tower reading a book. If I were to pick, I would have chosen the tower, too.

Since he'd acquiesced to train the Regulars, Vane had been grudgingly cordial—at dinner. He still drove us into the ground during training. I'd almost blacked out once or twice while he'd been yelling at me to try harder. Between class, training, and dinner we spent most of the day together. However, since the night of the festival, he hadn't even tried a peck on cheek. I sighed and played with the silverware.

As if he could tell what I was thinking, Vane cocked a very male eyebrow. I swallowed.

He leaned down to whisper in my ear. "Feeling dry?"

Issuing one magic command, Vane filled our goblets with ale.

Another knock pounded on the door. Vane sighed. "What do you do, Dorothy? Post dinnertime on a billboard?"

The door flew open.

Matt stumbled inside, one hand clutching his head like he had a terrible headache. He glanced around the dinner table. He didn't seem surprised to see the large gathering. He motioned at the flat-panel TV that hung on the wall. It switched on.

A news reporter stood next to the giant stone. "This is Anders reporting live from Trafalgar Square where—" The camera expanded to show a boy holding a sword in his hands.

"—this young man has just pulled King Arthur's sword."

THE DECOY

Oliver sprang up. "It's not possible!"

"Who is he?" Grey said.

"Quiet," Vane told them.

On TV, the reporter stuck a microphone in the boy's face. "How do you feel?"

"It's crazy. I came out here on a dare from my buddies." He pointed behind him to a group of guys wearing University of Boston sweatshirts. "I was just fooling around. I almost left when they closed off the square to clean it, but I was first in line… and I don't know… it just came out."

"And nothing unusual happened? You know that is supposedly King Arthur's sword. It fell out of the sky. Some people have said the blade feels tingly, like touching something with an electric current. Several young men have died from heart attacks—all with no prior history of any medical problems—after trying to pull it."

The boy shrugged. "Nope, I didn't feel a thing."

"Nothing... magical?"

The boy laughed. He held up the sword so it gleamed in the sunlight. "It's pretty cool, but nothing weird, as far as I can tell."

"So nothing magical, but you did get an interesting offer from this man." The reporter motioned the camera over to a smartly dressed man in a black suit. "Aurelius Ambrose, a representative of the British Museum. They have offered this man fifty million pounds to sell the sword to them."

"Aurelius? He's buying the sword?" I said.

Aurelius spoke. "The sword is a legendary artifact and should be studied, but it is also at the core of our history. We wish to ensure that it remain here."

"But fifty million pounds? How could the British Museum procure such a sum?" the reporter demanded.

"We've been preparing for this eventuality since the sword first dropped. A number of private donors have made this possible. The sword will belong to the people. It will remain home."

The reporter swung back to the boy. "Have you accepted the museum's offer?"

The boy nodded. He smiled. "I call it magic."

The camera returned to the reporter. "And there you have it—one for the history books. The shortest but undoubtedly the most lucrative possession of King Arthur's sword."

Vane switched off the TV. He arched a brow at his brother. "Explanation, Merlin."

"It's a decoy," Matt said. "The Council has moved the stone to a more private location."

A chorus of ohs followed. Oliver sat down, relief clear on his face.

I wasn't at all relieved. I'd been happy to see the sword in the boy's hand. My stomach clenched with a thick knot of tension I hadn't even realized I'd been carrying.

"Fifty million pounds just to move the stone?" Blake said. "Is the Council using magic to print money?"

Oliver snorted. "No, just selling it at outrageous prices."

I got up and went to Matt. His face was worn, his skin a sickly pallor. I steered him to the sofa to get him off his feet.

Vane's razor-sharp gaze locked on Matt. "It's time."

Matt nodded. "My vision confirmed it. I knew the season from a previous vision, but I had to guess at the day. Today, the vision told me I was wrong. It's going to happen earlier than I thought." Matt glanced at me. "I've been hoping to see this for months."

"I didn't know your visions had clocks," said Vane.

Matt leaned back on the sofa, closed his eyes, and yawned. "I've just spent the last few hours mapping the positioning of the stars into this." He held up the iPad. "I had to get it down before I forgot it."

"What's so special about now?" I asked.

"It's tomorrow," Vane said, studying Matt's research on the iPad. "I've been wondering if the sword fell according to the lunar calendar. The full moon is not until next week."

"I had originally thought so, but no. Tomorrow night is not

a full moon. But it is a red moon eclipse and—" Matt closed his eyes and yawned again.

"And?" Grey prompted.

"Tomorrow." I glanced at the small window in the kitchen. It had darkened early.

"Tomorrow night is the shortest day of the year. It's the winter solstice," Matt said.

"Wizards are weakest on the winter solstice," Blake said, "since we draw our power from the sun."

Matt nodded. "The sword may be magical, but it was not necessarily intended for a wizard. The winter solstice gives advantage to the gargoyles. A solstice combined with an eclipse, however, gives advantage—to Regulars."

Vane let out a laugh. "Of course."

Matt glanced around the flat at the candidates. "Get ready. Let everyone know. We leave in the morning."

The room cleared within minutes. Gia looked a little ill as she stumbled off to the bedroom. Matt snored slightly, already asleep on the sofa. I repositioned his head. He stopped, but didn't wake.

I put a blanket over him. "He's exhausted."

"Intense visions drain him," Vane said.

Most of the food had been left untouched. I didn't care. I'd lost my appetite. Vane sat down at the table. He ate slowly, savoring each bite.

"How can you be so calm?" I demanded.

Vane took a loud swallow of some ale. "Shouldn't you be

getting a bag together?"

"Shouldn't you?"

He got up and wiped his mouth with a napkin. He flicked his hand and the dishes started floating one by one over to the kitchen sink. Seeing the chore done only irritated me—as if I'd be around to enjoy clean dishes later.

I sank down on the sofa on the opposite end from Matt. "You are going with us, aren't you?"

Vane stilled. "Do you want me to go?"

"Yes," I said simply.

"Why? You've been trained. I know you won't lose your head. You don't need me."

I lowered my eyes at the sudden intensity of Vane's gaze. I didn't have a good answer, so I took the offensive. "The better question is—why not? I can't see you sitting on the sidelines."

"You didn't answer my question," Vane said lightly. "But I'll answer yours. I'm afraid I have no ticket to get to the final game."

I glanced at Matt snoring away on my sofa. "Matt and the Council want to keep you out?"

"I may have been tolerated for training purposes, but they don't trust me. My brother has it all figured out. He will take the candidates to the secret location. No one knows where the sword is being kept except him and the First Member."

"First Member?"

"The head of the Council."

I frowned. "I thought Aurelius was the head of the

Council."

"Aurelius is Second Member. He's more of an operations head. Think of it as the difference between the one who makes the rules and the one in charge of carrying them out."

"Who is First Member?"

"Apparently no one knows," Vane revealed. "The First Member is not elected like the rest of the Council. He is a descendant of the very first wizard family. He and the Council communicate by using a special seeing stone. I have seen it used."

"What? If no one knows who the First Member is, how can we trust them?"

"Believe me, the seeing stone can only be used by the First Member. Merlin used to be First Member. I tried to use the seeing stone when he wasn't looking. It nearly killed me."

"Merlin was First Member." I looked at Vane. He had a carefree smile on his face, but I was starting to know better. I quietly said, "Tell me, did you get anything in your time?"

A flicker of surprise lit Vane's eyes. He masked it with a smug smile. "Well, there was Guinevere."

"Ugh." I grimaced. "I thought she loved Lancelot and Arthur."

Vane glanced at Matt. "And a few others."

I grimaced again. "Please, forget I asked."

Vane rose. "*You* should get some rest."

"I'd never fall asleep. My mind is running." I pointed to the giant magic textbook Matt had given us. It sat on the coffee table. "Maybe I'll read."

Vane crossed the room and flopped down on the sofa in between Matt and me. He waved his hand. The TV switched on and a game console appeared on the coffee table. Picking up a controller, Vane put his feet up.

I gaped at him. "What are you doing?"

"Passing the time." He scrolled through the game's menu. It looked to be another sword and sorcery fantasy RPG.

"Are you crazy?" I said. "This is the night before the biggest final exam of our lives. Shouldn't you be giving me some last minute advice or training or something?"

"Would you listen?"

"Probably not."

Vane put down the controller. He stretched, showing off tight muscles. He leered comically. "Are you offering a different way to… amuse me?"

"Matt is sleeping on the couch!"

"Am I to infer that you would offer if my brother were not here?" he said.

Elbowing him in the stomach, I moved to get off the sofa.

He pulled me back.

"I need to pack."

"I'll do it for you. You have such interesting undergarments in this century." Light reflected off his cornea, making his eyes sparkle. He leaned me back against him.

"Forget it," I said weakly.

Our noses brushed.

"You should know I usually get my way." Vane touched a

finger to my forehead. "*Svapati.*"

Warmth radiated out from that spot and spread down my body. Suddenly, my eyes became heavy. I fought to keep them open. Vane's face blurred. He'd put a sleeping spell on me.

I yawned loudly. "Why?"

Strong arms went around me. Vane carried me to bed.

"What happened to her?" I heard Gia demand. I didn't hear Vane's reply. I felt covers going over me just before I fell deep into sleep.

***

Heat emanating from my amulet prodded me awake. Moonlight streamed in through the window in my bedroom. On the other side of a small nightstand, Gia slept, breathing loudly in her narrow bed.

I threw the covers aside and got up in a panic, cursing Vane. I hadn't gotten anything ready for tomorrow. I crossed to the dresser Gia and I shared. In the attached mirror, I saw I had on a nightshirt. *How had that happened?*

I smoothed down the out-of-control bed hair coming out in all directions from my head and told my reflection, "You don't want to know."

"Why are you still here?" Matt said loudly from the living room.

I padded along the wood floor to the bedroom door. It was partially open.

"I want to talk to you about Ryan," Vane said.

I stopped at the door.

"Where is she?" Matt demanded.

"I put a sleeping spell on her."

Matt harrumphed. "I don't want to talk about her with you."

"Then listen. Have you seen the One yet?"

"No. It's not like it was with Arthur. I saw him clearly."

"Because you're too close to this one. What if it's her?"

"It's not," Matt exploded.

"Would you sacrifice her?"

"Would you?" Matt retorted.

"Absolutely not."

"Why?" Matt said. "You fought against letting the Regulars train. Now you're helping her. Befriending her. Eating dinner with her. What's your game, Vivane?"

I could hear Vane grind his teeth, but he replied in an even tone. "You can guess why."

Matt paused. "She is not Guinevere."

Vane snorted. "Definitely not."

"You would risk the sword for her?"

"She could have left me in the basement. At that bloody festival. I would have died that night. I should have. But she came back for me. Do you know how long it's been since anyone's done that for me?"

"You never tried to protect Guinevere."

"Guinevere and I amused each other. Who do you think told Arthur about us? She did. He sent the knights to hunt me

MY BOYFRIEND MERLIN

down. Why do you think I came to stop you at the cave? If Mordred hadn't taken on Arthur, I would probably be dead."

Matt snorted. "What happened to the noble motive of wizard solidarity? You encouraged Mordred to challenge his father to restore the wizard's power in the kingdom."

"My personal goals coincided with the good of all. I don't see anything wrong with that."

"You wouldn't. That's why we can't trust you."

"Fine, don't trust me. But don't do this," Vane said. "Don't risk her."

"Listen, Vane. Don't you think I've had the same thought a thousand times? If anything happened to Grey or the candidates, she would never forgive herself. She would come to hate whoever stopped her."

"Let her hate me. She would be safe." He paused. "Or let me come with you."

"Finally, we come to what this is really about," Matt said with a harsh laugh. "Using Ryan to get to the sword. How do you live with yourself?"

"At least I'm not running scared like you. You can tell yourself that the visions are keeping you from her, but deep down you know the real reason. I've seen you do this over and over again. All for what? Camelot is a dream and you've sacrificed everyone for it."

"No one will find us," Matt declared. "I know what I'm doing."

"Don't be stubborn. The cave proved it. The boy in the alley proved it. Our powers are tied somehow. We are stronger together. She will need *both* of us."

"No," Matt said.

Vane cursed. "Forget it. I'm taking her out of here."

I opened the door and stepped out. Focused on their argument, it took the two brothers a second to realize I was there. Vane saw me first. He sat on the sofa. Matt's back was to me as he paced along the coffee table. Matt almost fell on the table when he turned and spotted me.

I locked eyes with him. "Let Vane come."

Matt's jaw tightened. He stuck fisted hands into trouser pockets. "There are only two choices. Go with me or stay with him."

Biting my lip, my eyes flickered over Vane. I touched the amulet.

"Have you picked?" Matt prompted.

Vane stood up. "Yes, she has."

***

The world surrounded us in high definition picture perfect clarity. Short stubbly trees swayed with lonely moans. The colors, an array of different hues of brown and grey, melded into a tapestry proclaiming a cold harsh landscape broken here and there by small ponds of sparkling blue-grey water.

If the windows of the car had been open, I'm sure I would have been overwhelmed by the pristine scent of winter. As it was—the mix of deodorant and lotions mingled with desperate anxiety filled my nostrils. We rode through the rolling countryside and I'd never felt more alive... for all that I might be driving to my death.

I sat beside Matt. We'd taken off in a caravan of black vans before first light. Matt had done a number of cleansing spells on the vans before we'd left. We were free of any tracking spells. He'd also done an electronics sweep. I'd been a little surprised because it wasn't like Matt to think of technology. He'd found a few tracker spells (planted by councilmembers, Matt suspected) and a cell phone (planted by Vane, I suspected) to GPS track us.

Matt and the other guardians had also put some kind of glamour on the vans. Apparently, we were invisible. I'm not sure how that worked with other cars on the road, but I decided not to worry about it.

Councilmember Thornton—minus his apple—drove us. I would have rather had Vane along. I stole a glance at Matt. In my mind, I replayed the conversation between him and Vane. Most of it left me confused.

Why had Vane offered gallantly to take me away? Why hadn't Matt?

I glanced at him. We'd been in the car for hours and he'd spent the whole time flipping through a giant book of frayed parchment pages that looked about a hundred years old.

We had reached the outskirts of London when I finally asked, "What are you reading?"

"My grimoire," he said absently.

He'd rather read a book that had been around for a thousand years than talk to me.

"How did you find it?" I asked.

"The Council kept it."

I gnashed my teeth. "What are you trying to find?"

Matt shut it carefully. "Spells to help us if we run into any trouble."

"You told Vane there would be no trouble."

"One must be prepared."

I said sharply, "Why didn't you let him come?"

"He's done his part. Despite Vane's conceit, we don't need him."

"What about the combined magic he was talking about?"

Matt smiled. "I have a lot of trained candidates to help me. I don't need Vane."

The tension in my shoulders increased. "What if you do?"

"Vane's good at convincing you that you need him. The problem happens when you start depending on him—he will fail you."

"Harsh, much?" I muttered.

The cars navigated around the gulley-like streets of London. A thick grey cloud, a combination of smog and winter weather, covered the city.

Matt traced a finger on the frosty windowpane.

"Did I ever tell you about what happened when I took Arthur to the sword? It wasn't like today. We didn't have a decoy. The journey was treacherous. Arthur and I used a jousting tournament as a cover. Vane was supposed to participate in the tournament. Arthur was to be his page. If anyone had found out Arthur's true identity as the dead king's son, he would have been killed. The prince had been declared lost on the battlefield and the nobles were all too eager to take the kingdom. They would have done anything to cement their power. Vane never showed for the tournament. We had to use Arthur's cousin Kay at the last minute. Kay hated Arthur. The day we were trying to get to the sword, Kay betrayed us. Of course, at the last moment, Vane swept in as a hero. And instead of Arthur clapping him in chains, he was made a knight."

"What was his explanation for not making it to the tournament?"

Matt said, "He said the gargoyles attacked him."

"And they didn't?"

"They said they hadn't," Matt said.

"Wait. What?" I squawked. "The gargoyles *said* they hadn't attacked Vane and you just believed them? Over your own brother?"

"You don't understand. The gargoyles aren't like us. They have a caste hierarchy. The king is at the top. He has several lieutenants. If someone in that chain issues an order, the lower ranks have no choice but to obey. Not listening causes physical agony. The gargoyles would not have dared to attack Vane. The king had already ordered us safe passage."

"And they couldn't have found a loophole or something?"

Matt frowned. "A loophole?"

We came up a quiet street into an open pavilion. A crowd gathered in front of large black gates. They held up pickets proclaiming, 'SWORD PULL A HOAX,' 'WE KNOW WHAT YOU DID,' 'EXPLAIN THE TOTAL TREMOR,' and on and on. There must have been a few hundred people gathered. They chanted, "*We still want our chance!*"

"How did it leak out?" Grey said.

Matt dialed his phone. It connected. "Aurelius, did you know about the protest?"

I couldn't hear what Aurelius said back to him. But the answer must have been unsatisfactory because Matt cursed.

"We don't have time for this, Aurelius. We proceed as planned." Matt hung up the phone. He tapped our driver's shoulder. "Get us through. I'll clear the crowd."

"*Atikram,*" he said.

A breeze swept through the angry crowd, and somehow a slim path opened between them. The driver hurried the car into the void. I glanced out of the blackened windows at the angry chanting faces. It wasn't until we got right up to the huge black gates that I realized where we were.

A giant seal on the gates declared "HRH." My eyes went wide. The gates opened. A man in a red uniform waved us through. Another red-liveried footman rushed up to open the car door. Matt sprang out. The rest of us followed more slowly. I stepped down and gaped at the massive building complete with sweeping buttresses, flowing gardens, and one ornate entrance.

"You must be joking," Blake said in awed tone behind me. "The sword can't be here."

"That is why it's the perfect place," Matt said.

I had to agree with him. We'd arrived at Buckingham Palace.

A CHRISTMAS PARTY TO REMEMBER

A thin man in a grey tweed suit and pencil moustache came out of the palace to greet us.

"I am Charles Dawson. I will be your emissary. I am afraid that the First Member could not greet you personally. As you can see, the palace is facing quite a crisis with these protestors. However, the staff Christmas Party will still take place tonight. I have arranged for all of you to attend. Until then, you may pass the day at a private residence on the grounds. Please follow me."

Dawson started to walk off, but we all remained in place, trying to absorb the barrage of information he'd thrown at us.

"Mr. Dawson!" Aurelius halted him. He emerged from one of the other cars. Instead of a robe, he wore a regular suit—white, of course. Even in a suit, he couldn't resist showing off his elevated station.

"Over the years of our correspondence with the First

Member we suspected that they were part of the Royal Household." He told Matt, "This is the closest any councilmember has been to the First Member since your time." He looked at Dawson. "When do we meet him?"

Dawson's mustache thinned even more. "The schedule is not something I am at liberty to discuss—for the candidates' safety as well as the First Member's. We must be very careful. As secure as the palace is, it also has many eyes."

"We have not come for games," Aurelius said. "We must meet with the First Member immediately."

"Nevertheless, those are my instructions. Be assured the First Member knows the importance of your mission," Dawson said with a steady expression. "You may follow me or you may leave."

Councilmember Thornton jumped out of the SUV. "How dare you speak to Master Aurelius in such a manner?"

"I am certain the First Member has good reason to be mysterious." Matt cut Thornton off. "However, Master Aurelius is correct. We do not wish to waste time."

Dawson nodded. "We have already gone through much to get the queen's party moved to tonight. You can imagine what a feat that was. We are lucky it was not too far from the original date." He glanced at Matt as if he was unsure about him. "You are certain about tonight?"

"Absolutely," Matt said. A soft breeze flew through Matt's longish hair. A shadow flitted across his face. His eyes blazed, becoming blue-black with power, and for a second, he looked like something otherworldly, something unreal, something not human.

Dawson lowered his gaze. "Of course. Of course. I apologize, Master Merlin."

Matt's eyes returned to normal. "Good. Then we shall wait as you ask."

Dawson gave a visible sigh of relief. With a quick nod, he led us past the palace toward the Royal Stables. A small manor stood to the side. Trees all around the grounds had been decorated for Christmas. Dawson opened the manor door and led us into an airy foyer. Thick red drapes had been pulled aside, allowing the room to be bathed in light. The furniture looked delicate and I winced as some of the candidates flopped down on sofas which were probably priceless antiques.

"There are five rooms upstairs. Multiple sitting rooms downstairs." Dawson pointed to a small hallway. "There are also two water closets. One up and one down. You will need them to get ready for the party. It is a formal affair—clothing has been arranged. You will find it in the rooms with your names on them. A dressmaker will be here in a few hours for any last minute adjustments." His gaze raked over the group. Most of us were dressed in plain jeans and serviceable long-sleeved T-shirts. "Also, a hair stylist will be here closer to the evening."

"We're not here to go to a party," Grey said in a sneering voice. "What we need to do to is prepare for the trial."

I kicked him in the shin and said to Dawson, "Do you have any other instructions?"

Dawson gave me an appreciative look. "The First Member

has not shared anything else with me." He walked to a pair of glass-paneled doors that led outside. "However, this house was especially chosen to allow you access to this."

We rushed to the doors Dawson swung open. A huge terrace had been enclosed by dense evergreens. Delicate ornaments and silver garlands decorated the trees. Practice mats lay across the cobblestone terrace. Small wooden racks filled with different weapons lined the edges.

"A training area," Grey said.

Gia jumped down the short stone steps onto the terrace. "It's cold."

Matt uttered a word. "*Agni.*"

The wind shifted. A soft glow formed all around the terrace, forming a bubble. I stepped out. I no longer felt the wind. The whole area had been insulated.

Matt said, "Glamoured to hide the area from prying eyes and protect you from the weather."

Dawson looked at Matt, impressed. "The First Member gained special permission to prepare the manor, but didn't have enough to draw on to do an insulation spell."

We could still see the palace in the distance. Gia asked, "*Who* is this First Member?"

"Most likely a steward or someone of the sort." Blake let out a groan. "I just hope no one put a spell on the royal family."

Dawson's mustache twitched. I had the distinct feeling he was laughing at us.

Grey raised his brow. "Do we get food?"

"The pantry is stocked. Tea will be served, of course." He gave a little bow. "If there is nothing else, I will take my leave."

Matt nodded in dismissal.

"It is an honor to meet you, milord," Dawson said. With a last awed look at Matt, he left.

"I need some food," Grey said.

A few others followed him into the house.

Aurelius sought out Thornton. "The Council will be wanting an update."

Aurelius and Thornton went inside.

Gia and Mark went to the swords. Gia picked one up and swung it in an arc.

"Nice." She stepped through a first-level sword form. The sword seemed to sing as it cut through the air. She whistled. "Very nice."

"Want to practice?" Mark looked at me.

Mark had thawed considerably since the night of the festival. Vane often put us together to spar, but I was still surprised he'd ask me on his own.

"Not a chance," Gia said for me. "Mark, you're with me first."

The remaining candidates filed out onto the terrace next to Gia and Mark and started picking through the weapons.

I remained beside Matt. "Why did he call you milord?"

Matt's lips quirked up. "You don't miss anything, do you?"

"That's not an answer."

"The First Member has a title—Lord Protector."

"Arthur made you Lord Protector? Isn't that the real ruler of the country?"

"I was the head of the wizards."

"But he was king, so it was just a title to pacify you? He doesn't sound like the best king to me. I don't even get why he passed the trial."

Matt colored. "He was the best candidate. Vane and I trained him."

"Vane trained him, too?"

"I asked Vane to do it. No one compares to him."

"I see. Arthur used magic to bring the kingdom under his rule. Then, he turned his back on it because it became a threat to him."

Matt cocked his head. "He gave me the title when he was young. Later, he feared I wanted to take over. I never did. Then, when he found out about the gargoyles, he lost all reasoning."

I frowned. "I don't understand."

"I never told Arthur there were other supernatural beings in the world. He found out that wizards had been holding a truce with the gargoyles and decided that we were amassing a supernatural army. It wasn't true, of course. The gargoyles wanted to be left alone in their mountains. Many of them are in the Pyrenees, Southern Europe, and some in the Scottish Highlands."

Matt watched the candidates spar for a minute. "I had hoped that Arthur would bring a new light into the world where wizards, Regulars, and gargoyles could all walk free without having to hide from each other."

"You wanted Arthur to be the bridge." I said. "Why him?"

"He had a way of bringing people together. He always seemed to know what to do." Matt looked up at the sky.

"What would the sword bearer do today?"

"So much has changed. The world is smaller. I'm amazed at how adept the gargoyles have become at blending in. The wizards in this century should learn from them. Instead of hiding in remote areas and relying on spells for money, we should aspire for more." Matt turned amber brown eyes on me thoughtfully. "I am hopeful it will happen."

I sent him a narrow glance. "You didn't answer the question."

"You mean besides keeping it from the gargoyles?" he said. "I'm not sure yet."

Reaching out, he tucked a stray curl behind my ear.

I moved away from him. "Don't. You wouldn't want to risk the curse."

Matt stilled. He said after a pause, "I didn't ask for the visions, Ryan. I'm doing this for you."

I snorted. "I thought it was for the world?"

"The two are the same—"

"Personal goals coincide. Didn't you just blast Vane for that?"

"You overheard quite a bit." He moved closer to me. "You made the right choice, Ryan."

I looked out at the candidates as they practiced. Grey had come out of the house and was now sparring with Oliver. I touched the amulet on my neck. "I made the only choice."

Vane. I called him silently. A faint heat emanated from the amulet. In a trickle, the heat slowly expanded and grew stronger.

Matt put a palm over mine and pushed the amulet back down. Cold stone fell against my chest. My heart banged against it. "Don't start depending on him, Ryan."

I looked at him. "How did you know I was thinking of him?"

Matt's lips quirked into a half-smile. "I know you. And I know him."

I looked at Matt for a long moment. "I didn't kiss him, Matt. He kissed me."

Matt's jaw tightened. "Maybe not then, but would you now?"

I hesitated. Over the past few weeks, I'd seen much more of Vane. I'd seen how much he held the world at bay, but how much he wanted to fit in. And I found... I liked him. I liked how he didn't hide what he wanted. Something of what I was thinking must have shown on my face because Matt's expression darkened.

"Forget him. You can't help everyone, Ryan. Vane will take everything and give nothing."

"And you're the kind who always thinks he's right, but

doesn't believe anyone else can be!"

Matt's face puckered.

I took a quick breath. "Given that you both have only each other left in this century, don't you think you're being harsh? He's your family. You don't like it, but he's a survivor, Matt. So are you. You don't want to see that. *You* don't want to see that you and he are not all that different."

"No," Matt said vehemently. "Vane does what he does for Vane. I'm—" His voice dropped to a whisper. "I'm struggling every day, every minute, not to reach for what I want."

Matt moved until his body just brushed against the back of mine. I wanted to lean back on him, to let everything fall away, to not worry about what came next. But I held myself stiff. My throat parched from a never-ending thirst, I forced myself to ask, "What happens after the sword, Matt? Will you give up the visions then?"

Matt put his hands on the sides of my upper arms. A soft tug and I would fall back against him. I held myself in place.

He sighed. "I can't say. I don't know what will be needed from me."

My hands moved to cover his. "I don't need a promise, but I need a possibility."

"I don't know what will be needed from me," he repeated.

My shoulders drooped.

His hands tightened on me. "I can find a way."

"No. Save it, Matt. I may not have much time left and I want to spend it with someone who cares."

I pulled away. He let me go.

Grey grinned at me when I walked up to him. Without a word, he threw me a sword. I caught it easily with one hand.

***

The day passed all too quickly. Matt ducked away to who-knows-where. I spent the morning sparring with various candidates. By late afternoon, I'd slipped on a gorgeous silver gown cut to emphasize every curve I had. A red cashmere shawl covered the skin shown off by the scoop-necked dress. Gia wore a green gown in the same style. Two other girls wore similar gowns.

The hairstylist finished with Gia's hair. With a shy nod, she left. Grey came in. We had taken one of the bigger rooms. I stood at the window looking out across the front of the manor. The sky darkened bit by bit, throwing the palace grounds into black.

Grey came up beside me. He wore a breathable black suit and a red button-down shirt. He tugged at his collar and loosened a white Christmas tie. He arched a brow at us. "How are you supposed to take the trial in those outfits?"

"We look awesome. Thanks for the compliment," Gia said with a snarky grin.

I pushed aside the strap on my shoulder to reveal a black tank. "We've got these stretchy suits on underneath." Gia pulled up her skirt to show black leggings.

Grey shook his head. He turned back to look out the window.

"Think there's still time to change our minds."

"Do you want to change yours?" I said.

He shook his head. "Emrys was right. They're never going to stop attacking us. And you were right. This is our fight now. I just hope whatever happens tonight ends it."

I looked out the window. The palace loomed ahead of us. The fading light made the shadows seem sharper. I took his hand and squeezed it tightly. "We're in this together."

"Did I ever tell you how annoyed I was that Mom wanted to adopt you?"

I let out a laugh. "Don't overwhelm me with sentiment."

"It's the best thing that happened to me," Grey said. "I would have never gotten through the past few months without you."

I ran my hands along the line of his shoulders, brushing off imaginary dirt from the tight line of his fitted suit jacket. "Alexa would say you look too hot for your own good."

He put a hand around my shoulder. "Alexa would have loved this. The party. The palace."

I nodded, my eyes bright. Grey hugged me hard.

"Sorry to break this up," Gia said.

She didn't look sorry at all. I suppressed a smile at the sour expression on her face as she glanced back and forth between Grey and me.

"It's time," she said.

Grey strode up to her. "One thing before we go—"

Gia squeaked as he swept her up in a smoldering kiss.

I watched them with mixed emotions. I was happy for

Grey, yet I yearned for the same thrill.

I touched my amulet. The gemstone heated.

A breeze flitted around me. I thought I heard a whisper.

"Dorothy."

***

The group gathered in the foyer of the manor—a tide of black suits, neatly swept back hair, and sober faces. Matt, Aurelius, and ten other wizard guardians herded us into the black SUVs. We rode along the cheerily decorated pathways up to the palace.

Twin Christmas trees framed the entrance and invited us inside. Matt kept me close by his side as Dawson led us in. Blake, Mark, and Grey followed behind us. The nearly forty other candidates all trailed behind them. Wind rushed around us. Above us, the sky held an eerie blood moon that stood out against a blanket of dull stars.

My mouth opened in awe as we stepped into the palace. Lush garlands, delicate ornaments, fresh, bright red poinsettias, and soft-white water fountains decorated the hall leading up to the lush grand staircase.

"Welcome." Dawson greeted us. He pointed us over to the security line. "You are all on the list to get inside."

We were early for the party, but the line was already a hundred or so long. Women swirled about in beautiful gowns and men in finely cut suits. They all talked and laughed and warmed the gargantuan, hollow chamber hall with comforting chatter.

It took forever for all of us to pass through the metal

detectors. The last security guard surprised us by surreptitiously searching us with a magical amulet built into a metal detection wand. I passed by Councilmember Thornton.

He looked me over from head to toe, then oddly enough, he winked at me. "Lovely gown, Ms. DuLac."

Before I could frame a startled reply, Dawson motioned for our attention. Gathering us around, he led the group up the red-carpeted staircase into a beautiful gallery. Everywhere, Grecian marble statues, elephant-sized oil paintings, and gold filigree crown moldings decorated the opulent interior of the palace.

The main hub of the party spanned two rooms—a supper room and the biggest ballroom I'd ever seen. Throne-like chairs sat under a red, domed canopy overlooking the entire ballroom.

I peered into the supper room. Long tables adorned with white tablecloth and centerpiece garlands and candles had been set up. There seemed to be about a few hundred place settings.

I elbowed Matt. "Think we'll get to eat?"

Matt rolled his eyes. "Is food all you think about?"

I whispered. "Lunch was three hours ago."

I eyed a beautifully set up punch bowl. It had a gurgling fountain in the middle. I started to gravitate toward it. "How about a small drink?"

Matt grabbed my elbow and pulled me away. "Later."

Several of the queen's staff eyed our group curiously. They greeted Dawson, who casually explained we were a special services group. This got an even wider-eyed response, but no one asked any further questions.

Dawson led us inside the ballroom. He pointed at a panel on the wall. "There's a hidden door there and a secret passageway that leads down. We had the ballroom especially opened for this reason. I can tell you the First Member said Her Majesty was not thrilled about it. But it is the most convenient way for you to slip away a few at a time."

"Did you relay our message to the First Member?" Aurelius asked.

Dawson inclined his head. "The whole country is watching the protests. The First Member hopes that once the sword is actually pulled, we can bring the stone out again. It might satisfy some of the unrest—" Dawson broke off as another guest came up to greet him. He hustled the guest away quickly and turned to Matt. "Master Merlin, you must go first."

"What do I need to do?" Matt asked.

"The vault is directly beneath us. You will need to open it."

The noise level in the room increased as music started. Brightly dressed people glittered like shiny jewels under the teardrop chandeliers as they milled around in celebration. They laughed and drank while we stood next to the door that might lead us to our deaths. Appropriately enough, the hidden door showed a mural of a lion with wings. For the first time, I truly noticed the depictions of lions tucked into every corner of the palace. The royal symbol itself had a lion. A light bulb went off in my head.

My eyes widened. I said, "Matt."

Horns blew loudly. The sound bounded down to us. A man in a deep voice announced, "Her Majesty, the Queen."

I didn't hear the rest of the announcement as I stared at the diminutive yet radiant woman who stepped out from a closed room at the other end of the banquet. A crown tucked neatly into her hair bun, the queen had dressed in a sedate gown for the celebration. Except for the crown, she could have passed for a commoner.

I drew Matt aside and whispered, "Is that the seeing stone on her crown?"

THE TEST

From the window, the clouds flitted across the reddening moon, marring its luminosity.

"That ruby looks like the one on my amulet." I pointed to the queen's head. A flash of jet-black hair at the queen's side caught my attention. A woman watched the queen with a hungry gaze. The woman turned and saw me. She looked down quickly to hide her face, but she wasn't quick enough. It was Marla, Sylvia's assistant.

I went cold.

"Matt." I grabbed him and pointed at her. "Marla!"

"Impossible," Matt said. He mumbled a spell under his breath. A whoosh went through the room. Several men and women clutched their faces. I noticed one by Marla. One minute he looked like a nondescript man, the next minute his face changed into that of a beast.

"Gargoyles!" Matt said.

"Get the queen!" Aurelius said from directly behind us. "She's the First Member!"

I realized Aurelius had heard our whole conversation. Matt and I turned just in time to see Aurelius clasp his hands together.

"*Agni*." His voice boomed through the ballroom.

Fire blew out across the room. Matt raised his arm to stop it.

"*Nimita*," Aurelius shouted and the walls trembled. The whole palace shook.

Screams rent the air as half the ballroom's floor collapsed.

Matt floated several hundred people in the air. I could see the concentration on his face as he moved them to the sides of the room away from the giant hole in the floor. As soon as they touched ground, the hapless guests scurried under the dinner tables that lined the sides of the ballroom. Before Matt could turn on Aurelius, he and all of the guardians who came with us directed a barrage of blue fire at Matt and the queen.

Matt wavered under the onslaught. The queen fell to the ground. I caught Matt before he could fall. Paul and Oliver came up beside me and caught Matt's other side. Oliver took the brunt of his weight.

Below the destroyed ballroom floor, a square vault, the size of a semi-truck, stood bared.

"How?" Matt gasped as we stood looking down at the vault from the sidelines. "Even combined, you are not strong enough."

"How do you think, Master Merlin? I channeled the gargoyles' strength," Aurelius said with a smug smile. I looked across at Marla. Her face changed into its beast form. She smiled at me with large pointed incisors. Forty other guests standing around her had also shifted into their gargoyle forms. Several hundred Regulars cowered under the tables. They huddled together, their terrified eyes locked on the monsters who had been among them.

Aurelius said, "The gargoyles are at their height tonight, while you are—"

"Diminished by the solstice," Matt concluded weakly.

"Exactly. With their power, we do not need you anymore." Aurelius raised his hand. Blue fireballs glowed in his palms. "Good-bye, Merlin."

Thornton strode forward, but it was not Thornton's voice that said, "I wouldn't do that."

The voice sent a shiver down my spine. My heart skipped a happy beat.

Aurelius squinted at him. "Who are you?"

Thornton's face morphed into Vane. He winked at me.

"Glamour," Matt said.

"Catch him," Aurelius shouted.

"Nice vault," Vane mocked loudly. "I see a powerful protection spell around it. Alas, how does one get in?"

The other guardians who'd accompanied us all turned on Vane, ready to attack.

Aurelius laughed. "They are all pledged to me, Vivane. You

are outmatched." He commanded the guardians. "If he moves, kill him."

Vane laughed. "Do the gargoyles really believe you can get them the stone?"

In a blink, Marla crossed the room to grab Aurelius by the neck. She put a long nail on a pulsating artery. "You promised us the stone, wizard. If you don't deliver, we will rip apart everyone in this room piece-by-piece, starting with you."

"You betrayed us, Marla," I said. "Did you send the dragon?" My voice lowered. "Did you send Morgan?"

Marla's laughter filled the hollow room. "Who else?"

Beside me, Grey let out a sound and moved to attack her. I held him back. I hissed, "We have no weapons."

"We don't have time for your reunions." Aurelius threw Marla's hand off him with a quick magical blast. "Patience, or neither of us will get what we want."

Aurelius strode to the queen. He held a fireball in front of the queen's face. "How do we get past the protection spell?"

A few of the guests tried to crawl out from under the tables to help the queen. Aurelius whispered to the fireball and tossed it at them. It roared loudly and expanded into a fountain of fire, blasting a guest across the arm. He screamed and dropped to the floor to stamp out the flames. Shaken, the other guests scurried back under the tables.

The queen shook her head. "I will tell you nothing."

Marla grabbed the queen by the neck. The queen's wizened face turned purple.

"Killing me will only make the spell stronger," she choked out.

"A life force spell," Aurelius said.

Marla dropped the queen into a chair.

Aurelius mused, "But what is the key?"

"You're a traitor, Second Member," the queen said calmly.

"I am your *savior.*" Aurelius pointed at Matt who was almost collapsed on top of me. "It's your ancestor who is the traitor. If it weren't for him and your support of his ridiculous notions, we wouldn't be in this mess. I'm not about to change our whole way of life because some old relic woke up with some idealized vision of what we should be."

"Merlin is a far greater wizard than you could ever hope to be," she said. "We are approaching a war, Second Member. Merlin's visions have been our best hope of averting it."

"His visions are nothing," Aurelius spat. "If we had stopped selling magic, we would have become weak ages ago. Where would we get the money to train our children? Do you have any idea how much it takes to keep ourselves hidden?" He waved his hand in the air. "Allow me to reply—no, you don't. Because you don't actually *do* anything. I do. I make the plans. I arrange the details. *I* should be in charge. Period."

"Greed has clouded your vision," the queen said.

"You know nothing!" Aurelius screamed. He blew her backwards until she toppled to the floor. "Open the vault."

The queen shook her head.

Aurelius thrust out a hand. He blasted Dawson, who'd been

standing at the periphery. Dawson let out a scream of pain so loud it seemed to shake the room. He collapsed to the floor.

I put my hand to my mouth. I took a step toward Dawson.

"Cease, candidate. He's already dead," Aurelius barked at me, then turned back to the queen. "How many of these guests do you think I can take out with one fireball?"

"No." Matt pulled away from us and shouted a spell. Swords appeared in every one of the candidates' hands. The forty candidates all fanned out. They faced off against the gargoyles who'd done the same.

Matt slumped backwards. I moved to try to catch him. Paul blocked me. Matt's back hit the floor. Before anyone else could react, Oliver hit Matt and knocked him out. Oliver stood over Matt's limp form, his expression cold. "Training is over, Master Merlin."

I stared at Oliver in shock. "What?"

Paul's face morphed into that of a gargoyle's. For the first time, I really looked at him. He smiled. It was oddly familiar. I whispered, "Morgan?"

"Finish her," Marla snarled.

My eyes on Paul, I asked Marla, "Why target me?"

"Your boyfriend still hasn't told you?" Marla laughed. "Paul, restore your family's honor. Finish what Morgan could not. Do not fail your queen."

"Time to die. My brother deserves as much," Paul said. Within the flicker of an eye, he lunged at me.

Vane cursed. "*Vitisthate.*"

A burst of wind blew Paul across the room. His head struck the wall, emitting a loud crack. The guardians shot a spell at Vane; bright light surrounded him and held him.

"Enough! We don't have time for this. The red moon will not last." Aurelius crooked a finger and a guest from below one of the tables floated out. "Will you sacrifice this one next, Your Highness?"

The queen hurled a ball of light at Aurelius.

Aurelius deflected it. It bounced back on the queen. With a strangled cry, she collapsed.

"No." Blake extended his hand with a fireball and lobbed it at a gargoyle.

The gargoyle screamed as the fireball hit him. He rolled on the ground to put out the fire, then got right back up. The other gargoyles held out their swords in readiness. They formed a line like experienced soldiers ready for battle. Oliver turned to stand at their head, his face alight with anger. His lips curled with bloodthirsty eagerness. I sucked in a breath. We were outnumbered and inexperienced. I prayed that this wasn't going to be a massacre.

"Stop!" Vane said. "I know how to open the vault, Aurelius. Release me and I will get it for you."

Marla and Aurelius glanced at each other.

"Vane, don't do this," I pleaded.

Vane looked at me with an insincere smile. "I am sorry, Ryan. The sword is the most important thing." He pointed to a dark window. The pink had deepened into red. His eyes locked on Marla. "Time to play or go home. Do we have a truce or do you want to keep wasting time?"

"Hurry, wizard," Marla commanded.

The guardians released Vane, but the candidates moved to stop him. Grey reached him first and put a sword to his chest.

"Trust me." The words in Vane's voice whispered at the edges of my hearing.

My gaze jerked to his. He gave the barest hint of a nod of acknowledgement. I had no idea how he was talking to me. Vane turned his head and looked deliberately at Matt.

I looked at Blake, Gia, Mark, and all of the candidates. They all watched Vane, prepared to strike. I glanced at Matt. He lay on the floor, his body still, but his chest rising and falling. I saw Blake raise his hand to attack. A gargoyle poised to intercept him if he did.

"Blake, stop," I said. "Merlin would want us to go for the sword." I moved to face the candidates. "Let Vane do this. Stand down."

Surprise filled Grey's eyes. The expression echoed in Gia's, Blake's, Mark's, and the rest of the candidates.

"Are you sure?" said Blake.

Grey's lips thinned. He glanced at Marla. "Do you understand what you're asking? She killed your mother. She was behind the dragon. She killed Alexa! I won't give them what they want."

"And what about the world? Sylvia? We're here for a reason." I locked eyes with him. "This is how this stops. Once and for all." I turned to Vane. "Do what you have to do."

Stepping away from Grey, Vane walked to the queen.

"What are you going to do?" Blake asked. An edge of anxiety colored his voice as we looked at the fallen monarch.

Vane put a hand against the queen's head. He took a vial out of his pocket. "Lake water. If she's the lock, this is the master key."

"But she's unconscious!" I said.

"That just makes it easier." Vane poured the vial down the queen's throat.

***

The square vault unwrapped as neatly as a Christmas present. It revealed the stone sitting silently inside. Light from the chandeliers caught the hilt of the sword, and for a second, the stone shone like a beacon in a storm. Half of the gargoyles jumped down into the pit. They rushed to the stone.

Lights flickered. The massive stone shot into the air. It crashed into the ceiling.

"What happened?" Aurelius shouted.

In a blink, Marla stood in front of Aurelius. She grabbed a guardian standing on Aurelius's right. She snapped his neck and dropped him at Aurelius's feet. She grabbed another guardian from his left. "Figure it out, Aurelius. You don't want to see me angry."

Vane ran to Matt. He poured the remaining Lake water down Matt's throat.

Matt stirred.

Aurelius put out a hand to blast the stone.

"Stop," Matt said. "It's seeking a power source."

"The moon," Vane said.

The stone tore through the ceiling.

"Get to the roof," Marla commanded the gargoyles. Like spiders, they started climbing the walls. They went up into the hole.

"Matt, what do we do?" I said.

Vane arched a brow at Matt. Matt gave a grim nod.

Together, they said, "*Upari.*"

We all floated in the air. Matt and Vane levitated the candidates up through the hole onto the roof. We got up at the same time as the gargoyles. Vane and Matt set us to the side. The stone spun like a top just above the hole. It glowed softly beneath the hauntingly red sky.

Every gargoyle reverted back from beast form into regular human. One gargoyle, who had been climbing up the hole, slipped and started falling back down. Some gargoyles caught him and pulled him back up.

"What's happening to us?" Marla said. "Why can't I change?"

The sky darkened into a black blanket of nothingness.

"The eclipse," someone said.

The stone spun faster. A wave of light shot out from it. It hit us like a tsunami. I stumbled. The buzz rounded my lobes and stabbed into my eardrums. I fell to my knees. Everyone around me—including the gargoyles—went down, too.

A soft ooze of liquid dripped down my ear canal onto my

cheeks. Sticky and wet it coated my skin. I touched it and then, held up my hands. It was blood.

"Ryan!" I heard Matt cry out from a distance before I blacked out.

***

The world appeared to be an odd shade of oblivion when I woke. I saw no color anywhere, only black, white, and an in-between grey. I saw no clouds or stars, only a hazy blankness above.

The stone still spun on the roof. All around me everyone lay on the rooftop like they'd fallen asleep. I sat on stone pavestones. A ring of black monuments, a replica of Stonehenge, surrounded the outer edge of the rooftop, penning us in. More of the light haze that made up the sky stretched beyond it.

People started getting up. I didn't see Matt, Vane, Aurelius, Marla or the other guardians. Only the candidates.

A gargoyle got up and ran to the stone. He pulled on the sword. He let out a great scream and caught on fire. He ran to the rooftop's ledge and stumbled off.

I jumped up and ran after him. Others followed me. We stopped just beyond the stone circle.

Blake looked over a ledge. "What is this?"

The rooftop ended. And beyond it was... nothing. No street. No people. No building. Nothing at all. Only the rooftop existed. It floated in the air like a lost cloud.

"Limbo," someone said.

Grey grabbed my arm. "This is the trial."

A great rumble sounded. The edge of the rooftop started shaking. We backed away from it. The black monuments shuddered. As we watched wide-eyed, the monolithic replicas of Stonehenge broke and fell backwards into limbo. We all jumped back toward the center.

"I guess there's a time limit," Mark said from somewhere behind me.

It was my worst nightmare. We were completely alone.

We all turned back to the stone. The sword beckoned us.

"I still can't change," a gargoyle cried.

Oliver stood at the center of the gargoyles. He said, "The sword is only way out of here. We have to get to it before this whole place collapses."

The gargoyles rushed toward it.

"Candidates, get to the sword first," cried Mark.

Most of Vane's candidates followed him to the stone.

The gargoyles and candidates, two battling teams, crashed into each other. Each time one tried to reach the stone, someone from the other team who was covering them would attack.

"What do we do?" Blake looked at me.

I never got the chance to answer. I spotted Paul. He didn't look any worse for getting slammed hard against the wall. He made his way toward me with a determined look. I picked up a fallen sword from the ground just before he charged me.

Locked into a macabre dance on the rooftop, we fought

each other. At least with the gargoyles unable to use their strength, everyone was more or less on a level playing field. If Paul had been at his full strength, I was pretty sure I would have been dead.

A candidate made it to the stone and tugged at the sword. He let out a scream and collapsed.

"He's dead," someone pronounced.

Paul's attention wavered. With one quick move, I knocked the sword out of his hand. I put my blade at his neck. "Why is Marla after me?"

Paul laughed. "You won't kill me."

In my best impression of Vane, I cut into Paul's shoulder. "I can hurt you much worse."

Somewhere in the fight, I heard Grey yell in pain. With a curse, I hit Paul across the head. I ran to help Grey. He was trying to hold back two gargoyles from the stone. One stabbed him in the shoulder and ran past him to the stone. The other one was Oliver.

Grey stumbled and fell to the ground. I ran and placed myself between him and Oliver.

Oliver smiled. "I knew I would get my chance with you."

Blake hurried to Grey to help him with his wound. As I fought Oliver, the other gargoyle reached the sword and pulled at it. His body shuddered as a current seemed to go through him. He, too, screamed and collapsed.

"One caught fire. Two collapsed," Blake shouted above the fray. "What does it mean?"

I ducked as Oliver tried to take off my head. One of Vane's candidates, a gargoyle, and a Regular made it to the sword on the giant stone at the same time. They touched it. Light from the sword reflected off the large amulet ring Oliver wore. The gemstone glowed for just a moment.

Out of the corner of my eye, I saw the trio with their hands on the sword. In the next second, they all disappeared.

My eyes went wide. "That's it."

The rooftop shook as another layer of stone fell off the edge. Oliver stumbled.

I moved quickly. My sword caught Oliver by the neck. I held it just against his skin. "I could kill you right now, Oliver, but I won't. I'm going to believe that your mother sent the dragon, not you. I'm going to believe that you had nothing to do with my mother's death." I eased my sword just a fraction away from his neck. "Now, do you want to live or not?"

Oliver faced me warily. "What have you figured out?"

"Matt told me Arthur's sword is a bridge between all races. Did you see the two candidates and gargoyle? They touched the sword together and they didn't collapse or catch fire. They disappeared. That is the doorway out of here."

His lips curled. "You still want to kill me."

"You betrayed us," I said, not disagreeing.

"Why should I trust you?"

"You'll never figure it out without me," I said bluntly. "While I might not care if you live or die—" My eyes flickered over Grey and the other candidates. "I care if they do."

Oliver's lips thinned. Another row of pavestones at the rooftop edge fell. The ground we stood on see-sawed.

I looked at him. "We don't have a lot of time. Order the gargoyles to stop."

Oliver glanced back and forth between the edge of the shrinking rooftop and the spinning stone. Reluctantly, he dropped his sword. He shouted, "Gargoyles, stand down."

To my shock, the gargoyles all lowered their swords at once.

Mark and the other candidates blinked in surprise.

"I know the way out," I announced.

Oliver pushed away the sword I held at his neck and stood up. "What next?"

"We do a test," I said. "We need a gargoyle, a Regular, and a wizard. Only all three can pass. If they touch the sword together."

"It makes sense," said Blake. "The energies of all three might open a doorway."

Oliver crooked his finger at a gargoyle. The gargoyle came forward. Oliver looked at me. "This one goes first."

I turned back to the candidates. "I can go for us."

"No." A Regular candidate held up a hand. "I will. They will need you if this doesn't work."

"And I will." A girl wizard stepped forward.

Blake grabbed her hand and squeezed it.

The three strode to the stone.

"Touch it together," I said.

They did. They disappeared. Whoops of celebration sounded across the rooftop.

I raised a brow at Oliver in triumph.

Grey thumped my back.

"What are your terms?" Oliver asked.

I looked at the candidates. They all stared back at me. I felt the mantle of their trust come down to rest on my shoulders.

My chin rose. I faced down Oliver. "We can get out of this together. But what's the point if we're just going to kill each other on the other side? If you really are their leader, you will agree to stand down."

Oliver's lips curled. "Or what? You'll sacrifice yourselves? I don't believe it."

Grey and Blake moved to stand behind me in a visible show of support. Gia followed Grey. All the candidates except those with Mark moved to stand behind me.

Mark frowned at Gia. I could see the decision warring on his face.

"You need all three," I told him. "Without the Regulars, you will fall here."

I held my breath. Mark gave a tight nod. His sword gleamed in the dull light as he moved to stand beside Gia. And just like that, I had the rest of Vane's candidates.

The rooftop shook again. Another fat layer of stone tumbled off. The roof had become so narrow that we huddled together, barely fitting on the remaining stone. The candidates standing at the edges of the stone held hands, fearing any sudden movement.

I turned back to Oliver. "Do we have a deal?"

"I agree to stand down if you do the same," Oliver said.

"Agreed," I said.

"Do you have enough pairs to cover everyone?" Oliver asked in a lower tone.

My heart thumped. The rooftop shook as another layer of rock fell off. Cries went up in the air.

"We need to go," I told him. "We'll figure out if we don't. Gather the gargoyles."

I turned to Blake. "Group the wizards together."

Between Grey, Blake, Oliver, and myself, the candidates grouped into loose sections. Oliver and I sent a trio pair one after the other. Finally, we were down to the last three in each group.

Grey caught my hand. He hissed in my ear. "There are four Regulars left."

"We draw straws," a Regular said.

"We don't have straws," I said. "I will stay."

Blake nodded at Mark. With one command, they turned the swords into pens.

"Now we have straws." He took out the ballpoint in one and threw it away. He held it up and pushed the top. Nothing happened. "The short straw."

"Test the other pens," Grey said.

Blake tested each one, then held them out to us.

I reached for one first. Grey grabbed it from me. "I pick this one."

"No," I cried.

Grey pushed the pen's top. No ballpoint came out. He stared at it with a half-smile.

"I knew you'd try this." He held up the pen to the other two Regulars. "I stay."

"Grey," Gia sniffled. "I'll stay, too."

"We had a deal," Oliver reminded us. "No one else remains."

The roof rumbled. We all jumped. Only two rows remained on the roof. We all huddled next to the stone.

Grey thrust Gia on the stone. "Go, now."

She went. So did the next pair.

Finally, Blake, Grey, Oliver and I remained.

The last layer of the roof dropped. We jumped onto the stone together. The rooftop completely disappeared.

I pulled Grey in for a hug. Grey grabbed me tightly. "Tell Mom good-bye for me."

I shook my head. "You tell her."

Oliver hit Grey over the head. He caught Grey before he fell off the stone. They teetered toward limbo. I pulled them back.

Blake gaped at us. "W-what?"

"I'm making sure Grey gets home," I said, handing him to Blake.

"He's going to kill me," Blake muttered. Holding Grey in one hand, he pulled me into a one-arm hug and squeezed tightly. "We'll never forget you."

Then, without another word, he carried Grey away. I bit my lip, trying not to cry.

Oliver stared at me. "I should kill you, but I have a feeling you'll suffer worse alive."

I grabbed his sleeve. "Why do you hate me?"

It was my last chance to ask him anything. It was my last chance to ask anyone anything. The enormity of what I was doing hit me. I would be totally alone. I would die alone...

Oliver's mouth twisted into a bitter smile. "I've been watching you from the beginning. The candidates didn't pick you as their leader because you are smart, DuLac. They picked you because you would sacrifice yourself if it came to it. Looks like they were right."

My fingers tightened on his sleeve. "Our bargain?"

"I knocked out Ragnar for you, but I can't guarantee what happens on the other side." With a sneering smile, he pulled away from me.

Blake, Grey, and Oliver touched the sword. They disappeared. I sat down and stared out over the never-ending expanse of nothingness.

I was alone.

THE SHOT HEARD AROUND THE WORLD

Completely, totally alone.

I sat on top of a floating rock, and the cold metal gleam of the sword was the brightest thing in the universe.

My body shook. An icy blast of wind sent a draft straight through my sheer gown. My body shook harder, but I didn't move to stop it.

It was as if I'd distanced my mind already. There was nothing left to hold on to.

It would have been easy to step off the stone and let myself float away.

I touched my amulet. A sudden burst of heat pulled me back. The charm spread warmth across my skin. The red gemstone burned brightly.

A white horse thundered along limbo, straight up to me. It

stopped just parallel to the stone. Matt sat on top.

Another horse appeared to the left. A jet-black stallion with an ornate saddle carried Vane.

"What are you doing here?" Matt demanded.

"About damn time you touched the amulet, Dorothy," Vane said. "I see you made it to the witch's castle."

I gaped at him. "I'm losing it," I muttered.

"Stop wasting time, Vane," Matt said. "Ryan, if you fall into limbo, you lose the trial."

I blinked. "How are you here?"

Vane smirked. "We're not really. We're talking to you the same way we've been communicating back in the real world. In your head. It took me a while to figure out, but apparently my ingenious brother put a little safety into the amulet—mind reading."

"Something you weren't supposed to know how to use," Matt muttered.

"My powers are tied to you," Vane said.

"W-what?" I sputtered. "You can read my mind?"

Vane smirked again in confirmation. "If you want to kill him, you have to come back."

"How?" I looked at the sword. "If I touch it, I die."

The stone wobbled and stopped for a second. My heart paused along with it. The stone restarted with a sputter.

"This is not going to last much longer," Matt said grimly. "Listen, there is another way than the three working together. You have to show the sword sacrifice."

I stared at him. "I'm the last one here! What other sacrifice is there?"

Vane's horse snorted in agreement. He snapped at Matt, "What have you seen?"

Matt ignored him. "You have to pull the sword."

"How is that sacrifice?" I asked.

Matt reached out with a translucent hand to touch my forehead. My eyes widened as images of what he wanted me to do flooded my mind.

"Oh." I swallowed. "What happens on the other side?"

"Whatever you do here will probably follow you through."

"Oh." Blanching, I swallowed harder this time. "I don't know, Matt."

Matt watched me with soft brown eyes. "Trust me. There is no other way."

Vane jumped down off the horse.

Matt's jaw dropped in surprise. "You shouldn't be able to dismount."

Vane came up to me. His hands cupped my face. "Whatever he's told you, whatever he doesn't want me to see, I want you to understand one thing—the trial is yours. Only you know what to do. Don't do something because he says you must; do what you feel is right."

"Get back on the horse, Vane, or you'll be trapped when this place collapses," Matt said. "We have to be on the other side to catch her when she comes through."

The black horse neighed with corresponding urgency.

PRIYA ARDIS

"You go," Vane said. "I'm staying with her. Catch us both."

Matt made a noise of frustration. "It doesn't work like that. If we want to save her, we need to go."

Matt's eyes locked on me. Unchecked emotion shone from them. It made me catch my breath.

"It's all right," I told Vane. "You can go. I know what to do."

Vane didn't budge. "I'm not leaving."

I sighed. "You are impossible."

"It's my way." His fingers tightened on mine roughly.

I almost smiled. For the first time since Alexa's death, my heart felt full. I squeezed Vane's hand and then let it go.

It took me three strides to reach the sword.

The giant stone came to an abrupt halt. I was out of time.

"Vane, now!" Matt called.

Vane crossed and pulled himself onto his skittish stallion. "We'll be waiting."

They disappeared.

I pulled out Arthur's sword. The ground gave way under me.

I plunged the sharp blade into my stomach.

***

Excruciating pain spread out in an expanding wave. Then, black curtained my eyes. Breath left me. For a second I was stateless, nowhere and everywhere at once. My body split into a million pieces; then each particle slowly reattached.

I couldn't scream.

Only the sword tethered me to myself. Slowly, my body reformed. My mind rose back into consciousness. I opened my eyes. I stood on the rooftop again. Yet this time, the red moon shone down brightly, illuminating the stain of blood on cream stone.

A battle raged in full color.

Whatever truce we'd made to exit the trial had been lost.

Matt, Vane, and the other candidates stood backed up to the stone, surrounded by Marla, Aurelius, and the gargoyle candidates. On the front lines, Matt dueled with Aurelius. The other wizard candidates were taking on the traitor guardians. Many of the candidates who'd been alive just a few minutes before lay broken and bloodied on the unforgiving stone.

No one had noticed my appearance. I fell on my knees.

"Ryan," Grey shouted.

"The stone stopped spinning," someone said.

Vane leaped onto the stone. I barely noticed as he pulled the sword out of my stomach. He laid me across the black stone's smooth surface.

"She has Arthur's sword." I heard Oliver scream. "Get it!"

"Grey," Matt shouted. "Keep them away." Then, he appeared over me, next to Vane.

I tried to keep my eyes open.

"Do something," Vane shouted at him.

Matt grabbed me. Burning heat climbed into my stomach. I cried out as fire consumed me. My mind threatened to cave in. Then, my vision clouded.

My breathing slowed. My body slowed.

"You're losing her!" I heard Vane cry somewhere far away. "If we don't do this together, she'll die!"

"Fine!" I heard Matt snap.

I closed my eyes. Every corner of my existence fell away, leaving me free to float in peace.

A powerful jerk yanked me back. A hammer shattered through the calm. With a gasping cry, my eyes flew open. The sudden centering left me nauseous. The smell of blood and sweat seeped back into my pores.

"Matt? Vane?" I said.

Vane laughed. A faint glow of blue and red fire around me dissipated.

"You're back," Matt said.

He touched my face and lay down next to me.

"Matt!" I pushed myself up. Matt lay still on the stone.

"He'll be fine. He's just spent," Vane said.

To my surprise, Vane grabbed me up into a hard kiss. "No more dying, DuLac."

"I died?" I said.

I touched my stomach. The skin on it stretched out smoothly without even a scar.

"Ry!" Grey yelled.

My attention turned abruptly back to the battle. The candidates and gargoyles hacked away at each other. The two sides seemed equally matched. I glanced at Arthur's sword.

Your sword. The wind whispered.

I picked it up. It burned with yellow fire.

A beast-like howl sounded from behind the gargoyles. Oliver looked up from in front of the gargoyles. Although my bones still felt hollow with weakness, I forced myself up.

I lifted the sword high. "It's over, Oliver. I have the sword."

The gargoyles paused as they absorbed my words. They looked uncertainly to Oliver.

"The gargoyles will not be defeated today. You are no one, Ryan. I will be king. The sword will be mine," Oliver shouted.

Beside him, Marla nodded. Her gargoyle face became feral and lit with excitement. "The others will be here soon. They don't have a chance."

An army of gargoyles streamed over the walls of the palace and onto the rooftop, surrounding the stone.

Oliver stood at their head. "Give up the sword and no one else has to die."

Matt stirred behind me.

Vane helped him, putting Matt's arm over his shoulder to hold him up. "The gargoyles have come to play. Any bright ideas?"

"Stand behind Ryan," Matt rasped. "Ryan, keep holding the sword, no matter what."

Matt put his hand on my right shoulder.

Vane put his hand on my left shoulder.

"Just a small spell," Matt said.

"Are you sure? We could take care of them today," Vane

replied.

"I'm not killing off a whole race," Matt retorted. "Besides, I don't have enough magic to do much more."

Vane sighed. "If you say so."

The gargoyles advanced on the candidates. Oliver lunged at Grey with a loud battle cry.

I gritted my teeth. "Can you stop arguing for a sec and do whatever it is you're going to do before we get slaughtered?"

"You'll need to focus us, Ryan," Matt said.

"*Svapati,*" Vane said.

"*Svapati,*" Matt repeated.

I gasped as a shock of energy ran through the sword. I had to resist the urge to drop it. A wave of translucent color spread out across the rooftop until it covered hundreds of gargoyles.

Within seconds, the gargoyles lay fast asleep. All except the few gargoyles who had also been candidates.

Matt and Vane let go of me. Matt sat down.

My heart racing, I lowered the sword.

Oliver jumped past Grey. He tried to lunge at me. Vane knocked him down. Oliver fell hard on the rooftop.

"It's over, Oliver," I said. "What will this be? The fourth time you've failed to kill me?"

Oliver growled in frustration. He yelled at the remaining gargoyles. "Get her!"

"Stop!" An older man stood on the roof's ledge. He was about the same age as Marla with a shock of blond hair.

The gargoyles stilled.

Four other gargoyles stood beside him, two on each side. I recognized one of the gargoyles. He was the one we'd captured in the alley at the festival. The one who'd escaped.

"Who are you?" I demanded.

The blond man spotted the sword in my hand. He walked closer until he stood only a few feet away. "You pulled the sword?"

"Yes," I said.

Vane came up beside me. "And she has shown she can use it. Do yourself a favor and leave."

The blond man let out a dry laugh. "You dare to command me? Do you know who I am?"

Vane lazily folded his arms in front of him. "By the way they followed your command, I would say—the king?"

"My name is Rourke," he said with a nod. He glanced at the sleeping gargoyles on the rooftop. "Gargoyles, wake!"

To my dismay, the army of gargoyles began to wake up. The candidates gathered together and lifted their swords in readiness.

Unperturbed, Rourke continued. "It seems I am a little late to this event, but then I was never even invited as I should have been." He hooked at finger at Oliver. "Son, I order you to tell me why I am just finding out about tonight, after the battle appears to be over—"

"No, this is not over. We will have it. The sword bearer will die," Marla said. In a flash, she threw a dagger straight at me. On instinct, I held up the sword. The knife struck the blade instead of me. At the same time, Aurelius let loose a fireball straight at me.

Still sitting on the giant stone just behind me, Matt fired back with a stream of magic. Vane did too. They deflected the fireball. It boomeranged back on Aurelius. He screamed as he burned. The fire blazed with such heat that within seconds, his body charred down to just bone.

Marla took out another dagger and let it fly. I deflected the dagger just inches before it reached my face. Vane caught it and sent it sailing back. The dagger struck Marla in the head.

"No, Mother!" Oliver cried out. Marla fell to the ground. Oliver ran to her and picked her up in his arms. He sobbed into her neck.

Rourke, his face changing into a hulking blond beast, turned on Vane. "You have killed my consort, wizard. There will be retribution."

"I don't think so." I lifted Arthur's sword high. "This seems to have a lot of power over all of you. You've lost, gargoyle. Care to test me?"

Rourke's eyebrow rose. "I would see what the sword bearer thinks she can do."

"As you wish," said Vane.

I winced. Throwing the gauntlet at Vane never led to anything good.

"*Tagka.*" Vane slapped his hand on my arm. I felt Arthur's sword heat.

Rourke's right knee lifted and the gargoyle king stood on one foot. To my surprise, all the gargoyles followed the king's actions. They all lifted the same knee and stood on the same foot. Every gargoyle except the candidate gargoyles, like Oliver.

Vane lifted a brow. "Would you like to jump, too?"

Rourke's face turned bright red.

Matt put his arm on my other side. "*Tagka-apte.*"

Rourke's leg lowered. Every subordinate gargoyle's leg lowered.

Matt cleared his throat. "As my brother so aptly demonstrates, you have already lost, Rourke. Don't push us. With one small command, we can end the life of every gargoyle on this roof."

The gargoyle from the alley, who'd been standing unnoticed at Rourke's side, held up a cell. "Sire—"

I frowned at him. "You work for Marla."

"No, lass. I serve the king first. I helped the queen only as long as I believed it to be in his interest." He said to Rourke, "Sire, the First Member has rallied more wizards to her. They will be coming."

Wizards floated up from inside the palace through the hole in the roof. The queen stood between them. She walked though them to the front. Hundreds of wizards fanned out behind her.

"Actually, we are here," she said.

"You're a little late," Vane told her.

"I would say entirely on time." The queen looked at the gargoyle king. "Rourke, your consort and your son conspired to gain Arthur's sword for themselves and usurp your throne. They have lost this battle for you. If you wish to save the gargoyles this night, you will leave."

Rourke didn't look at the queen. He watched me. I glanced up at the sky. The red moon had started to wane—and along with it, the gargoyle's advantage. I raised a brow at him in silent challenge.

Rourke's eyes lit with surprise. He turned back to the queen. "We came for the sword. We have lost it. We concede— for now. However, I would not get too comfortable. The sword's allegiance is not yet fixed."

"You'll stop hunting candidates?" I asked.

Rourke inclined his head. "Not that it is necessary to say, since the sword has been taken, but the order is rescinded."

With a final nod at me, Rourke bowed to the queen. She inclined her head in regal acknowledgment.

I glanced around at the gargoyles. They watched the candidates with alert eyes, but their swords had dropped down to their sides. The gargoyle from the alley moved to pick up Marla. Oliver snatched her up before he could.

"Come, Oliver." Rourke walked to the edge of the rooftop. "We have much to discuss."

Bending his head, Oliver carried Marla to his father's side. As he passed, he shot me a look that burned with hatred. The glow of the moon angled off the gargoyles as they lined the ledge of the rooftop. A high-pitched whistle sounded.

The gargoyles all leaped off the roof and into the night.

***

I put down Arthur's sword and leaned on its hilt. "It's over."

"Ryan," Paul yelled. "A brother for a brother."

I whipped around to see Paul run a blade through Grey's back.

It pierced through his chest.

"No!" My scream tore through the night. *Grey.* The stench of fresh blood hit my nostrils.

I crossed to Grey. I moved fast. Faster than I could see or think.

Triumph lit Paul's face. Grey fell to the ground. Paul pulled the sword out of Grey and blocked me as I swung my sword at him. His sword glanced off mine. My hand swung again without even thinking. I connected with the hard bone of his neck. His smiling head came off in one neat slice. I didn't waste any more time on him. I dropped the sword and knelt down beside Grey.

MERLIN

The red moon was waning; only a trace remained. Clouds moved rapidly across the sky. A soft kiss of rain started to trickle down on the rooftop. I clutched a blood-soaked Grey to me.

Vane knelt down beside us.

I choked out. "H-help him."

Saying nothing, Vane touched my shoulder. He put a hand on the wound on Grey's chest. It healed, but Grey remained still.

I let out a broken sob. Gia came up beside me. Silently, she touched Grey's face.

Matt stumbled over to us and dropped down to Grey's side. He put his hand on Grey's heart. He shook his head. "I am sorry, Ryan."

"No." I touched Grey. He still felt warm to the touch. My

amulet surged with power. I caught Matt's shoulder. "Do something. He's not gone yet; I know it."

Matt's dark eyes clouded. "The blade went through his heart, Ryan. He died in seconds. It's too late."

The same words he'd said when Alexa had died. My fingers tightened in anger. I shoved Matt in the chest, knocking him on his butt.

"It's not too late!" I stood up. I looked down at him. "If it's too late, then what was all this for? I didn't get the sword to watch Grey die. We have it now. We didn't have that when Alexa died. Don't tell me you can't do this. The candidates did what was asked. Now it's your turn." I picked up the sword and held it over Matt. I swung it around in front of his face—either an avenging angel or a deranged lunatic. I didn't care.

"Are you the greatest wizard in the world or not?" I yelled at him. "If you are—prove it now. If you aren't—you may as well go back into the tomb you came from."

Vane stood up. He put himself between Matt and me. "He doesn't have enough power left to do much. I'm nearly used up. The red moon is gone. There is nothing left to draw from."

"There must be another answer," I snapped. "Think. Whatever it is, I don't care. If you don't fix this, Vane, I will never forgive you." I stared at Matt. "Either one of you."

"There is another way." The queen strode past a group of wizards to the three of us. She glanced up at the wet, dark sky. Nothing penetrated through the clouds.

"She has the blood of three." The queen looked at Matt. "Does she not?"

Matt nodded.

"What?" I blinked at the queen in confusion.

"The sacrifice in limbo worked because you have dormant gargoyle blood," Matt told me. "It is not active, but it is there. Sacrificing yourself brought the blood in contact with the sword."

I stood in shock for a moment. I stared down at Matt. "You lied to me again!"

Vane grabbed me. "Leave it, Ryan. Grey needs you now." He looked at the queen. "What else do we need?"

The queen nodded at the wizards surrounding us. Nearly two hundred or so wizards took up the wide expanse. "She must channel every wizard on this rooftop."

"It will kill her," Vane said.

"It is still the solstice," the queen said. "It has its own power."

"She is the sword bearer. She can handle it," Matt said dully. "But should she? To bring him back now would be unnatural. We don't know where he would come back from. What it will do to him. Who he'll be."

I knelt down next to Grey and put my palm to his cheek. It had started to turn cold. Tears flooded down my face.

No one said anything. Quiet filled the rooftop where there had been a cacophony of battle sounds before. We were up high, yet not far enough for escape. Stray noises from the streets beyond the palace wiggled up. My shoulders started to slump.

Gia stood up. "We're with you, Ryan."

All of the candidates gathered and formed a circle around us in a silent show of support. Matt looked at them without expression.

"P-please, Matt. I know this is right. It has to be." I begged him. "Please, do this for me."

Finally, Matt gave a slow nod.

Vane handed me Arthur's sword. I held it close.

Matt chanted one word. "*Invati.*"

Vane repeated it.

All of the candidates—Regulars and wizards alike—shouted the word.

The gemstone on my amulet warmed. Everything around me warmed. The sword glowed blue in the dark night. The sky seemed to deepen with shadows and the full power of the winter solstice flowed through me to the sword. For a moment, the whole world stood still. A bright flash burst from the sword. I saw Matt and Vane direct it at Grey.

Grey rose up in the air.

My whole body burned, overheated like a too-taxed light bulb. A million lines of disparate energy hit me. I became the central source of power. The synapses of my mind fired with unbelievable speed, trying to process all the separate threads at once. My mind couldn't handle the load.

Grey rose higher.

Then, in one loud burst, the light bulb fused. A loud crack of lightning flashed across the sky.

Grey fell to the ground.

I let go of the sword. I touched Grey's chest. It rose as he took a breath.

Gia squealed from beside Grey. "He's all right."

"Ha," I said, unable to say more past the mush that was my mind. Cleansing rain fell in glorious rhythm.

Vane laughed. Matt sat beside Grey with a tired half-smile.

Cheers broke out over the rooftop.

The queen watched us silently. She went to Matt and touched a hand to his chest. The wizards chanted a word. Matt blinked, suddenly looking more alert.

The queen turned to me. "Good work, sword bearer. You show as much promise as Merlin had pledged." She gave me a keen look. "Despite your dubious blood, you have fire." To my shock, the queen took my hand and declared, "And we quite like you."

She arched a brow at Matt and Vane. "You two will have to train her up, of course."

The queen's wizards gathered the guardians who'd sided with Aurelius. I'd almost forgotten about them. They wore resigned expressions. "Excellent work on capturing the collaborators. However, I suspect we have not entirely cleaned house. I will gather the Council. I believe I need new leadership." She glanced at the giant hole in her palace. "First, though, we shall get everyone to the infirmary. Then, I think we will start with my poor staff. They have seen entirely too much." The queen started to leave. "It has been a most interesting night."

"Wait—" I said.

She stopped.

My fingers tightened on Arthur's sword. "You're just going to let me keep this?"

"The sword has chosen you, my dear." Her wizened face lit up with bright eyes. "I cannot take it away. You are now the owner of its fate."

Matt bent his head. "For Camelot."

The queen bent her head. "For Camelot."

The other wizards cried, "For Camelot."

A sizzle of energy went through my amulet. A sudden flash of lightning twisted through the clouds. It struck the stone... where the sword used to be.

***

Two days later, I stood inside Buckingham Palace looking out at one of the side gardens from a second-floor window.

"Have you gone crazy?" Grey demanded from where he lay resting in the middle of the giant bed the queen had arranged for him.

"Don't sit up," I said.

"I doubt you would be lying still if you were in his place." Sylvia sat on the other side of the bed.

"I'm getting up," Grey said. "I need to stop this insanity Ryan is bent on."

The door opened. Matt and Vane entered.

"It's time," Matt said.

"Are you sure about this?" Vane asked.

"This is the best way to keep it safe," I murmured, glancing at a nearby mirror hanging on the wall. I'd found myself doing it more than I liked. Something inside me needed assurance I wasn't going to sprout fangs... or beastly facial hair.

Vane put a hand on my back. "You look fine."

"There has to be another way," Matt declared.

"That's what I said," Grey said grumpily.

"She always was headstrong," Sylvia said.

I smiled at Sylvia. It was nice to have her by our side once again.

"I should go." I leaned over the bed to hug Grey one more time.

"No matter what, you'll always have us. Remember that," he whispered into my ear.

I squeezed his shoulders so tightly he winced. I let go.

Matt and Vane led me out. Guards—some in stylish black suits that gave them away as royal protection officers and some in white mage robes—followed us. We walked down the hallway and into a small waiting room with two sets of doors.

A young, smartly-dressed man, Darcy—Dawson's replacement—waited for us inside. He dropped his eyes when he saw me.

"Her majesty will be here in a few minutes," he said to Matt. He glanced at me again and swallowed visibly.

"I'll wait outside," he mumbled and scurried to the door.

My status as full-fledged freak was confirmed.

"Awe-inspiring angel," Matt corrected.

Grimacing, I touched my amulet. "Stop reading me or I'm taking it off."

Matt crossed his arms and looked at me steadily. "You can still change your mind."

I took his cell phone and flipped on the news feed. It showed the angry mob outside of Parliament. It panned again to a similar looking crowd outside Buckingham. I went to a nearby window. The sky sat still in a hue of soft periwinkle-blue. But on the grounds of the palace, a storm raged.

"They haven't figured out what's going on, but the gargoyles will keep driving them. I went through the trial to protect my family, and now we're in more danger than ever. This way—at least—anyone trying to get to me will have a harder time of it."

Matt came up to stand behind me. "This is exactly what I didn't want for you. You'll leave yourself wide open."

"If I don't do this, can you promise me I won't be buried inside some bunker? I don't want to live like that." *I don't want to lose my mind.* The memory of how easily I'd killed Paul haunted me. I put a hand on the cold glass pane. The world seemed so vast. I touched Matt's cell phone. Yet, it was smaller than ever.

I watched a news clip about the decoy student who'd supposedly pulled out the sword. He had been murdered in his Boston townhouse. "The gargoyles killed him to fuel the conspiracy theories. If the sword is revealed, it will save lives."

"By sacrificing you," Vane interjected from behind us.

"By not isolating myself," I corrected.

"Arthur said something similar to me once about forming a Round Table and spreading the power," Matt added. "As I recall, it didn't work out as he planned."

I grinned up at them. "Arthur wasn't a girl. This story will work out differently."

"It had better." Matt's dark eyes deepened with emotion for a brief moment, making my pulse race. Then a veil fell between us as Matt drew away.

He went back to the middle of the room where Vane lounged on an uncomfortable-looking settee.

Darcy peered inside the room. "Second Member, if you please, her majesty wishes for you to give the Council a final update before we begin."

Matt gave Darcy a curt nod and looked at me. "I'll be right back. Stay put."

He said to Vane, "Keep her safe."

"I'll watch for trouble," Vane replied.

"That's not what I meant." Matt turned on his heel.

He and Darcy went back out into the hallway. Darcy closed the doors behind them.

"After all we've been through, he still doesn't trust me." Vane got up and paced back and forth. I watched him, my eyes drawn to the lean, graceful movements of his body. Finally, he sat against the edge of a writing desk, but his fingers kept fidgeting.

"Want to make out? It'll pass the time." I said lightly.

Vane stilled. "It's not nice to tease."

I batted my lashes. "I'm not."

Vane moved in a blink. He stood inches from me, not touching, yet the heat of his body warmed mine despite the tight layers of my dressy suit. "Is this what you really want?"

Am I the one you really want? he meant.

I stared at the strong line of Vane's jaw. I touched the amulet around my neck. It was Vane who I heard in my head, not Matt. It was Vane who forced me to fight. Around him, I found myself. I couldn't quite believe I'd fallen for Vane, but somewhere along the way, I had.

"Matt and I will always have a connection,"—When Vane's expression soured, I suppressed a smile—"but I want you."

"Why?" he demanded.

"Because you helped save Grey."

Vane raised a brow. "You're so grateful I saved your brother, you want me."

"Helped save," I corrected.

Vane smiled. The same smile that snuck under my every defense, examined the real me, and still refused to leave. My fingers tightened on the amulet. "Because I trust you."

"You shouldn't."

I let out a loud sigh. "Because you're a pain in the ass."

"Your ass is a good place to be," he deadpanned. A rare genuine smile lit his face. He yanked me to him and lowered his mouth to mine. He kissed harshly, as if he couldn't believe I was letting him do it. His hand fingered the edge of the short skirt of the suit. I shivered despite the fact that I wore thick black tights. The kiss gentled as I continued to respond.

Finally, he broke away. "I shouldn't let you do this."

I opened my mouth to protest.

"But unlike my brother, I'm not that unselfish." His fingers untangled some of my upswept hair. "You're making a mistake encouraging me. I won't let you go now."

I smiled. "The queen's hairdresser is going to be annoyed you messed up her 'do."

Vane brushed a thumb across my lips. Stormy eyes locked on me. "You have my brother fooled, but do you really know what you're doing?"

I moved away from Vane and took a step toward the other set of closed doors in the room. I could hear the shuffling of people from behind the painted wood. My heart jangled inside my chest. "I'm afraid."

"You should be." Vane came up from behind and wrapped his arms around me.

I inhaled his dark scent. "Shut up and just tell me it will be all right."

"As you wish." He nuzzled my neck.

The doors I'd come in through opened again. Matt strode in with the queen. They stopped short at the sight of us.

Vane released me slowly.

The queen marched up to me. "Give me one reason why I should let you do this. Why I should let you risk exposure?"

I walked back to the window behind her and pulled the drapes aside. The protesters sang *Silent Night*. Simply, I said,

"They don't need to know about wizards. They need to know about the sword. They're afraid. I can give them hope."

A smile broke across her face. The heat of it made the sun appear pale by comparison. She straightened and the smile dimmed. "Well, then, do make sure you keep it to that. I refuse to have a thousand-year secret leaked on my watch."

The queen held out her hand to Vane. "I will go first. You may lead me."

Vane walked with her to the closed doors. Noise in the other room hushed when he opened the door. They went through. The doors closed behind them.

Matt held out his arm. I crossed to him.

I blurted out, "Vane and I—"

"I know. I have eyes, Ryan." He glanced at the *Dragon's Eye*, my amulet. "And ears."

I flushed and glared at him. "This mind reading is getting irritating."

"You'll get used to it." Matt's hand tightened on my arm. "He's not the right one for you."

"At least I know who he is," I replied softly.

A knock sounded from the other side of the door. It was time.

I took a breath. Matt pulled open the door and pushed me through to the other room. On shaky heels, I crossed a small stage to the podium. Vane and the queen sat at a nearby antique desk.

Matt came to stand behind me. I laid my palms down on

the wood podium and faced the crowd. Rows and rows of reporters filled the queen's pressroom. Flashes exploded from what seemed like a thousand bulbs. A line of television cameras took up the back of the packed room.

"Hello." Silence fell across the room.

The enormity of what I was about to do hit me. My life would never be the same again. Anxiety tightened around my throat. A warm hand settled to support my back. *Matt.* He moved to stand at my right.

I leaned into the mike. "My name is Arriane DuLac and I am here to settle a question about who pulled the sword from the stone."

Matt handed me the sword. I held it up, blade aimed down. The cold metal winked in silver beauty for everyone to see. I twisted the sword and lifted it straight up.

Gasps and the snap-click of shutters reverberated around the room.

Several of the reporters jumped up. One said, "How does she have it?"

"Why is it in the palace?"

"I want to see for myself," someone else yelled.

They scrambled out of the rows of chairs and headed straight for me. I had a sense of *déjà vu* from a Frankenstein movie as the reporters stormed the podium with their microphones like villagers coming at me with pitchforks.

Unconsciously, I took a step back.

Matt grabbed the sword from me. He put himself in

between the reporters and me.

"Matt, what are you doing?" I hissed at him.

"Saving you," he said to me.

He looked at the reporters and declared, "The sword is real."

"Matt!" I said.

Matt held the sword up high. It glowed bright blue.

"The sword *is* real!" a reporter whispered.

"Is it magic?" another said.

The queen stood up in alarm.

Matt continued, "The sword is called Excalibur and it belongs to me."

I touched my amulet. *"Matt, why?"*

"Because I love you." His reply reverberated in my head.

Matt stared straight into the cameras. "My name is Merlin."

***

MY MERLIN AWAKENING
BOOK 2

If you haven't broken the rules, have you really lived?

Excalibur has been pulled from the stone, but what does it mean? Arriane (aka **Ryan**) DuLac's got bigger problems—as student president, she's got to put on the Prom. While the Wizard Council debates their next move, she leaves the craziness behind and heads home. But she can't hide forever. Sooner than she'd like **Merlin** (aka Matt) has her chasing mermaids on the trail of the **Fisher King**. The wounded king, defeated by Merlin's brother, **Vane**, in the past holds the key to save the future.

On the journey, Ryan begins to realize the friends she thought she knew, she may not know at all. At a time of shifting alliances, she must decide whose side she's on—the brother who struggles to do right or the brother who dares to break the rules? And Ryan must decide who she is—a regular girl or a champion?

One wrong decision and her family falls apart. One wrong decision and the world falls apart. No pressure.

Continue the adventure and get more Ryan, Vane, and Matt in the second installment of the My Merlin series!

EVER MY MERLIN
BOOK 3
THE CONCLUSION

He was the right one, the fated one, but was he right for her?

The end of the world. The day of reckoning. The final battle.

It is a time of great strife for Arriane (aka Ryan) and Merlin (aka Matt) as they struggle to stem the flood of destruction unleashed upon the world. Their only hope rests in the one object that can restore their greatest ally: **the Healing Cup**.

With every scrap of life hanging in the balance, Ryan must convince both friends and enemies that the key to survival rests in the plans of a sword-toting girl of only eighteen. She must reconcile a fifteen-hundred-year rivalry between two brothers, and be ruthless enough to break a heart—and a life—in the process. And at some point, she really needs to get herself to Prom.

Find out who will win and read the conclusion to Ryan, Vane, and Matt's story in the last chapter of the My Merlin series!

ABOUT THE AUTHOR

Priya Ardis, loves books of all kinds—but especially the gooey ones that make your nose leak and let your latte go cold. Her novels come from a childhood of playing too much She-Ra and watching too much Spock. She started her first book at sixteen, writing in notebooks on long train rides in India during a hot summer vacation. Her favorite Arthurian piece is the poem *The Lady of Shalott* by Lord Alfred Tennyson.

A hopeless romantic, she is a longtime member of the Romance Writer's of America.

***

Please support this book by leaving a review at your retailer. Your efforts are greatly appreciated!

And look for more information on upcoming books stay connected at the following sites or sign up for notifications of new releases on the author's website (http://www.priyaardis.com). To read deleted scenes, articles, and listen to the soundtrack, follow the blog: http://blog.priyaardis.com.

Talk to Priya at the following hangouts!
Twitter: http://www.twitter.com/priyaardis
Facebook: http://www.facebook.com/priyaardis
Goodreads: http://www.goodreads.com/priyaardis

Made in the USA
San Bernardino, CA
27 July 2014